Amanda Brookfield

Amanda Brookfield was born in London in 1960. She was educated at Godolphin School in Wiltshire and University College Oxford from where she graduated with a First Class Honours degree in English in 1982. After working in advertising for three years she accompanied her husband on a posting to Buenos Aires where she worked as a freelance journalist and wrote her first novel. She now lives in London, dividing her time between writing fiction and looking after her two young sons.

SCEPTRE

Also by Amanda Brookfield and published by Sceptre

Alice Alone
Walls of Glass

A Cast of Smiles

AMANDA BROOKFIELD

SCEPTRE

British Library C.I.P.

Brookfield, Amanda
  A Cast of Smiles. – New ed
  I. Title
  823.914 [F]

ISBN 0-340-62449-3

Typeset by Hewer Text Composition Services, Edinburgh
Printed and bound in Great Britain by
Cox & Wyman Ltd, Reading, Berkshire

Hodder and Stoughton
A division of Hodder Headline PLC
338 Euston Road
London NW1 3BH

For my parents

The Wedding

'Dearly beloved, we are gathered together . . .' began the
sing-song holier-than-thou voice of the Very Reverend
Peachy. Julian looked at the light squeezing through the
tiny cracks in the stained-glass windows behind the vicar
and wondered if Veronica secretly felt as unsure about
the whole business as he did. The original decision to get
married, which had seemed so simple, and something that
he very much wanted to do at the time, had long since
been overtaken by events. The small announcement had
triggered such an avalanche of activity and commitment
that the original conviction behind his proposal now lay
buried in heaps of arrangements and lists of people and
things. He thought the conviction might still be lurking
there somewhere, but he had lost touch with it.

The idea of trying to talk to Veronica about his doubts had
occurred to him on more than one occasion. She was very
keen on 'sharing their feelings' and, especially in recent
weeks, had taken to chiding him for keeping things too
much to himself. But Julian did not have the courage to
begin. He would have liked a sensible, objective discussion

as to whether their decision to get married really was in the interests of both their happiness. But a circumspect stab at this – a flippant comment about understanding the freedom of bachelorhood – caused an emotional explosion. Veronica had promptly accused him of not loving her any more; which meant he felt obliged to swear that he did and consequently ended up promising more ardently than ever that she was the only person he wanted alongside him in his journey through life. The atmosphere in their – (or rather his) – small Primrose Hill flat, which had been ricocheting between tense and very tense ever since they had got engaged, grew almost intolerable. The phone assailed them with batteries of congratulation and impossible requests as to which shade of pink they would prefer for the tassels on the place-name cards. Talking to Veronica became a minefield of trying-not-to-say-the-wrong-thing. It had been a positive relief to get away for a twenty-four-hour stag session with Teddy followed by a day in which to recover and write his speech.

'. . . if any man can show any just cause, why they may not lawfully be joined together, let him now speak . . .' Julian found himself half-hoping that there would be a cry from the back of the church. But after the statutory awkward split-second of silence – during which, as he often thought, no one had a decent chance to interrupt anyway – the Very Reverend Peachy turned his holy gaze upon the happy couple. Julian sneaked a look at Veronica. She was staring raptly back into the eyes of the preacher, as if she had had a revelation of the holy spirit. No bride could ever have looked more convinced of her actions. Much more reassuring to Julian was the fidgety rustle coming from his other side, from dear old Ted, hunting for the ring no doubt, having a last-minute fumble and panic. Perhaps he really has lost it, thought Julian, suppressing the urge to turn and look. I ought to concentrate, he told himself; this is it; I'm getting married; this is happening. But any sense of the reality of his situation eluded him. More vivid than the warbles of the vicar and the sound of his own voice quietly committing himself to a lifetime with Veronica Kembleton, was his awareness of the hundreds of eyes behind him, boring into his back, watching his performance. The feeling was familiar. It took him back to the first of his rare appearances on stage – aged seven, as a mostly silent Roman general. Teddy had been at his side then too, digging him in the ribs with the tip of his cardboard spear to try and make him laugh. Then as now, parents in large hats, with tense faces, had made up the bulk of the captive audience; Julian's leading the way in the centre of the front row. Now it was only his father, accompanied by the lady-friend of the month, who perched self-consciously next to Veronica's parents in the nearest pew. Julian's mother had fled shortly after her son's theatrical debut, worn down by years of pretending that life with Lionel Blake was enjoyable. Having little confidence and no money, she had left Julian with his father and made her way to America to begin again. Her original plan had been to win the right to have her son back once she got settled. But she met a nice lawyer with two children of his own, England gradually became a hazy memory and somehow she never got round to it. Neither Julian nor Lionel ever heard from her again.

At seven, the sense of those hopeful, terrified gazes pinned on his every move had caused him to muff his lines. Now, twenty years later, it did not affect his performance at all. He carefully repeated the vicar's promises to love and cherish Veronica for the rest of his life, slipped the ring, warm from its stay in the hot palm of Teddy's hand, on to her finger and then stood listening to a long diatribe on the woes of married life.

The Very Reverend Peachy was not very enthusiastic about marriages these days. Couples whom he had never seen before booked him up like some sort of dating service. Their sole attendances in his church were for his mandatory premarriage chat followed by the wedding itself. He had long since given up trying to make converts of them all. Now he merely nodded his head when they confessed – as most of them did – that they weren't quite sure what they believed and that, no, they had not thought about religious instruction for their children. He tried not to mind when their eyes glazed over as he explained about the sanctity of matrimony and he enjoyed the panic in their faces when he said he did not believe in rehearsing the service. It was during the actual ceremony that the reverend finally got his own back. Long sermons on the difficulties of married life were his speciality: the temptations of the flesh, the need for compromise, the frequency of disagreements – nothing was left out in his catalogue of the hurdles that awaited them.

A row of Julian and Teddy's friends – most of them from the rugby club – placed bets on how long the vicar would talk for. Mrs Charleston, the best man's mother, wondered where Mrs Kembleton had got her hat from. Except it wasn't really a hat; it was more like a sequined veil, draped over the side of her head, like a dead seagull she thought. At least it should have looked like a dead seagull – it certainly would have done perched on the side of Marjorie Charleston's flat grey head – but, infuriatingly, it didn't. Lavinia Kembleton was a tall, elegant, fashionable woman. The hat had been made to her own exact specifications; each tiny sequin, sewn on by hand, glinted in the shafts of light falling into her side of the church, picking up the louder glints of the jewels in her ears, round her neck and on her fingers. Lavinia Kembleton looked exactly as she intended: a wealthy, attractive, stylish woman-of-the-world. Suddenly sensing she was being watched, she glanced along the pews across the church to see who was staring. Marjorie quickly turned her head back to face the vicar and dispelled her envy by admiring her son. Darling Teddy, so smart and handsome – better looking than the groom even.

The length of the parson's talk to the couple was causing trouble amongst the herd of bridesmaids and, more particularly, to Gloria Croft, Veronica's chief bridesmaid and oldest friend. The smallest of the silk-clad little bundles, each with huge pink Easter egg bows round their waists, had begun lifting up her dress and trying to pull down her pants. The rest were giggling and tugging at the fresh flowers in their hair. The only aspect of the duty which had attracted Gloria in the first place was the opportunity to wear yards of sky-blue taffeta and to have cream-coloured freesias interlaced in her auburn curls. Why Veronica wanted to get married remained a complete mystery to her. Julian was a decent enough guy, but why stop all the fun by getting married? Gloria lived for the thrills of the ritualistic attraction, chase and discard of men. It was why she got out of bed each morning, why she skimped on meals to keep her figure slim and why she wore shoes that were slowly deforming her feet. High heels, narrow fittings and pointed ends characterized all her footwear. They looked lovely, but squashed her toes together so tightly that after long periods of standing they would go numb. She wiggled them vigorously now, feeling a slight ache where what looked terrifyingly like the start of a bunion pressed against the patent leather. Veronica was good looking too – not the sort of girl who should have felt in the remotest hurry to find a permanent man. It had all started with her job, decided Gloria, as she bent down to rearrange a fraction of the bride's long train as a way of ignoring the antics of the small people around her. Whereas Gloria was quite happy temping in advertising agencies – a dense grazing ground for handsome hungry men with big expense accounts – Veronica had somehow landed a job with a small publishing house. Having begun as a general dogsbody, she now seemed to be doing some quite high-powered executive stuff. Gloria was not sure exactly – the books seemed to be mostly rather boring and educational so she didn't ask too much about them. But Veronica had her own secretary now and far less time for drinks after work, so she must be doing pretty well. The child pulling her pants down started to cry loudly. Gloria, at her wits' end, looked round for help. A woman with a shiny pink face at length emerged from the throng of hats, pinstripes and padded shoulders to lay claim to the wailing infant. She scooped her up, mouthed 'sorry' at Gloria and tiptoed down the aisle, trying not to make a noise with her stilettos.

By now the entire congregation was a mass of restless rustles and coughs. A vague sense of outrage and protest had descended. Really, it wasn't on – either for a vicar to paint a picture of such gloom and doom at a wedding, or to take so long doing so. Only George Smithers was grateful to the preacher. His long-shot bet of fourteen and a half minutes for the sermon was already the winner. The Very Reverend Peachy had long since overtaken this mark and several five pound notes had passed down the line and into his pocket.

'. . . and so . . .' the vicar put on his winding-up tone of voice; the congregation stopped coughing and sat up to attention.

'. . . Julian and Veronica, two strong, brave people, you know the dangers of the voyage you are about to undertake and you know, that with God's help, your love will be mighty enough to overcome those dangers, to ride through those stormy seas and, one day, to arrive safely on the beach beyond. God bless you both. In the name of the Father . . .' The collective sigh of relief was audible. Veronica squeezed Julian's hand and he dutifully squeezed hers back. Then she turned her face to his for their first married kiss.

2

The Reception

The Kembletons knew how to throw a good party. Armies of dapper little waiters had been recruited to keep the line of guests well watered with champagne. In case of rain or sun, a long elegant pergola-type walkway had been constructed in the garden. It wound round the flower beds, past the swimming pool and the summer-house, through the cherry orchard and out into the field where it met the yawning entrance of an enormous marquee. Like some frilly white snake, thought Jack, the gardener's son, from his hideout high amongst the branches of an enormous oak. And as he watched the guests arrive, the snake seemed to come alive: it bulged with coloured hats and ribbons, it hummed with chatter, clinks and laughter; and the little flags dangling along the sides of the white canvas roof fluttered in the teasing, gentle breeze. He pulled the squashed cigarette from its hiding place in the back pocket of his jeans and settled down to enjoy the afternoon.

Greeting the guests was taking longer than Lavinia Kembleton had anticipated. She caught the eye of Geoffries, the head waiter, who came scurrying to her side, his face puce with exertion.

'Such lovely weather Lavinia – how did you organize it?' said Mrs Charleston, trying not to look at the hat, as she took her turn along the row of shaking hands. 'The shade of that lovely archway is a positive godsend in this heat – so clever of you to think of it . . .'

'Darling thank you . . . But do please excuse me a tick while I see to it that all those poor people don't die of starvation while they're waiting.' She stepped back out of the line to talk to Geoffries who had been hovering patiently behind her. They were among his best clients, the Kembletons. Regular thrashes, lots of guests and big tips.

'Get some trays of food taken down the line could you Geoffries. None of the really fancy stuff – just the sandwiches and pastries. Give them napkins, but don't bother with any plates. Ease up on the champagne for a bit and get your men to do the food instead.'

'Right away, Mrs Kembleton.'

Lavinia stepped back, smiling, to shake hands with the vicar's ninety-three-year-old mother. So far so good she thought. It wasn't really concern at the hunger of her guests that had prompted her orders to Geoffries. Just a fear that too many people would pour too much champagne into empty stomachs and then throw it up all over her pretty flower beds.

'Well, they're certainly not holding back are they?' said George Smithers, helping himself from a passing tray of smoked salmon sandwiches. 'Mind you, if I had old man Kembleton's bank account I might throw a good party or two as well.'

George was supposedly addressing himself to Peter Sidcup, with whom he shared a flat in west London. But he was raising his voice and trying to catch the eye of the girl standing behind and a little to one side of Peter. She did not appear to be with any particular escort and was wearing a mesmerizing combination of tight-fitting black and white dots. A mini bowler hat cocked roguishly on one side of her head with a large black feather sticking out behind it hid most of her face from view – as if she wished to remain unrecognized.

'I say, Peter,' he lowered his voice, 'don't look now, but you don't happen to know the name of the charming creature standing just behind your left elbow do you? A real little stunner.'

Without a moment's hesitation Peter turned his head and stared down at the jigging black feather until he caught a glimpse of the face beneath it. Two large brown eyes peeked at his for a split second before looking quickly away again. Peter turned back to his crimson-faced companion.

'You oaf,' spluttered George, 'you really go too far some-time, Sids – I mean, that was just bloody rude.'

'Try not to get so excited, dear boy,' said Peter languidly. 'I think she's called Katherine. I think she's one of Julian's ex-ladies – from a long time back mind you. Waiter, get some more champagne down this end of the queue, there's a good chap. Smoked salmon never was very good at quenching thirst, was it, Smithers?'

George laughed, already forgiving his friend, whom he admired enormously, for his behaviour over the girl. Peter Sidcup was endowed with a confidence about life which George found baffling and admirable. He did not fear, as George did all the time, the opinions of others. This sometimes made him arrogant – rude even – but it also made him honest. He was one of those beings effortlessly accepted in pools in which George spent every moment just trying to keep afloat. Without seeming to care or try, Peter managed to get himself invited to all the parties that mattered and quite often afforded the luxury – or so it seemed to George – of deciding not to go. The mantelpiece of their rented flat in Thurloe Road was always laden with gold-embossed invitations to things like country parties and weddings. And if the function demanded a female escort, some willowy, glamorous girl would appear magically at his side, behaving as if she would lay down her life for the man.

As far as George could make out his flatmate never struggled to make things happen. Whereas he, George, struggled all the time, making a tough, conscious effort to be charming and to be accepted. In spite of this, he lived with the sneaking feeling that he would never be a fully-fledged member of the club – (for so it was that he regarded his circle of acquaintances) – that he would always be knocking at its door. Quite what the club was, or how one qualified for membership was something to which he had devoted many fruitless hours of study. It certainly wasn't money – because Peter Sidcup never had a bean. Nor did it depend on success with girls. Julian had always produced a steady stream of girlfriends, but Teddy never had and Peter often seemed happier on his own. It was more to do with a certain attitude to life – like Sids just turning round and staring at that girl for instance and getting away with it. George had tried, ever since having the good fortune to fall in with their set, to emulate their approach to life, their inner confidence or whatever it was that made them seem so free and so good at enjoying themselves. This good fortune had arisen from landing in the same chambers as Peter, whose cool exterior hid a very warm centre. When he heard that the bumbling new clerk was commuting every day from a bed and breakfast in the East End he immediately offered him the spare bed in his newly acquired flat at a very reasonable rent. But in spite of being able to watch from such close quarters, George Smithers, son of Henry Smithers of Electrical Components in Brentford, found he could not make life work for him in the same way. After a couple of years of slog, he did now get invited to some of the same parties. But usually the invitations came scrawled on the back of Peter's – 'bring George if he's around, we're short of men' – or via Peter himself: 'Come along old man, I'll get you in. You can't stay moping here on your own all night, it's too tragic for words.'

As for George's girlfriends it was one long round of painstakingly organized, excruciatingly expensive candlelit dinners that never seemed to get anywhere. What he would have given for Peter's nonchalance, Teddy's charm or Julian's looks. As it was, being OK-looking, sensible and polite seemed to be a recipe for disaster. By the middle of the main course the girl was usually stifling yawns; at which stage George's confidence would plummet to such depths that he abandoned all secret plans of whisking them off for a whirlwind tour of London's best nightspots – wrung from a disinterested Peter – and offered to drive them straight home instead. At the door he rarely found the courage to plant even the most innocent of goodnight kisses on their lightly rouged cheeks. Nor was he ever invited to meet their parents – as was always happening to Peter and Julian.

Take Veronica's parents for example: George knew for a fact that Peter had once badly scraped one of her father's Porsches after drinking the best part of a bottle of vintage port one Sunday lunch-time. But here he was now having his hand shaken by Mr Kembleton like some favourite son, while Lavinia was positively beaming with delight. Whereas when it came to George's turn in the queue they appeared to lose interest; indeed Mrs Kembleton couldn't even remember his name.

'So glad you could make it er . . .,' she said, placing a limp white hand in his, and then moving quickly on to his neighbour:

'Ah Katherine, isn't it? You look so charming . . .' George

moved quickly along the line after his friend. He would go and talk to Gloria he decided, who was a few yards away and full of beans as usual. Then he would think of a way of introducing himself to Katherine.

Everybody agreed that Teddy's speech was brilliant. Rude enough to make the boys laugh and yet subtle and quick enough not to cause offence to the ladies. There had been some talk of Lavinia wanting to see the final draft beforehand in order to censor it. Teddy's reply had been that since it was still fermenting in his head it would be difficult to comply with such a request. In fact it was only after the service that he got round to jotting down a few brief thoughts, with several glasses of champagne to oil the wheels. Making speeches was something which Teddy had been doing at debating societies and dinners ever since he could remember. Unlike Julian, his appearance on stage at prep school had been the first of many dramatic ventures. He was too lazy and disorganized ever to embark on acting in a serious way, but had successfully appeared in several university productions as rebellious butlers and gallivanting bachelors. In truth, going on stage or speaking in public always tortured his nerves horribly – especially now he had built up something of a reputation for being funny. Large slugs of whisky – or whatever else came to hand – had become a prerequisite for his performances. But somehow he always pulled it off in the end and Jules's wedding was no exception. Part of Teddy's secret lay in his face. He only had to look at people in a certain way and they wanted to laugh. He had a sort of outraged well-what-do-you-expect look that never failed. Then, once he had heard a few snorts and giggles, he was away, the nerves melting in the enjoyment of the moment and the powerful feeling of holding people's attention. His penchant for ad lib – usually prompted by not knowing his lines – had made him a difficult person to work with on stage; but it ensured his success as a speech-maker.

The telegrams he was given to read out at Julian and Veronica's reception struck him as so dull that he altered their wording as he went along and then made up a couple of his own to finish with. It was such a good performance that not even Lavinia could mind.

'You're a wicked, wicked boy, Teddy,' she said afterwards, 'and I love you dearly.'

'And you're a wicked, wicked woman Mrs K and I love your champagne,' replied Teddy, kneeling at her feet and kissing her hand.

'Teddy dear, what are you doing?' It was his mother. Lavinia, flashing her even white teeth, slipped away, leaving Ted on his knees.

Mrs Charleston patted her son's head. 'Do get up, darling. People are staring.'

'Don't fret, mother,' replied Teddy good-naturedly. 'Hang on a minute, you look as though you're going and the thing's barely started.'

She took hold of his hand. 'Don't be cross, sweetie. It's a long drive and I'm worried about your father. He pretends not to mind being alone, but of course he does. Though just as well he decided not to come – it would have been jolly difficult with the heat and everything.' Mr Charleston had suffered a stroke during Ted's last year at prep school, which had left him almost completely paralysed from the neck downwards. People said that he had been very spritely before the accident, but Ted could neither recall nor imagine such a thing. He was a poor, grey shadow of a man, kept at the rituals of maintaining a life by the will-power of his wife alone.

'Well, I won't force you, mum.'

She reached up and kissed him. 'Lovely speech, darling. I'll tell your father how they all laughed. He was quite a

performer in his day you know . . . ring me soon, darling.'
She kissed him again, before squeezing her way through
the throng of guests and setting off across the paddock to
her car. She had to walk on tip-toes to stop her heels from
sticking in the grass. She went carefully and determinedly,
as she did through life, negotiating the problems, not letting
herself feel down.

3

Marriage In The Making

Veronica was honest enough to admit to herself – though not to anyone else – that it was Julian's good looks which had attracted her to him in the first place. She hid this attraction very well; several months after meeting him, she would still only allow her face to light up when they fell to discussing books. She went around in the same crowd, secretly making sure which invitations he had accepted before accepting them herself, but always refusing to go out with him on his own. Julian – as she had intended – became, by gradual degrees, curious, fascinated and, finally, besotted. Anyone privy to Veronica's campaign might have thought of all sorts of unpleasant words to describe her behaviour. But when she first laid eyes on him she really did get a tingly feeling that told her here was a man whose looks and brain were such that she might never tire of waking up to them in the morning. It was a serious attraction, she decided at once, full of potential, and above all to be handled with care. Never having lacked admirers herself, she did not have to worry about feeding her own confidence during those months of wooing Julian Blake. And if, during that time, she had come across something she truly did not like about him, she would have stopped immediately. But everything she heard and saw fixed her heart more strongly in his favour. It was a slowly constructed love therefore, but solid nonetheless. Like a detective, she sought evidence to assemble her case and – though Julian never realized it – she put him through all sorts of little tests in the process. All of which he passed with flying colours. And when the moment finally came, when at last he reached for her hand across the table where they were celebrating their first anniversary of going out together, she had no qualms whatsoever about accepting his offer of marriage. She had done her research well. She was sure that the man opposite her was one of the ones – for Veronica was a realist about such things – with whom she could happily spend the rest of her life.

When Veronica Kembleton first appeared on the scene Julian had begun to wonder if he wasn't losing his touch. He had grown used to believing that if he put his mind to it he could persuade almost any girl to fall in love with him. Ever since Katherine Vermont. Katherine had been his First Love. That is to say she had been the first girl whose admiration he had really concentrated on winning. She had been shy and freckly then, the devoted shadow of her brother Tommy, who for a while had been Julian's best friend at school.

In the whole business of getting a girlfriend, Julian, like any green sixteen-year-old, had nothing to go on except the blatantly fictitious stories of his friends and things he read about or saw on the screen. And wanting a girlfriend – rather than wanting Katherine Vermont – was very much why it all began. Having noticed the way she looked at him sometimes from under her bushy fair hair, he quickly realized that she was his best option. Apart from anything else, spending so many weekends out with her brother meant he saw her more often than any other female. It also ensured a lot of publicity over the affair, vital in the schoolboy race for credibility.

First he wrote her a letter, dutifully delivered by Tommy one half-term. In it he was quite romantic, describing the sunlight playing in her straw-blonde hair and the number of times his heart beat per second whenever she appeared. A timid little notelet came back in Tommy's blazer pocket; neat, upright handwriting revealed that she too 'liked him very much'. And so it went on – at least a letter exchanged a week – until the dreadful business of actually meeting for the first time since the written communication began. Carried away by the role of ardent lover, Julian had allowed his letters to become more passionate each week. Fancying himself an unrecognized expert on Eliot and Keats at the time, all his prose was liberally punctuated with words and phrases from *The Wasteland* and *Ode to a Nightingale*. Was Katherine, 'a vision or a waking dream'; 'memory and desire were stirring his dull roots' and so on. The focus of his desire reciprocated in kind, although without the literary cross-references. The initial 'from Julian' and 'from Katherine' rapidly got promoted to 'love from', 'lots of love', 'tons of love' until, in the letter Julian sent the weekend before he went to stay with Tommy, he allowed his ardour to reach the dizzy heights of 'all my fondest love'. The noughts and crosses accompanying this declaration took up the best part of half a page. After such epistolary extravagances the actual meeting between the star-crossed teenagers had a lot to live up to.

'Hello,' said Julian, his heart beating at twice its usual rate from terror, not love, 'I brought you a present.' He handed over a bottle of bubble-bath, stolen from matron's bathroom and topped up with water. That afternoon the three of them went off to the cinema. At least Tommy went to the cinema, leaving the lovers to get to know each other a little better. Even as they sat in the Bay Leaf

Tea House on that first rainy Saturday together, Julian had the vague sense that he had bitten off rather more than he could chew. As with his letters, he concentrated on saying what he thought he ought to say in such a situation, rather than on what he really felt. It was all a big game to him. Katherine on the other hand was clearly genuinely moved by their relationship. At first he thought she was just acting out her part better than he was managing his. But as the months passed, it became clear that when she said she loved him she meant it. Although floundering in the vilest years of adolescence, Julian knew in his heart of hearts that this meant it was wrong of him to carry on. Perhaps a diet of nannies rather than motherly love was to blame, but he was simply incapable of caring more for someone else's feelings than for his own. Katherine presented an opportunity that was too good to miss. Sexual experience. The initial tentative touchings, the first speedy, disappointing climax and then on to the less hurried discoveries of how to get pleasure as well as satisfaction – all this Julian learnt with Katherine Vermont.

What's more, it earned him considerable admiration amongst his less fortunate sixth form colleagues and cemented his own sexual confidence.

As often was the case in the years that followed, getting out of the affair proved much more difficult than getting into it. Even knowing that Katherine's frequent professions of love were more heartfelt than his, Julian was astonished at the violence of her misery when he finally decided to call it quits at the beginning of his A-level term. First he tried a let's-be-friends scenario, but every time he saw her it was worse. She never stopped crying and the dreadful, pitiful entreaties to have her back became unbearable. So in the end he simply had to refuse to see her at all. He lost Tommy as a friend in the process – although he was never entirely sure if this was the reason – and took himself off on a pre-university grape-picking season in the South of France to get the whole episode out of his system. Which, with the help of the feline wife of the vineyard manager, he did very successfully.

What Julian came to refer to as 'my fling with Katherine' affected him barely at all compared to the body-blow she suffered. But it made him sly: he became one of those people who make a show of emotional honesty, just to cover themselves. From then on, he readily admitted to every girl he liked the look of: 'I'm very selfish when it comes to women – I always end up hurting them. I wouldn't have anything to do with me at all if I were you.' And having made such statements, felt purged of all moral responsibility for his actions. The girl had been warned. If she was hurt it was her lookout. Unfortunately many females rose to such statements as if to a great challenge, so Julian was never short of lovers. Then along came Veronica – stoic, calculating, a tower of self-possession. Julian was perfectly primed to react to her stratagem; after that first easy collapse of Katherine, the hardest to get was always going to be the one he wanted most of all.

Julian was not in the habit of analyzing the whys and wherefores of his behaviour. At the last minute he had decided it would do no harm to invite Katherine to his wedding, especially since hordes of Veronica's ex-boyfriends were on the list. But when he saw her a vile doubt crept into his mind . . . perhaps he was making a similar error with his bride as he had with his first lover; namely, committing himself to something in which he did not fully believe. His trouble, he decided, was that he was too much of a romantic. He said things he wished were true and imagined he felt things because it would have been nice to do so. While all the time a selfish voice in the back of his head sneered at his efforts to be sincere, about love especially. As early as the second day of their honeymoon Julian began seriously to wonder if his father's philosophy – 'love means getting them where you want them' – wasn't the right one after all.

* * *

'Teddy – hello there. It's Julian. How are you, old man?'

'Fantastic.'

Teddy sounded rather drunk.

'I thought I'd show up at rugby training tonight. Wondered what your plans were?'

'How was Lanzarote?'

'Fine, except it was Miami.'

'Sun, sand, sea, sex and all that stuff?' His words were very slurred indeed.

'All that stuff was just great thank you, Teddy. Now are you going to take a cold shower and get your butt along to the club or not?'

'Oh God, Jules, I don't think so. I've been on the bottle since lunch – celebrating a big deal you know, all very confidential of course . . .' Teddy was a banker in a small Dutch firm and quite often found pretexts for long lunches.

'Don't start boring me with your business secrets Ted, I'm not interested. Look I'm coming round to pick you up. You'll feel better for a good sweat . . .'

Teddy groaned loudly.

'I'll be there in half an hour.'

Teddy groaned again, but Julian had already put the receiver down. He threw his kit into a bag and roared off to Thurloe Road where for the last year Teddy had been 'temporarily' lodging with George and Peter.

Since the flat was small, its inhabitants messy and Teddy's bed the sofa, its condition was fast sliding from acceptable chaos towards unacceptable squalor. How the three tenants emerged from it each morning in their pinstriped suits and spotty ties, with their hair brushed and their faces shaved was almost miraculous. Julian, who was rather keen on himself and his surroundings looking spruce, had always been clever enough to find obliging ladies to look after him – sometimes employed, sometimes not. Having been careful to enter a career that immediately paid quite well, squalid living quickly became a student memory. Added to which, his income as a stockbroker was supplemented by a generous monthly allowance from his father. It had started when he was at university and somehow never been stopped. The only recompense the old man seemed to expect was that Julian paid for every other of their weekly lunches. These took place after a game of squash or real tennis and were invariably expensive. But not so expensive that he could not afford to take out a large joint mortgage on a three bedroomed house south of the river with his new wife.

Julian was disgusted anew each time he entered Thurloe Road. The only event which prompted any semblance of order was one of their impromptu parties; in which case all larger objects were thrown into George's bedroom and all smaller ones – like Teddy's socks and handkerchiefs – were stuffed either down or under the sofa. No such tidying up was in evidence as Julian entered now. Peter lay reading on the sofa-bed, apparently oblivious to his squalid surroundings. His head rested on a large greying silk cushion; suspended a few inches above his book was the one light in the room, directed towards this point with the aid of several wires and a considerable amount of Sellotape. Coils of thin blue smoke from his cigar hung below the lampshade like some motionless sea of vapour. He raised one eyebrow at Julian's entry, but otherwise continued with his reading.

'Hi Sids. Is Ted around?' asked Julian.

Without taking his eyes off the page Peter pointed towards the far corner of the room. In it was the one valuable piece of furniture in the flat, a baby grand piano inherited by Peter from a great aunt. Since nobody knew how to play it, its mahogany surface – like every other surface in sight – was covered with mugs, half-empty glasses and full ashtrays. What could be seen of the once polished wood was now a mass of white circles and smudges. Teddy lay underneath the piano, with his eyes shut and a lit cigarette stuck into the corner of his mouth. The ash on it was very long and ready to fall.

'You're a bloody fire hazard, Charleston,' said Julian, gently kicking one of the legs that protruded from under the piano.

Very slowly, Teddy took the cigarette from his mouth and stubbed it out in a saucer beside a half-eaten piece of fruit cake.

'What are you doing here, Jules?'

'I thought we were going to do some running at the club . . .'

'Running?' Teddy laughed, although from his prone position, it came out more as a gurgle. 'My dear chap I can't walk, let alone run. You always were a bloody optimist.' He swivelled out from under the piano and gently manoeuvred himself into a sitting position, with his back against the wall.

'Want a drink, Jules?'

'No thanks, Ted.' Julian flopped down into an armchair, on top of a pile of Teddy's clothes.

'You haven't got a cigarette on you have you, old man?' Teddy made a fumbling show of patting his empty pockets.

'No, Ted. I don't smoke.' Julian sighed quietly. It didn't make him angry to see Ted like this. He didn't really care about the rugby training. They were both well enough ensconced in the club to get away with skipping it every now and then. Nor was it disapproval that made him sigh. Getting drunk was a vital part of all of their lives, once in a while. They didn't plan it that way, but every so often they would find themselves at a party or in a pub when the mood would take them. The hangovers seemed to get worse with age and getting home sometimes caused problems, but it was still fun. Ted had always put away more pints than the rest of them. Just as he had always smoked more than anyone else, told more jokes than anyone else, stayed up later than anyone else and slept in longer the following morning. He was that sort of person. He lived by extremes, dangerously, but somehow always getting by in the end. Like doing their finals for example. Julian, always a keen party-goer, had put his foot down the night before exams. Two days before, yes. But the night before, never. But Teddy had kept going through it all, as if the exams were mere interruptions to the parties in between. As he was quick to point out, he didn't have as much to revise as everyone else because his files were so pathetically thin from lack of work. To this day Julian marvelled at how his friend had got away with it. Even given his belief that English was an easier exam to pass than history – which had been his own subject – Ted's third seemed to him an academic miracle. It was his imagination and energy that carried him through, thought Julian. Although, looking at the crumpled figure slumped in the corner, this was now hard to believe. Ted's own reasoning during that term had been that if he had stopped – to sleep for more than a couple of hours or generally to be sensible for a few days – he would never have started again. And of course they all admired him tremendously – for taking such risks, for drinking brandy at breakfast to get him through a paper – and above all for managing to pull it off.

Now Julian was not quite so sure. There was some aspect to all Ted's drinking and horsing around which, almost imperceptibly, was changing. Some element of control, or at least of choice in the matter, seemed to be fading. Or was it just that being an alcoholic lout was all right as a student – when everyone expected you to be irresponsible and reckless – but not quite so acceptable in an adult? Julian wanted some sort of reassurance from his friend.

'You normally save your benders for a Friday night, Ted. Did you miss me while I was on my honeymoon or something?'

'Leave off, Jules, can't you. Here I am sitting minding my own business, trying not to feel as sloshed as I know I am, or at least as I think I know I . . . oh shit . . . give us a cigar, Sids.'

Without glancing up from his book Peter drew a small packet of panatellas from his breast-pocket and threw them in the direction of Teddy. They landed rather neatly just beside the saucer with the fruit cake in it.

'Good shot, Sids. Now all we need is a small brandy and things are beginning to look good again.'

'Are you being serious?' asked Julian.

'Deadly.' Teddy attempted a resolute stare at his friend, but his eyelids kept flopping shut, ruining the effect.

'If I may say so,' came a lazy voice from the sofa, 'you are being very boring this evening, Julian. Married life obviously does not agree with you.'

'Oh, fuck it,' Julian got up and picked his way through the mess to the kitchen where he rinsed out two wine glasses and located a half bottle of brandy.

'And where's mine?' asked Peter, putting down his book and removing a pair of small round spectacles from the end of his nose.

'You're an affected old woman,' said Julian, pouring a brandy for him in one of the many dirty glasses on the coffee-table beside the sofa.

'At least I'm not an affected boring old woman though, Jules, which would be far worse, don't you think?'

'Cheers,' said Teddy, raising his glass to the piano leg.

The brandy was a good one. Julian lay back amongst

Teddy's clothes and felt its warmth move down his throat and into his stomach.

'A nice tipple this,' he said. 'Whose is it?'

'George's,' said Peter and Teddy in unison, and they all laughed.

'Poor old George,' drawled Teddy, who was better at being kind to George than the other two. Peter was as gentle with him as he could be, but his sharp mind and wit – which made him suffer less articulate mortals with difficulty – often got the better of him. One could hardly not like George Smithers, but he found it hard not to keep pity out of the affection. Julian, who liked their missing flatmate least of all, said 'stuff George' and emptied the contents of the bottle into his glass. The others were too drowsy-drunk to stop him.

George, when he came upon the scene a little later, was torn between pleasure at finding his brandy had been so appreciated and disappointment at not having been included in the session.

*   *   *

Julian knew from the vigour with which Veronica threw herself out of bed the next morning, and the tone of voice in which she told him it was already well past eight o'clock, that she was not very happy. What he did not know – because his eyes had closed heavily the moment his head touched the pillow some time around midnight – was that she had spent half the night yanking meaningfully at the double duvet and heaving significant sighs in a vain attempt to get his attention. Just so as to leave him in no doubt at all as to the state of play, she left the house without saying goodbye and banged the door behind her.

His hangover slowly gathered force during the morning. At first he just felt a little thick-headed; but the grogginess steadily converted itself into a real, throbbing pain which no amount of black coffee and Disprin seemed able to alleviate. It was a day full of briefings from his superiors on what had been going on in his absence, so he chose to pretend that it was too much rugby training rather than too much brandy which made him somewhat weary. Mercifully his suntan hid what would otherwise have been an ashen face. By the end of the day the muscles round his eyes and mouth ached from holding fake expressions of concentration and interest. His hangover followed him home on the tube, like a mangy dog. He was not looking forward to seeing Veronica, knowing, from past experience, that the previous evening had to be talked about in some way.

As usual he was the first to get home. So there was time to recover slightly with a hot bath and several slices of bread and jam. A little before eight o'clock his wife made a big show of struggling through the front door with a full briefcase and several bags of groceries.

'Sorry I'm even later than usual,' she said, in a tone of voice that suggested he was the one who should really be sorry, 'but I thought I had better make sure there was something to eat in the house. I hope you haven't eaten as I thought we'd have a chilli con carne for supper.'

'Just a small snack,' said Julian, wishing he'd put the jam jar away. He went and put his arms round her, but she stayed stiff and said she had to unpack the shopping.

'What's the matter, darling?' he asked, as sweetly as possible, while helping to empty the shopping bags.

'Nothing, nothing at all,' she huffed. 'Julian, for God's sake, the tinned food doesn't live down there it lives up here.' She jerked open the relevant cupboard with such force that the handle came off. She slipped backwards, falling against the kitchen table and knocking a packet of spaghetti onto the floor. The bag split on landing and spaghetti went everywhere. Then she burst into tears.

'Darling, darling, please don't cry.' Julian folded her in his arms, full of gratitude to the cupboard handle for giving him the opportunity. Veronica clung to him, sobbing for several minutes while he made soothing noises in her ear and kissed her hair.

'I know you had rugby training . . . and I know you would have wanted to stay for a bit afterwards . . . but you were so late that I couldn't help . . .'

'I know, I know, shush now, don't cry.' Julian could not decide whether to tell her the truth or not. Things were going so well that he did not want to ruin them. But the thought of the scene that would follow if Veronica ever did chance to hear that he had not been anywhere near Tadfield Rugby Club the previous night was too awesome to risk. Fear made him honest.

'It was awful of me not to ring, I know, darling. But I'm afraid I was even more evil than you imagine.' The sniffles stopped, although she kept her head buried in his jumper. 'I never got as far as the rugby club. I went to pick up Teddy and he and Sids gave me a welcome home party instead – just the three of us. Like a post stag-night sort of thing.'

Veronica actually laughed. 'No wonder you slept so bloody soundly. Go on, give us a hanky.'

Women were incredible, he decided. All the clichés about them were true. It was simply impossible to know how they were going to react to anything. They were always full of surprises – most of them unpleasant or disconcerting.

'Come on, let's ditch the stupid chilli and go out for a bite instead.' Before she could protest he scooped the broken packet and most of its contents into the bin and gave her her handbag.

'Darling I can't go out like this, I look ghastly – all red-eyed and puffy-faced.'

'We'll go to a dark restaurant then. The Chinky would do perfectly don't you think? All those dim lanterns and things; no one will notice us at all. In fact we'll probably have trouble attracting the attention of the waiters . . .' As he spoke he steered her towards the door. Since Veronica was still blowing her nose, she could offer little resistance. When they got to the car, she turned and flung her arms around him.

'I love you. I suppose that's why I get so upset.'

'And I love you too, which is why I hate to see you so upset,' he answered glibly.

4

Katherine

Anyone acquainted with the shy, introverted Katherine Vermont who tagged along behind her brother Tommy and then clung limpet-like to his best friend would have been amazed at the neat, self-possessed little lady who later emerged. The scruffy straw-blonde hair was now guided every two or three days – with the aid of curling tongs – into an orchestra of curls that neatly framed her face. She carried her petite, perfectly proportioned body with all the poise of a girl who had spent three years at modelling school rather than studying general sciences at university.

Katherine had spent the early part of her adolescence, when it really mattered, convinced that she was extremely ugly. Then, on one of Julian's innumerable weekends out with Tommy, she tried brushing her hair differently and smiling a bit more. Julian smiled back, a lot. And followed up the smile with the first of his wonderful letters. If he had only paused for thought, he might have registered an unusual intensity about the girl that would have warned him off starting anything.

Until Julian, Katherine had lived in an imaginary world of

fictional heroes whom she could not conceive ever finding in real life. They made up her secret inner self – the same self that had developed a private language for her dolls, that worked fanatically hard at any project she set her heart on and which ensured that she spent most of her spare time on her own. Her parents got so concerned at one stage that they tried to persuade her to take less time over her homework and devote more hours to having tea with schoolmates. She did make an effort to be more sociable, just to please them, but a shadow of loneliness hung over her, even in the company of other people.

In the beginning, it was Tommy who had received all her trust, all her idolizing love; she followed him around like a puppy and was heartbroken when, at thirteen, he was packed off to boarding-school. Things were never the same after that. Tommy still let her tag along when he was home, but he was less kind and didn't talk to her as much or in the same way. He made her feel boring. So, as she entered the dark tunnel of adolescence, Katherine fixed her loving energies first on fantastic cavaliers and then on Julian Blake. His blue eyes, blond hair and bewitching smile captivated her from the first. All her frustrated, powerful images of love converged on the boy. Through him the hopes of her inner life and the gap in her real life merged into an incredible reality. As with all those afflicted by an infatuating love, she did not see the faults; nor was the relationship allowed to continue long enough for it to reach that point where she might have started to see them. She gave him everything; all the secrets of her mind and body she uncovered for him, reverently.

The effect of Julian's supposed undying passion converting itself – overnight apparently – into a desire to be friends, was nothing short of devastating. Even while she was intelligent enough to see how ridiculous it must appear, that to others it must look like just another failed puppy-love, she could not bring herself to regard it in the same light. Her misery did not feel ridiculous; nor did it feel like any other teenage romance. It felt like the real thing.

At first everyone, especially Tommy, was very understanding. Knowing she was upset, they made special concessions for her mopey behaviour. But after a while they got bored. Neither family nor friends could believe she was still slouching around behind a mask of silent glumness after so many weeks. Julian was old hat; she ought to put it behind her they said and get on with life. During this time, without really meaning to, she became very thin. She lost interest in food as she did in everything else. Her parents began to worry that she was anorexic and called in a specialist to talk to her. In short, it all got so unbearable – all the pestering attention of people telling her to cheer up and get better – that she found herself with no recourse but to lock her misery away as best she could and pretend to the outside world that she was all right. Control became the watchword of her life. Control over how she looked and behaved, only letting show what she wanted people to see. Control over what she ate – enough not to get too thin (so no one could accuse her of starving herself), but never too much of anything, since she seriously believed that her tiny figure was rather on the plump side. In this way Katherine assembled the pieces of herself and her life and concentrated all her efforts on keeping them together.

Shortly after Julian jilted Katherine, Tommy went peculiar. The whole of his year was in a last-minute flurry of preparation for A levels and applying to universities. (Pressures of work had been one of Julian's main pretexts for breaking up the relationship). Amidst all this, Tommy, much to everyone's amazement, opted for a late protest against the system. While even the most anarchic of his peers had decided to capitulate and play the game by the rules, Tommy made a last stand. He brought novels into the examination room and walked out after only an hour without having written a word. And then, after term ended he secretly applied for voluntary work overseas and rang his parents one weekend from London to announce that he was going abroad for a while. He did not even return home to pack any of his belongings. Losing her brother so soon after her lover was another blow for Katherine. But the looks and whispers of worried disappointment from her parents at his behaviour made her feel more compelled than ever to present a brave face to outsiders. With Tommy gone, she felt all the pressure was on her to be the good, non-disappointing child.

She managed very well. In the job-hunting fever that seized all her friends during their final year, Katherine chose marketing – just because it sounded like a solid, sensible sort of thing to do. Her intention was to abandon it as soon as she sorted herself out and identified where her real interests lay. But somehow that moment never arrived. As the months went by, the idea of switching to something else grew more and more remote. The familiarity of the office – the people, the subsidized cafeteria, the exact knowledge of what was expected of her – became too comforting to risk giving up for something else. She felt safe there. She came to believe that a job served the purpose of getting one through the days and weeks, and nothing more; it prevented one from having too much time to think and it provided money to make things comfortable. After all, everyone around her appeared to work for reasons other than enjoyment – money, status, perks and security were the things that kept most of them going. She was really no different.

Playing the role of the modern business woman constituted Katherine's greatest daily defence against the world. Rows of smart skirt and trouser suits occupied all her wardrobe space. Underneath them paraded an army of high-heeled shoes and natty briefcases which she would select according to mood and outfit. Every morning she savoured the process of getting dressed and made up, like an actor preparing for a part. To go with the briefcases and suits were various combinations of make-up. She had grown quite meticulous as to what went with what. Putting on Geneva Grape lipstick for instance, to go with the burgundy Jaeger suit and the wine-red Carvella shoes was vital. Everything had to match perfectly.

Her lipsticks lay in orderly lines in the left-hand drawer of her dressing-table. Arranged beside them was her collection of blushers and powders. The right-hand drawer was for all things to do with the eyes. To make life easier she kept all her eye shadows in a fixed rainbow of colours, graduating from a light cream, across the bottom of the drawer to the darkest brown on the far side. Each morning her immaculately painted nails traced their way across the rainbow until they fell on the choice for the day. To try out a new combination of make-up colours with a particular outfit was quite an event. She normally thought it all out the night before and set the alarm half an hour earlier. Not all her experiments worked; she needed that extra half an hour in case she had to cream it all off and start again with an old favourite colour scheme.

Katherine was very good at her job. It helped both her own confidence and that of her colleagues that she always looked so perfectly turned out. When she told the sales force that they had to get the shelves in their area stocked with a product, they believed her and tried their best. When she made presentations to her bosses about the recent performance of brand X and its future prospects, they trusted her judgement. They would have been astonished to know that while freshening up during a recent meeting on one of her burgundy suit days, this composed, confident lady had nearly screamed on discovering she had left her Geneva Grape lipstick sitting on the dressing-table at home. Back in the boardroom she was coolness itself. No one noticed that each time she turned her back to point to another chart she bit her lips to make them look as much like wine-red as possible. Nor did they see her slip off to Boots in her lunch-hour to buy a substitute colour to keep her going through the afternoon.

Her parents were delighted with their daughter's entry into the commercial world and full of admiration at the number of noughts which appeared after her salary. It helped make up a little bit for the scruffy, ten-word post-cards that appeared in Surrey about once every six months from their nomadic son. Their relationship with Katherine seemed, in their eyes, to flourish. The only slight shadow was that they could never persuade her to bring any of her friends home for the weekend. She always looked well and spoke as if her life was bursting with invitations and people; but her mother, in particular, suspected her of having some serious secrets. In fact it was Mrs Vermont's quiet anxiety about her daughter that prompted her to put her in touch with Veronica Kembleton. The opportunity came up nearly a year after Katherine had moved to London, when Lavinia Kembleton came to speak to the Charity Begins At Home group for the Surrey area. Mrs Vermont, as President of the Upper Horley committee, was designated to sit next to her at the lunch afterwards. The two women got chatting about the worry of having working daughters on their own in London. When Mrs Kembleton complained that Veronica appeared every weekend with car-loads of hungry friends, Mrs Vermont confessed that she wished Katherine presented such problems. (She was by this time convinced that Katherine's secrecy could only be the result of a liaison with a married man. After two glasses of white wine at lunch she confessed as much to Mrs Kembleton, and the two ladies became firm friends for the afternoon). As a result they exchanged their daughters' telephone numbers as well as their own and soon afterwards Veronica was instructed to invite a certain Katherine Vermont to her next party. Mrs Kembleton never called Mrs Vermont; but Veronica kept her word to her mother and so drew Katherine into the outskirts of her own social group.

All this happened many months before Julian met Veronica. Later, when, with his future wife on his arm, he bumped into Katherine at a cocktail party, he smoothly remarked how marvellous she was looking, politely enquired how things were going and moved on as quickly as he could. He told Veronica all about it – making her laugh with his disdain for the fiery passions of his first affair. But while she laughed she made a mental note not to invite Katherine to any of her parties. She let Julian invite her to the wedding because several of her ex-boyfriends were on the list, so it was only fair.

As for Katherine, she had been amazed to receive an invitation to the Kembleton wedding. Her black and white spotty outfit took as many weeks of preparation and hours of agony as the bride's handmade silk and chiffon creation. She rehearsed the few words she would say on congratulating the happy couple with more care than any of her lengthy presentations at work. And in the end it all went very smoothly; all her preparation paid off. She had kissed both the bride and groom fondly, said congratulations and wished them a long and happy marriage. It hadn't been too difficult at all.

When she let herself, Katherine did worry a little bit about her life. She spent practically all her spare time alone in her flat; hardly what was expected of a successful working woman in her mid-twenties. The less she socialized the more difficult it became to go out and act normally. She had almost forgotten what acting normally meant. It was so much easier not to make the effort; to eat her funny meals, watch her favourite programmes and give in to all sorts of indulgences that she would not have confessed to anyone for the world. Like changing the sheets on her bed every two days. At first she had tried to resist the temptation, knowing such a thing would be considered extravagant and unusual. But nobody saw how often she put the washing machine on in her tiny flat so there was no danger of being found out. And she so loved the feel of cool, crisp, clean sheets against her skin that after a few months of holding out at every four days, she let it slip right down to two.

Seeing Julian get married gave her quite a jolt. She resolved, as she had many times before, to break away from the fringes of his group completely and to start making an effort on her own. People at work were always inviting her out for drinks and lunches. She really ought to accept them more often, try and see if she could start letting herself go a bit. These thoughts descended on the Sunday evening after the wedding, as she sat eating a bowlful of her homemade chocolate yoghurt. Its cool sweetness soothed her throat and tongue, helping to ease away the creeping depression wrought by guilt at her own unsociability, the prospect of another Monday morning and memories of the wedding. She had long since given up any hopes of winning Julian Blake's affections back again. At the time of the break it had been plain that in his own mind it was for ever. But she had not, in all the intervening years, let anything or anyone fill the gap that his withdrawal left. There remained a large black hole deep inside her, hidden from the outside world by her polished appearance and all the accoutrements of success. Seeing him get married reminded her of how dark and cold she felt inside. She shivered in spite of the warm evening.

Her red telephone started bleeping. It was George Smithers asking her to have dinner with him.

George read out the words he had written down on the back of an envelope, having learnt from experience that if he trusted to inspiration he made a mess of it.

'Is that Katherine Vermont?'

'Yes' (very cautiously). 'Who is this?'

'Katherine, you probably don't remember me. My name is George Smithers. We met at the wedding yesterday. I got you a glass of champagne when we first went into the marquee. After the speeches I fetched you a piece of wedding cake and we had a brief conversation about your job in marketing. I was wondering if we could perhaps continue that conversation over a spot of dinner sometime?'

'Yes, I remember,' said Katherine. 'But, dinner, well I don't know to be honest. You see I'm frightfully busy.'

'Oh,' said George, who had nothing left to say on his piece of paper.

'How did you get my number by the way?'

'A friend of Veronica's who's a good friend of mine. I hope you don't mind.' In fact it had taken George the best part of the day, ringing round various suggestions of Peter's before he had finally found someone who could give him Katherine Vermont's number.

'No, I was just curious. Look, about dinner. Perhaps you could call me back in a week or so when I'm less tied up?'

He was too stupid to recognize a polite rebuff.

'Well, wouldn't it be easier to fix a definite date now? I mean before your diary fills up, sort of thing.'

Katherine gave up. She could always cancel nearer the time for some important business project or something.

'Right you are. Hang on, I'll just get my diary.' She looked down the unmarked, blank calendar hanging by the phone and picked a date suitably far in the distance.

'Gosh, you are busy aren't you? Are you sure it couldn't be some time the week preceding that . . . say . . . Thursday the 5th?'

Katherine was running out of steam. 'Let me see . . . yes, actually that does look all right.'

'I'll come and pick you up, shall I?' George had an old

MGB which kept him severely in debt but which was his one trump card when it came to trying to impress a girl.

'No,' she said immediately. 'I'd prefer to meet you at the restaurant. I'll probably be coming straight from work you see, but I've no idea exactly when I'll finish – it's generally late – so all in all I'd prefer to get myself to wherever we are going.' Her reactions were strong and instinctive – to protect her private territory from invaders. It was her den, where she changed her sheets as often as she liked and ate chocolate yoghurt. She didn't want anyone barging in on it, least of all tubby little George Smithers.

'Fine' he said, thrilled to have made a date. 'Let's say eight o'clock at the Black Duck restaurant in the Fulham Road then. Do you know where . . .'

'Yes, yes,' she interrupted, now very impatient to get off the phone.

'I'll see you there then. Bye.'

What Katherine did not realize until it was too late was that, in her haste to end the conversation, she had forgotten to ask George for his number. This meant that calling him back to say she could not make it after all was not going to be so easy. She could get hold of his number somehow, she was sure. But it was going to be a hassle.

5 ∫

Married Life Part One

Married life had a number of unpleasant effects on the relationship between Julian and Veronica. One of these was that they started to have lengthy discussions about the division of labour within the house. For the short time they shared his small flat there had been no problem: he did a spot of washing-up and cooked the odd curry to show willing (he didn't know how to cook anything else), while Veronica seemed quite happy to see to the washing and other aspects of domestic cleanliness. Both had been fired by that desire-to-please which inflames most courtships. Now that they had graduated to the dizzy, unglamorous heights of house-ownership and marriage, managing their domestic affairs was not proving quite so easy. It was a subject that made Veronica particularly anxious. Inwardly cursing herself for having set such a dangerous precedent of cooperation when they lived together in Primrose Hill, she was now prepared to fight hard to see that the household duties were divided equally; it seemed only fair, since they both worked all day and had little free time to enjoy at home. She was particularly wary because she had seen too many girlfriends – worn down by damaging, tedious arguments with their men about whose turn it was to do what – finally giving in and taking on everything themselves simply to make life's daily rhythms a little smoother.

A vague – very vague – socialism on Veronica's part made her at first resist the easy option of employing some domestic help. But the resistance did not last long. After several heated debates over how often the grime-mark round the bath and the hairs that miraculously wrapped themselves around the basin taps needed removing, they decided to be sensible and hire a third party. Julian was in fact more satisfied with this arrangement than his wife. As well as letting him off the hook, it made him feel like one of those 'liberated' men who do not expect their equally liberated spouses to waste time over domestic chores. Having an employee also gave him a certain sense of affluence.

The lady they found to 'do' for them was the daughter of the local newsagent. When Veronica went in to ask if she might pin a small advertisement beside the many others stuck in their window – most of them yellow and curling at the corners with age – Mr Jones had given her little choice in the matter. Instead of putting up her notice he disappeared into the back of the shop and re-emerged with Deirdre, the prodigal daughter recently returned from Liverpool and a failed marriage – as he informed her cheerfully. Deirdre, who looked puffy-faced from too many chips and too much sleep, stood there chewing gum while her father eulogized about her standards of cleanliness. She did not seem as enthusiastic as he was about the idea of employment. Veronica, feeling cornered, suggested four hours three times a week to start with, adding that it didn't matter when the hours were done so long as it was between nine and six o'clock. Deirdre perked up a bit at this. Only when the whole thing had been firmly settled was Veronica introduced to her new employee's two small children. She could not have been much more than seventeen herself. Visions of cupboards and shelves full of breakable wedding gifts flashed through Veronica's mind. But it seemed impossible to back out. It also seemed mean not to like Deirdre just because she looked fat and lethargic. A job was probably just what she needed. She could always sack her if she didn't come up to scratch.

Veronica came to suspect that Deirdre used their key to let herself in as often as she liked in order to use their phone, watch their colour television and drink their coffee. But between these activities she also walked behind the Hoover, rearranged the dust and ironed most of the creases out of the washing. Nothing was done very well. But it wasn't done too horrendously badly either. So after a while Veronica stopped running her finger along the window sills and looking under the sofa and just accepted it. Having the cushions puffed up made the place look neat enough and anything was better than the impossible challenge of trying to persuade Julian that cleaning the loo was more important than watching *Grandstand*. She knew that, because of Deirdre's incompetence, little piles of dirt and grime were slowly accumulating in corners. But so long as they kept their distance and stayed in their corners she resolved not to mind them. Julian never gave a thought to lurking heaps of fluff and dust. As far as he was concerned the usefulness of Deirdre's visits boiled down to having someone to blame when he couldn't find his rugby socks.

Another aspect of getting married which neither had foreseen and which disturbed them, was that they became lazy – socially lazy, that is. During their courtship, the two of them had gone out practically every night of the week, usually to meet each other. They only lived together for the last couple of hectic months before the wedding, during which a night in bed had been a welcome break. Now that they had merged their two lives completely, it was logical that so much rushing around was no longer necessary. But Veronica, especially, felt bad about it. It seemed middle-aged somehow. For several weeks running the only events on their social calendar were Julian's rugby and her swimming (done in revenge for the rugby rather than out of any real desire to spend forty minutes doing breast-stroke in Battersea Baths). Veronica decided that the situation had to be discussed and put back on the rails.

'You're right darling,' said Julian when she broached the subject, 'we spend far too much time slopping around at home. That's why I'm bloody glad I've got the rugby . . .'

'Yes, but apart from the rugby, we ought to be doing more things together.' She knelt down in front of him and took away the paper which he had open at the television page. 'Together. Otherwise we'll start forgetting how to.'

Julian thought she was probably right, but it was such an effort to talk about it, to bring it all out in the open and churn it around, irritating each other in the process. 'Well now we've talked about it, we can both make more of an effort,' he said, reaching for his paper.

'No, Jules, I don't think it will work like that. I don't think it will change anything. We've got to make some definite plans.' She held the paper behind her back.

He didn't like the sound of it. 'Well my first plan is to have a drink. I'll get you your usual.'

'See what I mean?' she snapped. 'Soon we won't even be talking to each other. You don't even ask me what I want to drink. It's just "my usual". The next thing, you won't ask – you'll just plonk a dry white wine beside me every night before switching on the telly . . .'

'For Christ's sake Veronica, you really do exaggerate.' He poured himself a generous splash of gin. 'I thought one of the nice things about married life,' he said lazily, 'was getting to know each other so well that you didn't have to spell everything out all the time. 'He threw a dishcloth over his left arm and put on his worst mock French accent:

'Well, tell me, what aperitif would madame like to whet her delicate little palate tonight – un petit Cointreau? Or perhaps a beer with a dash . . .'

'OK, OK – I think I'll have a dry white wine thank you sweetheart.' She laughed even though she wasn't sure whether she thought anything was very funny.

'But you do see what I mean, don't you?' she persisted. They were both sitting with their drinks, pretending they did not want to watch television.

Julian sighed. 'Yes, I do see and, as I said just now, being aware of it will make it all much better, I'm sure.'

But Veronica would not give up so easily.

'What about making it a rule that every week we go out at least once to the cinema – or to the theatre or something – and that we give a dinner party, say, every Friday?'

'But why do we have to talk about it like this? Why don't we just do it?'

'Because unless we talk about it we won't do it.'

'Right, fine, I agree.' Julian had had enough. 'Now can I watch the nine o'clock news?'

'Don't be like that, Jules. I'm only trying to make things better for both of us.'

'Yes, yes, I know. I'm just tired, that's all.' So Julian watched the news while Veronica made some chicken sandwiches and drew up a list of prospective candidates for their weekly dinner parties.

Neither Julian nor Veronica felt good about this conversation. It was one of many that teetered on the brink of full-scale argument, but mercifully toppled back into the arena of domestic harmony. Both had presumed that married life would bring greater security and assurance to their lives. It was disturbing to find that instead it was making them less sure, less happy with each other.

It was as a direct result of this discussion that they took themselves off to the cinema the next night. Not wanting to go into the centre of London because of the difficulties of parking, the expense of taxis and the dinginess of public transport, they opted for a lesser-known film at one of the South London branch cinemas.

They both regretted their decision immediately. The film was terrible. They should have walked out at once – or at least the moment the girl said: 'Just so long as you still respect me' and started pulling off her jeans with a hungry leer on her face. The problem wasn't that it was pornographic (although Julian found himself wishing that it was); it was simply a badly made, badly acted romantic adventure story with painful aspirations towards profundity. They sat there in the half-empty cinema without touching. Julian did not want to say anything because the film had been Veronica's choice (she was sure she had read a good review of it somewhere) and he felt it was up to her to suggest they leave. But Veronica kept her eyes fixed firmly on the screen. This was the beginning of their new regime of weekly trips to the cinema and she was damned if she was going to give up on the first one. It was just bad luck that the film was not as good as they had been expecting.

'Well, not exactly a contender for this year's Oscar,' he said as they emerged from the cinema into the chilly night.

'Most of those that win Oscars these days aren't much to shout about anyway.'

'Now, come on. What about *Gandhi*, *Chariots of Fire*, *Platoon* . . .'

'They're all pretty sensationalistic . . .'

'And what does sensationalistic mean?'

'Look, Jules, I don't want to get into some heavy discussion about twentieth-century cinema . . .'

'You could have fooled me.'

'All I'm saying is that the general standard of films is pretty low anyway, so the one we just saw wasn't that bad in comparison.'

'So tell me, what did that load of garbage we just wasted two hours staring at have to offer? What morsel of interest, validity or anything else did it have?' He slammed his foot down on the accelerator and they lurched dangerously out of their parking space and into the road.

Veronica pursed her lips. He was trying to annoy her with his driving, so she was determined not to say anything.

'Come on, Veronica. Tell me what you thought was any good about that film.'

'I thought it said something very true about the way women are treated these days.'

'And what was that?' His voice had gone all quiet and tight.

'That in spite of all this claptrap about giving women equal opportunities and things, they still end up getting a raw deal most of the time. I mean that guy pretended for a while that he respected something other than her legs, but in the end it was quite obvious what he was after.'

'Jesus Christ. All you ever see in anything is that one over-cosseted bloody subject about women's bloody rights. You're like those blacks who take everything in terms of a racial insult just because it's the only issue at the front of their own minds.'

'I don't see what racism has got to do with this . . .'

'I was just using it as an example of your rather tedious predilection for translating everything in terms of one single, solitary, boring subject.'

'Julian darling . . .'

'Don't call me darling when we're arguing.' He turned the car sharply into their road.

'We're not arguing, we're just having a discussion . . .'

His damp palms slid on the steering wheel. In spite of the cold night he was sweating.

'Face it, Veronica. We are arguing. We are arguing quite badly. We are not being pleasant to each other. We are not finding it easy being married to each other.' There, he had said it. He jerked the car to a halt, switched off the ignition and sat waiting for her to say something. She sighed heavily.

'Why are you being so melodramatic about this, Julian? Give us a chance. We're only just beginning to work things out . . .'

He let her talk. There didn't seem any point in interrupting. He thought back to his apprehensions in the few weeks leading up to the wedding. Had it all been one ghastly mistake? Not listening to what she was saying, he turned to her suddenly in a final bid to express some of his doubts.

'Do you ever regret it, Veronica – getting married, I mean?'

'Darling, no,' she said at once, throwing her arms around him as best she could with the gear stick and steering wheel in the way. She had interpreted his question as a cry for reassurance about her love for him, when in fact it had been the opposite. Julian would have felt much more comforted if she had admitted to not being sure herself. But she wasn't like that, Veronica. She set her mind on something and did it, believed in it, never wavered from it.

*   *   *

Julian was used to telling Veronica off for wringing the spontaneity out of life by thinking about it too much. Now he found himself unable to stop brooding over his own problems. Before, he had always sat back and let things happen to him, effortlessly watching them fall into place. Life had been the easiest thing in the world to enjoy. Now, after nearly a year of marriage, he found that he couldn't sleep, was constantly irritable and had lost his appetite for both sex and jam sandwiches. What was worse, Veronica did not seem to mind. When he finally plucked up courage to tackle the subject, after a couple of weeks of barely touching her, she had given him a hug, murmured some inanity about being ready whenever he was and promptly turned over and fallen fast asleep.

On the surface he knew he had little to complain of. His wife's reasonable behaviour over every little crisis that creased their daily lives would have been the envy of many a person. But it was driving him mad. So many times he wanted her to explode at him – in anger or love, it didn't matter which – instead of taking everything quietly in her stride and spouting clichéd reassurances about how 'things would work themselves out'. He thought sometimes that she kept all her problems in a tall filing cabinet in her mind. When she felt one needed reviewing, she simply opened the drawer, had a good look and a rummage around, made a few tidy alterations and then closed the drawer again.

Now that they were married, all the romance they had once enjoyed was fast slipping away from them, like sand through an egg-timer. Nasty, insistent stabs of boredom were beginning to jab at him – boredom at the whole business of trying to be good and nice all the time, of feeling he couldn't just let go as in the old days. The routine of living together scared and depressed him with its sameness. Sitting at the same place for dinner, asking each other the same questions after work; he could not believe they could go on like that for ever. But Veronica seemed to expect – and even enjoy – this establishment of a cosy, familiar routine. It was as if she had always thought that marriage would immediately transport them into a dark tunnel of sensibleness and tedium. Likewise, their habit of disagreeing so often – and refusing to admit they were doing so – worried him, while Veronica appeared to take it as a matter of course. It was all part of getting to know each other, she lectured. (If Julian had been able to look behind the scenes of her campaign to win him in the first place, he might well have been warned as to just how pragmatic his wife could be. But Veronica had only referred jokingly to her battles to secure his affections and he had always presumed she was exaggerating.)

The other major problem area which occupied much of Julian's soul-searching as he lay awake at night, concerned this wretched business of women's rights. He did believe in them – or at least in the idea of them. As he frequently reassured Veronica, he respected her intellect as much as the next man's and saw it as only fair that tedious tasks should be shared and work should be equally rewarded regardless of sex. He was firmly convinced of all these things. However, trying to put some of them into practice was confusing and not so easy. When Deirdre went sick, which she did at least once a month, he agreed perfectly with the theory that they should assume joint responsibility for the domestic chores. But what he did not understand was the urgency that Veronica seemed to attach to doing them. He failed to appreciate why the carpets needed to be Hoovered twice a week, when they barely looked stepped on (let alone dirty). Nor could he understand the panic to iron shirts as they were washed, rather than letting a good pile mount up and then attacking the problem in one fell swoop. The big issues, like not minding that she earned nearly as much as he did, were the easy ones. It was the minor details, like why on earth plates had to be dried and put away the moment they were washed, that were the real stumbling blocks.

At heart Julian was a man's man. A good game of rugby meant more to him than a clean house. It always would. Whether through social conditioning or the hazardous link-ups of his genes, this was his nature. And his manliness – although it was of the most conventional, text-book variety – played a large part in why Veronica had been attracted to him in the first place. But she was so immersed in her war for recognition and fairness between the sexes, that she could not step back for a second and see that her criticisms of him were often contradictions of what she was supposed to like about him. If, when she had first met Julian, he had projected himself as a man who scooted round the house with a mop and duster the moment he got in from work, she would not have been half so keen. In fact she probably wouldn't have given him a second look. But Veronica never made these connections. She loved his broad, strong back and the bands of muscle in his long legs. But she now resented the rugby playing that had developed them. She saw it only as an activity that took him for long periods into a world in which she played no part.

So Veronica, although she never once thought of it this way, was busy fighting for a world full of men whom she would not have liked very much. In fact, she was fighting for a world of what she would scathingly have referred to as 'wimps'. For what she failed to realize was that she wanted a man's man as much as Julian wanted to be one.

The question is, can preoccupation with dusting and dry plates fit in with the business of being manly? Julian, as he lay watching car headlights beam across their bedroom walls each night, was slowly coming to the conclusion that it could not. But Veronica, with all her sensible sharing and her dreadful reasonableness, was, he felt, in danger of persuading him otherwise. He could already feel his defences crumbling – she put her arguments so fairly, so calmly and so persistently that it was hard to resist. He was even beginning to believe, as she did, that he should consider turning his energies from rugby to a less time-consuming and more sociable sport that she could join in with . . . Julian turned on to his side for the umpteenth time that night, looking for the elusive comfortable position. Veronica was curled away from him, her legs bent up under her and her arms tucked neatly into her chest. She had kicked the sheets back and her long white nightie was bunched up round her knees. Gently, he ran his finger down the curve of her spine, but she didn't stir. Why didn't she howl in misery and lunge at him with frustration for his lack of sexual drive instead of being so bloody understanding? Why couldn't she act as if she was glad he was a man for once? He would want to make love to her then, he was sure.

After weeks of such thoughts, Julian, for the first time in his life, was bursting for someone to talk to. This was a notion entirely new to him. He had always sneered at people who felt the need to pour out their hearts to their friends, regarding it as a sign of weakness and the height of indiscretion.

That confiding secrets was something girls seemed to go in for more than boys lay at the heart of his prejudice. Veronica, he knew, had regular sessions with various close girlfriends, when they talked for hours about their feelings. She insisted it was purely therapeutic and quite harmless, but it always made him feel threatened. All his worst suspicions had been confirmed when one of these girlie-talks, as he called them, had taken place under his own roof. An old girlfriend had stayed on late after one of their weekly dinner parties. Feeling a little superfluous, Julian eventually excused himself and went to bed. About half an hour later, on a last trip from the bedroom to the loo, he heard his own name being mentioned and stopped to listen. This unhappy coincidence had resulted in thirty very uncomfortable minutes spent leaning over the banisters straining to hear it all. Veronica was in full, articulate swing on the subject of her husband's attitude towards sharing jobs around the house. Not all that she said was critical, and some of it was positively generous. What annoyed Julian more than anything was the ringing note of patronage in her voice, as if he was some child being schooled in the basics of correct behaviour. That and of course the fact of being talked about like that, dissected like some helpless specimen pinned down under a lens.

After much deliberation Julian decided he might as well have a go at talking to Teddy – just to sound him out for a bit of friendly advice and support. But there remained the problem, that in all their years of friendship, they had never really talked to each other. Not really. Ever since prep school being friends had meant playing sports, breaking rules, and later, drinking and having fun generally. When they talked it was more of a banter than any sort of exchange of feeling. They'd had good thrashes on all the major subjects of course – religion and politics and so on – but only ever after lots to drink. Open analysis of their emotions was something which they had, by tacit mutual agreement, avoided. Ted barely mentioned his father, just as Julian avoided the subject of his mother. Since he was only seven when she left, this was perhaps not so surprising. But there were moments, later on, when he would have liked to talk to someone, especially when it dawned on him that she was never going to visit, and when the first of his father's lady friends planted her gooey lips on his and said they were going to be great friends.

'It's you and me, little man,' his father used to say, 'and boys together always have a good time. Women only get in the way of things – though I'm not saying I wasn't very fond of your mother once upon a time. And of course it is healthy to have a lady about the place.' And sure enough there always was, one lady or another, about the Blake place. If ever Julian's mother was mentioned, it was always in terms that suggested she had died many years before. Nannies took care of the child during the holidays and boarding school saw to the rest of it. Only when Julian could wield cricket bats, tennis rackets and pints of beer did Lionel Blake start to take a real interest in his son. The two of them developed the same type of hearty relationship that Julian enjoyed with his friends. They played tennis and squash together and drank fine wines over lunch. At sixty his father was slim and well kept, with sharp blue eyes and a vicious backhand slice which meant he still won the odd set or two. Over their lunches they talked business or sport. Julian felt something akin to competition on both subjects, brought on largely by his father's ceaseless confidence and energy. Lionel Blake played everything to win and expected his son to do the same – whether the stakes were a bottle of scotch or a million pounds worth of business. Nurtured on such ethics, no wonder Julian had never learnt to talk about anything personal. Problems in Blake terminology meant tricky decisions at work and getting the knack of a good topspin, not washing-up and women. So it was with much hesitation and trepidation that he came to the decision to try and talk to Teddy. Apart from anything else, it was no secret that none of his friends – especially Teddy – had ever been very keen on Veronica, let alone the idea of him getting married.

* * *

'I seriously think I'm getting too old for it,' said Teddy morosely, staring into his murky pint of beer as if it might hold some secret answer to his problems. 'I swear I hurt more after a match than I ever used to.'

'Don't be absurd,' said Julian, but without much conviction. 'What about Dusty Hare? He's still as fit as hell and he's got at least five years on you.'

'I think something psychological happens after thirty,' went on Teddy slowly, ignoring Julian's efforts at consolation. 'Not when you're thirty – then you're still all right, just – but each year afterwards; it all gets more of an effort.'

'Of course it does, you ass. It's called middle age.' They were both on their seventh pint. Julian had bought most of the rounds with the aim of getting to a state of mind where he felt capable of bringing up the subject of Veronica. Instead, the drinking seemed to be pushing Ted into one of his philosophical, depressive moods and Julian was doing all the reassuring and cajoling. There was only half an hour or so till last orders.

'Ever think about getting married?' he ventured at last.

Teddy burped and shook his head vehemently. 'Not bloody likely. It's bad enough getting old, without getting bloody married as well.'

'Yup. It certainly presents a few problems – having a wife I mean.'

Julian eyed his friend hopefully, waiting for him to lift his head, look him in the eyes and ask him if anything was wrong.

'Of course it does. Everybody knows wives are a problem. I always said you were mad, Jules . . .'

'Actually you never said anything very much. And you agreed to be best man.' Julian's tone was almost accusing, like a child looking for someone else to blame.

'Well, it wouldn't have made any difference if I had, would it?' For a second Teddy sounded angry. But he quickly checked himself: 'And I couldn't turn down an opportunity to take to the stage again could I? In fact that speech was, I feel sure, one of my greatest triumphs before a captive audience . . .'

'So you definitely think I was wrong then, to marry Veronica?' Julian knew he was being pathetic, but he had the booze to blame and he felt very sorry for himself.

'I don't think anything, my dear chap, as you of all people should know . . . except, that is, that we've just time for another round before our jovial host shoves us out the door. My turn to do the honours I believe?' Teddy drained Julian's glass as well as his own and made his way, a little unsteadily, to the bar.

Julian felt defeated. He was sure Ted knew what he wanted, but the bastard just wouldn't cooperate. The thought of his life becoming nothing more than a daily challenge to pretend everything was all right appalled him. Then it struck him that that was precisely what Teddy had been doing for as long as he could remember. A surge of drunken compassion for his friend heaved somewhere between his stomach and his heart. But there was nothing he could do with it, nothing he could think of to say that was acceptable and would express a part of how sorry he felt – for Teddy, for himself, for everything.

'Here's a toast to friendship,' was all he managed, raising his refilled pint-glass.

'For God's sake drink the stuff and stop talking so much,' Teddy took an enormous gulp of beer and kept his eyes averted from Julian's.

6 ♪

George and Katherine

'You're mad of course,' said Peter Sidcup, as he carefully decanted a bottle of vintage port into a milk jug, using a handkerchief as a strainer.

'Don't tell me you're envious, Sids,' put in Teddy.

'Sometimes you are besieged by the strangest notions Edward. Of course I'm not envious. I am never envious. I'm just trying to warn our mutual friend here of the impossibility of the challenge that he sees before him.' He was referring to George, who, ever since his phone call to Katherine, had talked of little else but their prospective date.

George sighed long-sufferingly and put down his paper. 'And why, Mr Sidcup, am I mad? I can only think Teddy must be right. You've probably been trying to get Katherine for years. Only being the secretive so and so that you are, you've never told us about it. I would say "fortunate" describes my position more than "mad", wouldn't you agree, Ted?' George was riding high on a new crest of confidence. He felt more than a match for Peter's bantering, especially as Ted seemed to be on his side.

'Ted, come and hold this blasted handkerchief would

you?' A considerable quantity of the precious liquid was spilling over to join all the other stains on the piano-top.

'You are mad, George, because Katherine Vermont is a cold fish. Or, to put it more crudely, the dear girl is frigid. F-R-I-G-I-D. This means, George, that when you place your warm hand on her cold thigh between your sprinkling of artichoke hearts and your slivers of duck breast à l'orange, it will remain cold. Her thigh that is. She doesn't like to be touched you see.'

'And I suppose you know because you've tried have you?' asked George, trying to sound nonchalant but actually very annoyed. 'I can't say I blame her for rejecting you . . .'

'My knowledge in this matter is not based on what you might call first-hand experience, George, no – hold up the corners a bit more could you, Ted? – but it is nonetheless to be relied on.'

'You are a prig sometimes, Sids. What are you on about – I thought you hardly knew Katherine anyway?' said Teddy.

'No, I don't know her at all. But she's always been there, on the fringes as it were. And report has it – indeed many reports have it – that she is simply not interested in sexual relations. With men at least. As for other possibilities I don't know anyone that's tried.'

'Now you're just being bloody rude.'

'I can assure you, George, I do not wish to offend either you, or your new-found lady love. I am merely warning you not to be disappointed if your suit fails. And now shall we sample some of this nectar of the gods?'

Teddy followed Peter into the kitchen.

'Go easy on him, Sids. He's so bloody excited about the whole business. It seems a bit of a shame.'

Peter looked seriously at his friend. 'I do realize that. And for that reason he's going to be all the more disappointed. I only meant it as a gentle warning. He's such a twit about women.'

Back in the sitting-room, Peter was noticeably kinder to George. 'If you really want to make a killing, old chap, you ought to come along to the Beauchamps' do with us on Friday. It's fancy dress, should be rather amusing. Lots of nymphettes to go round for everyone. It's one of the Beauchamp girls' twenty-firsts – I can't remember which, there are so many of them. All called things like Felicity, Melicity, Duplicity, Electricity . . .'

'For God's sake,' said George, laughing, 'I think you need your brain looking at sometimes, Sids. Of course, I'd like to go – but, as usual, I haven't bloody well been invited, have I?'

'Well, I don't think it's beyond the wit of man to fix a small detail like that, George. Say "aye" and the matter is settled.'

'Aye, aye, aye,' said George, grinning. Peter smiled back and raised his glass.

'To the party then.'

'To the party!' agreed George heartily.

Teddy raised his eyebrows in mock despair and flicked on the television.

'It's only a bloody party,' he said, refilling his glass with port.

*   *   *

Everybody was going to the Beauchamps' party. Everybody, that is, except Katherine who had turned down the invitation as soon as it arrived – several weeks back when she had been going through one of her extreme retiring phases. Over the years she had noticed that there were some periods when she almost came out of herself again, when she felt nearly normal about accepting things like invitations to parties. Then, for no apparent reason, the pendulum would swing right back to where it started and the very idea of talking, about anything except work, to another person became abhorrent, terrifying.

Peter's diagnosis of Katherine's condition as a case of frigidity had been cruel, but indirectly correct. During her teenage romance with Julian she had learnt enough about the human body's capacity for sexual enjoyment to ensure that she never turned against the sexual act itself. What she had turned against instead was the entire human race. Frigidity on a grand scale. The coldness inside seemed to seek equivalents in the outside world, looking for elements that reflected rather than consoled it. Shunning human contact was just one facet of this. Cold sheets were another.

The fancy-dress party would not have been too difficult for her to handle. She knew this herself even as she had carefully, in beautiful italics, composed a formal refusal: 'Katherine Vermont thanks Felicity very much for her kind invitation but regrets . . .' Her whole life-style was a masquerade anyway. But on the day she replied the sense of acting out a part had been particularly burdensome. During these bad patches she needed her time alone, each evening, more than ever in order to refuel herself for the next day's effort. Like an actress recharging herself between the performances of a long, exhausting run.

Trying to fight her urge for solitude was something Katherine found very hard indeed. She did try and fight it, every now and then, but it made her more miserable than ever. Then she would ask herself what the fight was about anyway. Why pretend to want to go out, to talk to stupid people about stupid things, while eating and drinking stuff that she loathed? Why try and be 'normal' anyway? Whatever that meant. So what if she didn't like going out and seeing people? Given that the outside world was really rather a vile place, full of misery and meanness, it was much more natural to want to avoid close contact with it than to seek it. Some people sought happiness and comfort by talking to each other. Katherine did it by popping black olives dipped in brown sugar into her mouth while watching entire series of American soaps on her video. She was one of those rare people, she told herself, who had the courage to experiment with happiness on her own. That her private indulgences brought her nothing more than a few minutes of short-lived, physical gratification was an aspect that she tried not to dwell on.

When the time came she did suffer more than a pang of regret at having refused the Beauchamp thrash. Not because she really wanted to go, but because it would have been an opportunity either to tell George Smithers their date was off or at least to get his phone number from somebody so that she could call to cancel. But she had thrown the invitation away, the Beauchamp phone number was not immediately to hand – (Katherine made a point of not exchanging phone numbers) – and it all seemed too much effort. There was still a week or so in which to wriggle out of her dinner with George. And even if she didn't manage to contact him in time, she reckoned she could probably survive one meal. She could tell him she was going away for several months' break, or that she was secretly very involved with another man or . . . she pushed these thoughts to the back of her mind and removed her yoghurt carton from a half-hour stay in the deep freeze. She especially liked it when it was on the verge of freezing – it went sort of hard on the top, all squelchy underneath and deliciously cool to swallow. She closed her eyes in bliss as she ate, her tongue darting in and out of the soft brown mixture like a small snake; so much more pleasurable than using a spoon.

7 ∫

The Party

One of the things George Smithers envied most about his flatmates was that they could make other people laugh. Peter because he had an extremely sharp wit and Teddy because he could tell jokes. He did all the different accents and actions so brilliantly that no matter how bad the story people always ended up in stitches. George concentrated very hard when he heard a really good joke, storing it away for a time when it would come in handy. But, somehow, even if he related it word for word, exactly as it had been said to him, his audience never reacted in the same way. He was wise enough to steer clear of Teddy's variety of long, intricate tales; but even with the shortest one-liners, George's punchlines fell flat. Or else he had that most loathesome of feelings, that the laughter was at him rather than the joke.

These experiences should perhaps have warned him in some way as to how he should tackle his costume for the fancy-dress party at the Beauchamps'. But he was very busy at work that week and there really wasn't too much time to think at all. Peter and Teddy said very little on the subject and the night before the party they were both out until late. The main intention at the back of George's mind was to be original in some way. He stared hopelessly into his small, cramped wardrobe and racked his brains. No inspiration came. So he opened a tin of baked beans and watched television till close-down, hoping that Ted and Sids would get back so he could consult them on the matter. But neither of them appeared and he began to feel sleepy. Punk-rocker, cowboy, wizard – none of them seemed possible on the basis of two pairs of corduroys, two suits and twenty-five shirts. He got temporarily excited at the idea of putting a tie round his head and calling himself a Red Indian. But the problem of the feather proved too much. It was just as his eyes were closing that a magic thought did at last occur to him. It was all a question of making use of limited resources, he congratulated himself. And what better resources than his bed linen? Yes, George's imagination had finally exploded into a magnificent vision of himself as a Roman Emperor. With the image of him and Katherine, both in flowing white gowns, feeding each other grapes from a large bowl of luscious fruit, he fell into a deep, self-satisfied sleep.

* * *

'Gt cktail. Mt yu at pty. Addrs; 42 Egerton Mews. P and T'. The note was pinned to the loo door underneath an old postcard of Prince Charles and Lady Di.

George was a bit disappointed, or rather daunted. It was all very well for the others – they at least knew their hosts. Arriving on his own at all would be quite a test of courage, given the fancy dress aspect of the thing. Then he realized that the scribble said nothing about the time the party started. He would simply have to find the original invitation. Entering the normally forbidden sanctuary of Peter's bedroom, George saw immediately that he wasn't going to have any luck. The room was virtually bare. Peter tolerated negotiating Teddy's dirty laundry in the sitting-room, but his own quarters showed a tidiness that verged on asceticism. There were no papers, no ornaments and no clutter. If George got an invitation he kept it for years. But Peter's mantelpiece had nothing on it except for a gold carriage clock and a small silver picture-frame containing a photo of his sister Mary and their parents. The frame was worn and travelled, but the smiles on the three faces were as warm as ever.

Although he was annoyed and in a hurry, George had time to marvel at the strict, empty order of the room. What did Peter do with all the paraphernalia that choked everyone else's lives, he wondered. Yesterday's tie, the odd sock, half-read books, letters, blunt pencils, newspapers? It really was rather remarkable. He closed the door, almost reverently, and spent a few minutes rummaging around the sitting-room and kitchen. Both were passing through particularly squalid phases and his search lacked the dedication necessary for success. All he could come up with were several old invitations, whose average starting time – he actually worked it out – was seven thirty. It was already seven. He was going to have to hurry.

George was glad he had his own transport, parked only a few feet from the front door. But he still took the trouble to check the street was clear before gathering the sheet up round his legs, scurrying down the stairs like some timid ghost and making a dash for the car door. Once inside, it was quite a wrestle arranging his costume so that it allowed him to drive. The sheets seemed to get awfully tied up in everything. In the end he had to yank the bedding right up round his thighs – exposing two hairless, white knees – in order to give his legs the necessary freedom to work the pedals.

Getting the sheet to comply with his vision of a Roman Emperor had proved more of a challenge than he expected. An urgent need for safety pins had soon revealed itself. All George had was two single sheets, neither of which – either separately or in combination – 'draped' as he wanted them to. Several more rummages through the flat had produced the grand total of three safety pins, which was cutting things very fine indeed. After various failed experiments with Sellotape, he had resorted to tying knots in strategic places. But tying knots used up lots of valuable sheet, preventing it from hanging in the right way over the right areas. In the end, by using both sheets, all three safety pins and various knots, he did manage to arrange things so that one shoulder was bare and the rest of him covered, more or less. The finishing touch was a bootlace, swiped out of one of Teddy's rugby boots, tied round his head and intertwined with some green leaves which he tore off the only living plant in the flat. He was almost pleased with the result. It was such an improvement on his earliest efforts that this was not altogether surprising. What he did not realize was how far he had compromised his original vision in the process.

Fortunately Egerton Mews turned out to be not very far from the flat in Thurloe Road. George clambered out of his MG, so intent on getting to the front door without any passersby spotting him, that he failed to notice the lack of cars in the street. Once safely inside the porch, he took a deep breath, pushed his bootlace a little higher above his eyebrows and rang the bell. It was answered by a scruffy man in jeans.

'Jesus Christ,' said the scruffy man.

'Who is it?' called a female voice from upstairs.

'I think it's a guest, miss.'

George wanted to run away, but it was too late. A young girl with lots of freckles and a snub nose, also wearing jeans, came running down the stairs.

'Gosh, who are you?' she asked, unashamedly looking his sheet up and down and giggling.

The colour of George's face mirrored the depth of his embarrassment.

'I, I, I am sorry . . .' he stuttered. 'I'm George, a friend of Peter Sidcup's . . . are you . . . I mean . . . is this where the party is?'

'Oh, yes, it's my twenty-first. But you're just a teeny bit early.' She and the scruffy man were both laughing openly now. 'I haven't even had my bath yet . . .'

'Darling, who is it?' A woman, with an identical snub nose but a much older face, appeared from behind.

George tried to leave. He began backing off and excusing himself, but the young girl grabbed him by the arm and insisted he stay. Her mother agreed and so he was pulled into the house and told to make himself at home. The ladies disappeared upstairs and the man, who explained that he was the DJ, showed him where the kitchen was. The house was enormous – bigger than any George had ever been in in London. He took a bottle of beer from the fridge and went to sit, as inconspicuously as possible, on a rolled-up carpet at the end of the largest of the rooms. All about him, teams of workers were moving furniture, positioning lights, setting up microphones and covering long tables with glasses, bottles, and hundreds of trays of food. He tried to help himself to a miniature sausage roll, but got told off by a fierce lady in a waitress outfit. It looked more like the preparations for a major press conference than a birthday party. Every so often the disc jockey would glance over at him from amidst a maze of wires and machines, and crease up with laughter . . .

The party began at quarter past nine, by which time the swarms of workers had vanished, leaving glistening floors, laden tables and not a wire in sight. 'We're Having a Party' started blaring out of the speakers and the Beauchamp sisters came bustling down the stairs. There were three of them, all a mass of crinoline, elaborate wigs, beauty spots and plunging neck-lines. George could not believe his eyes. They looked ready for a film set or something. Felicity, clad entirely in green velvet and white lace, was Scarlett O'Hara; her elder sister, in blue velvet, was Marie Antoinette; while the younger one was decked out as a prissy-looking Snow White. They all thought George extremely funny, but fortunately got interrupted from telling him so by the doorbell which started ringing at nine fifteen exactly and kept going every few seconds.

Never had George felt more inadequate in his life. The costumes of every guest were truly splendid. He found himself cowering behind pillars, self-consciously hoicking up his sheet and fiddling with his bootlace. He hoped, more than anything else, that Katherine Vermont had not been invited. She was the last person in the world he wanted to see him like this. After several glasses of champagne he plucked up the courage to make conversation with a rather despondent Minnie Mouse. She turned out to be quite drunk and very depressed about someone called Hugo.

As discreetly as he could, George started flicking his eyes over her shoulder for any signs of Peter and Teddy.

'There's no need to be so fucking obvious about it,' she hissed. 'If you find my company tedious, why the fuck don't you go away?'

'All right,' said George, and sidled off into the crowd of Henry VIIIs, Mad Hatters, Anne Boleyns and Alice in Wonderlands to try and identify his friends.

*   *   *

Julian and Veronica quarrelled quite badly on the way to the party. On the face of it the argument was about Julian's choice of route for getting across London to Egerton Mews.

Veronica, the A–Z open on her lap, kept issuing instructions which her husband ignored. Then they got stuck in a bad traffic jam and she couldn't resist an 'I-told-you-so' remark which sparked the whole disagreement into motion. Actually, they were in bad moods with each other for quite different reasons. Underneath their petty quibbles about directions lay all sorts of steaming resentments which had been building up over the days and weeks before.

In spite of numerous discussions well in advance of the occasion, getting their costumes sorted out had been a last-minute rush which Veronica had had to manage all on her own. The previous weekend one of Julian's precious rugby matches had prevented them going to the fancy-dress hire-shop together. She had taken his measurements along and chosen a very elaborate Henry VIII for him to collect later in the week, since it needed a couple of minor alterations. She had gone for an Elizabeth I outfit on which she had paid a deposit and left to be collected at the same time. Julian had the car for his rugby and she did not fancy struggling with the thing on public transport. He had not exactly jumped for joy when she revealed her choice of costume for him, although he failed to come up with any definite reason why. When she suggested, jokingly, that it was because he had to wear tights and a wig he got very annoyed. Then he claimed to be far too busy at work to collect the costumes during the week, even though the shop was a mere ten-minute drive from his office. Furious with him, since she was frantically busy as well, Veronica ended up rushing over there last thing on Friday and carting the wretched things home herself, by taxi. For this Julian had been grateful. But by then the damage had been done.

On top of all that Veronica had very bad period pains. The last thing she felt like doing was squeezing her bloated, tender stomach into a tight corset and prancing round a dance floor, balancing a crown on her head. She told Julian how poorly she felt and he said he was sorry, but she knew he didn't really understand. Not really. The theory of the matter was clear enough: that there were a few days in every month when a girl felt like death and cried easily. But underneath his murmurings of sympathy she always sensed an intolerance. Ill health and physical weakness made Julian impatient, even with himself. It also went against Veronica's own principles to play on the biological differences between men and women. So, silently stuffing her small evening bag with Tampax and Disprin, she resolved not to complain any more. But her eyes shone with martyrdom and unacknowledged suffering, piling yet another layer of tension on top of all the others.

They had to park miles away from the right house because by the time they arrived Egerton Mews was already packed with cars. On the long trek to the front door Julian marched on ahead, his silence and his long stride communicating better than any words could, how annoyed he was. She knew her slow, tottering progress at his heels was only fuelling his fury. But she felt hard-done-by too, so she was damned if she was going to hurry just to please him . . .

They heard the music long before they got to number 42. And when they did finally arrive, the very walls of the house seemed to be throbbing with the vibrations. Veronica remarked that the neighbours would surely complain. Julian grunted in reply. Then the door opened and they stepped into the hubbub of lights and smoke and music and bodies. After they had found Felicity and wished her a happy birthday, Veronica rushed off to the loo to swallow some more Disprin and Julian said he would find them both drinks. But then Veronica bumped into Felicity's older sister, Marie Antoinette, who was much more her friend and they got chatting. Meanwhile Julian, swigging at both glasses of champagne, was beginning to think that he might be in the mood for a party after all. In spite of initial reservations he was rather proud of his Henry VIII gear, although it was a trifle hot. He'd hardly moved and already beads of sweat were creeping out from under his wig and slipping down his temples. But the champagne was cool and dry. He picked up a fresh couple of glasses and looked round for any sign of his wife. Instead his eye was caught by a figure in knotted sheets, trussed up like some unplucked turkey ready for the slaughter.

'My God, George Smithers, you're a braver man than I,' he shouted over the strains of 'I can't get no satisfaction'.

'I've had quite enough comments already thank you, Julian. The only person who's been half-decent is old Nell Gwyn here.' He indicated his companion with his glass, spilling most of its contents as he did so. The lady to whom he referred was Gloria Croft, former bridesmaid and best friend to Julian's wife.

'Gloria, you look ravishing,' said Julian, bending down to kiss her.

'Darling, so do you. And how thoughtful of you to bring me some more champagne.' She cheekily snatched one of the glasses out of his hand.

'Married life obviously suits you, Julian.' She looked up and down his tall figure, lingering exaggeratedly on the white tights. 'I never knew you had such nice legs,' she purred, blinking her cat-green eyes and shaking her auburn curls.

'Well, you never looked did you?'

'Well, you never asked me to did you?' She smiled at him.

'What?' said George.

Gloria linked her arm through George's and chinked glasses with him.

'We're feeling quite left out, us unmarried ones, these days, aren't we, George?'

'Oh, rather,' said George, not following her train of thought, but thoroughly enjoying the attention.

'It has its disadvantages you know,' said Julian, looking hard at Gloria's oranges.

'Like what for instance?' put in George, sensing that the conversation was somehow moving on to a level that did not involve him.

'Oh, I don't know, George, various things, like er . . . the tax position for a married couple isn't as comfortable as . . .'

Gloria burst into giggles and splashed some champagne down the front of her Nell Gwyn outfit. Julian insisted on offering her his handkerchief, over-ruling George's protestations that she make use of all or part of his sheet. After an inordinate fuss had been made of the tiny mishap Gloria carefully folded Julian's hanky and handed it back to him.

'There, is that better?'

Julian stared at Gloria's high, deep cleavage, rising out of a neckline so low that he could not help marvelling at how everything managed to stay packaged in its proper place.

'Yes, that's great,' he said. 'And, if I haven't said so already, I think that's a stunning outfit, Gloria. Are they real?' He pulled at one of the many oranges draped across her back and arms like a shawl, at the same time thinking that she looked rather like a round, ripe orange herself; juicy, ready to be peeled and eaten.

'Of course not, silly. It would weigh a ton if they were – and I'd pong of orange. George, darling,' she tweaked his ear, 'you couldn't be a love and get me some more champers could you?'

George rushed off to oblige, glad, for reasons that he had not yet worked out in his own mind, to get away from the two of them for a bit.

*　　*　　*

The whole thing was ridiculous of course. In spite of his last-minute doubts, Julian had never entered marriage with the idea of being unfaithful, or at least not so early on. At the back of his mind there had been the hazy notion that the odd slip-up was bound to occur sooner or later. But so soon – only a year after their marriage – never. But then he had not anticipated quite what a trial being married was going to be, nor how demoralized it would make him feel. Even a few months previously the idea of kissing Gloria Croft amongst the folds of some large velvet curtains would have been totally absurd. But by taking small steps, situations that would otherwise be unthinkable can be arrived at. It is the gradual approach, the gentle sliding downwards that makes them possible.

In the case of Julian and Gloria, both of them had been tiptoeing, unknowingly, towards the grope behind the Beauchamps' curtains for many months. When they had first met, a few years earlier, Julian only had eyes for Veronica. Perhaps, as a sensible lover, he subconsciously protected himself from the messy dangers of being attracted to best friends. But Gloria and Veronica's friendship was on the wane anyway, so she was hardly around for him to be tempted. When the moment came however, Gloria, as a person, was barely relevant; it certainly wasn't as if Julian had spent years suppressing violent passions for the girl. She just happened to be standing in the right place at the appropriate time. And she just happened to be in a certain frame of mind herself.

Gloria Croft was the sort of girl who recognized a good-looking man when she saw one, and Julian, with his fair hair and tall athletic body, had always fallen into this category. But one of the main precepts of her life when it came to boyfriends was to avoid competition if at all possible. The important thing for her was a clean, unchallenged conquest. If things looked threatening in any way she simply didn't compete. That way she could never lose. So she had closed her sexual antennae to Julian and let him and Veronica get on with it. Their wedding, apart from the service itself, had been fun: lots of admiring glances, flirtatious chats and several invitations to parties.

It was shortly after Veronica's wedding that Gloria first began to feel a flicker of uncertainty in her hitherto unbridled friendliness towards life in general and the male species in particular. She still rushed around with a posse of eager men in hot pursuit, but for some reason a degree of fun seemed to be fading from the chase. Although only twenty-nine, Gloria's face was beginning to show – unfairly early she thought – a few lines of experience. She seriously wondered if this might be the result of so many late nights of collapsing into bed without bothering to wipe her make-up off, leading to bleary-eyed confrontations with the mirror in the morning. Worse still, the small bulges on the side of her big toes had been officially diagnosed as bunions. This depressed her very deeply. To have bunions did not do at all. It did not fit in with her own image of herself, let alone the portrait she projected for her admirers. It added another complication to the business of sharing a bed with any of them; since now she had to make sure her feet stayed well out of sight, so as not to shatter any romantic moments with their deformity. Until the feet problem, the only nuisance had been diving for the bathroom in the morning – before whoever it was opened his eyes – so as to assemble an acceptable face out of the crinkled havoc wrought by the night before. But this was never too difficult. It was an early, useful discovery of hers that men seemed to expect women to spend hours in the bathroom at any time of the day or night.

So, Gloria was beginning, however ridiculously, to feel old. She was also – although the two do not necessarily go together – beginning to feel lonely. Married friends were not the same as single friends, she discovered. Something was lost; a common bond of experience simply disappeared. Until so many of her girlfriends got married she had no idea how much she relied on talking to them. Now they still talked, but without that thrilling, comforting sense of shared secrets. For they never opened up about their husbands as they once had about their boyfriends. Gloria came to recognize it as a tell-tale sign of a relationship that was getting close to 'solidifying' (as she put it), when the girl involved suddenly shut up like a clam. No more juicy tidbits about little squabbles and reconciliations; the subject became taboo overnight. That in itself would have been almost bearable, since Gloria was quite happy to talk to sympathetic ears, even if they did not respond in kind. The truly unbearable part was that she perceived increasing bristles of disapproval in their married voices and looks, for her way of life. Given that most of them had carried on exactly as she did in their single days, she found this especially riling and put it down to jealousy for their own lost freedom. But whatever it was – jealousy, hypocrisy or plain nastiness – there were now many more of them than her.

Invitations to things were never a problem, although it was mostly to big parties that she got asked these days. Married couples seemed to prefer inviting other married couples to share their food. If she was lucky enough to be summoned to a dinner table, there was usually some frightful yawning bore, with acne scars and thinning hair, who had been enlisted as her opposite number. It was all very trying. Parties were certainly easier: she could at least exercise some personal choice in the matter.

But now even the parties were getting to be tedious. She knew everybody so well and any new, interesting faces tended to be on very young shoulders. Gloria had not yet got so obsessed with her wrinkles that she dare not approach such youngsters. The trouble was simply that she found them very immature and not good for much more than a dance and a giggle. It was just beginning to strike her quite how small her social world was and how restricted its mode of development. Things moved in one direction only, like toothpaste through an endless tube. Everybody got squeezed along the same tunnel, gradually teaming up, pairing off and moving on, making way for the younger ones to enter the same tunnel and proceed in exactly the same way. Now a few of them, like Gloria, found themselves caught in an air bubble, suddenly left out of the mainstream. Obviously, this handful were all there partly because they had not found any answers in each other either, so they offered little real consolation. They looked after each other; took each other out to dinner, danced together, laughed together and sometimes slept together, but none of it was going anywhere and any of them with half a brain knew it.

It was as a result of this that one of Gloria's best friends during recent months had been Teddy. She had rung up one evening – to cancel a dinner that she had rashly agreed to with poor old George, who had been mooning around her for years – to find that only Ted was in and that he was in the mood for company.

'Have dinner with me instead – tonight,' he said. Gloria was surprised and even a little flattered. Ted was one of those men who seemed so wrapped up in his man's world of drinking and sport that he never had time to be interested in chasing ladies. He wasn't very attractive either, at least not in Gloria's terms. His body was large and thick-set, with what had once been hard muscle now visibly relaxing into soft, spare flesh. He made no secret of the fact that the social side of rugby interested him far more than the physical. But she liked his face which was interesting and elastic, and the way his kind eyes peered out, rather shyly, from under all that dark curly hair.

'Well, I am honoured I must say. What are we celebrating?'

'Nothing in particular. I'm just in the mood for a meal out and no one's around.'

'Well, perhaps I'm not so honoured after all. You really know how to make a girl feel wanted – I hope you don't speak to your sweetheart like that.' (Gloria was one of those who believed that since Teddy never appeared publicly with a girl he must be having a secret affair with a highly unsuitable, probably married woman.)

Teddy ignored the remark. 'What do you say? I'll even offer to pay.'

'Well, that definitely settles it then.' Ted's directness could be so refreshing.

So the two of them had found themselves eating spaghetti, drinking liberal quantities of house-red and thoroughly enjoying each other's company. Gloria was good at getting people to talk, especially men. And for both of them it was easier to talk to each other than to friends of the same sex. Their first outing was such a success that they repeated the occasion several times. Their dinners were always characterized by lots of talking and lots of drinking; they tended to drag each other down, but always felt better for doing so. Most interesting of all for Gloria was that this was the first truly sexless friendship she had ever had with a man. Until Teddy, all men who swam into her sights contained at least a germ of sexual potential. Sometimes it was just a speck, a hint in a grin, a quick exchange of glances or even, as with Julian for example, a knowledge that there could be a sexual development if circumstances had been different. With Teddy there was nothing. That first evening she wondered if he entertained any hopes about getting her into bed after the pasta. When he clearly didn't (he hailed her a cab outside the restaurant and saw her into it with the most brotherly of cheek-pecks), she tried to feel insulted.

But she soon gave up the effort, admitted to herself that it made a nice change and proceeded to enjoy the company of a human being who constituted no threat to her at all. To her surprise, she sensed that he needed someone to talk to. Behind that supple smile, she discovered, lay a hint of loneliness that she would never have expected or imagined possible in one so popular and busy. So I'm not the only one who struggles, she thought.

*   *   *

It was very hot behind the curtains. Gloria's auburn ringlets were all a jumble and her cheeks glowed with the heat of arousal. Julian was an even better kisser than she had imagined. She confided this thought to him and he kissed her again, but hurriedly. They had been too long already. He pulled his wig back on and fumbled with his shirt buttons.

'Here, let me . . . perhaps next time we could find a slightly more comfortable venue,' she whispered, as she attended to his shirt.

Julian nodded, speechless with the heat, the frustration and shock at his own behaviour.

'You could perhaps drop by my place one evening next week? Only if you want to of course – I mean I quite understand . . .'

'Thursdays are good,' he croaked.

'I'll be waiting for you.' She gave him a quick kiss on the nose and disappeared before he could say anything else. He continued sitting at the scene of their crime – on the window-seat behind the ample sweeps of curtain in the main dancing area. His blood was still racing; thumping round his body, beating with the heavy rhythms of the music. No one had seen them, he was sure. They had danced briefly, before slipping behind the curtains. No one could see anything out there. The place was a sea of flashing disco lights, gyrating bodies and unfamiliar painted faces. That's what had made the whole astonishing episode possible – the animal impersonality of it all. They had hardly said a word, as if it had all been obvious from the start what was going to happen. That had made it easier too – the not-talking. He had read in those green eyes of hers that she would let him kiss her if he wanted to. And he had wanted to terribly. And now he wanted even more, which was why he would go to her on Thursday, when Veronica thought he was going to rugby training.

Julian slipped out from his hiding-place and passed unnoticed through the mass of dancers back into the crowds of those still more concerned with eating and drinking. He spotted Veronica almost immediately. She was talking to Teddy and Peter and looked quite happy. He felt absurdly normal.

'Hello, darling, your champagne got warm so I've been dishing it out to other women instead. I see you're in good company with these two Al Capones here.' (His friends were rather thinly disguised as gangsters.)

'You look rather hot in that get-up,' said Teddy.

'Positively steaming I'd say . . .' put in Peter.

'Have you been dancing?' asked Veronica.

'In a manner of speaking. I took Gloria for a quick spin. But I don't recommend it at all – it's worse than a sauna in there.' This is easy, he thought.

'Oh, good, where is Gloria? I haven't seen her for ages.'

'She whizzed off somewhere . . . I really must get myself a drink or I'll die of thirst. Anyone else?'

'There she is,' exclaimed Veronica, 'right next to the bar. You couldn't post her over here while you're at it could you darling? I don't think she's seen me yet.'

'Sure thing.' Clutching several empty glasses Julian threaded his way to the bar.

'My wife wants to talk to you,' he said grinning stupidly,

'about nothing in particular, I think. She's over there.' They both looked in the direction of Veronica, who was beckoning at them with a white gloved hand.

'She's Queen Elizabeth I,' said Julian.

'I'd never have guessed. Well, I'll see you in a minute then.'

'Yup. See you in a sec.'

Without the animal spirits, there was just embarrassment. The whole thing was barmy. Thank God they hadn't done more than kiss. It would be rugby training on Thursday after all.

'Sorry,' said Veronica.

'What for?'

'Being such a beast earlier on. It was my period that did it. I'm feeling much better now, though tired. I shouldn't have had that dance with George, but I felt so sorry for him, the silly twit. Everybody laughing like that and him trying to look as if he didn't mind.'

George Smithers' humiliations that evening had reached an unforeseeable climax shortly after midnight. Felicity's father had taken over the disc jockey's microphone, first of all to make a rather sickening speech about how wonderful his daughter was, and then to hand out prizes for the best fancy-dress costumes. After Alice in Wonderland, Lord Nelson and Boadicea had received various boxes of chocolates and magnums of champagne for their sartorial efforts, Lord Beauchamp handed the microphone over to his wife. In a shy, quiet voice, Lady Beauchamp informed the scores of shining faces before her that she had decided to present a booby prize to the person whose costume she found most endearing. Her choice for this honour, as it turned out, was 'that tubby little ghost who arrived early'.

Everyone looked round, their hearts rising in gratitude that it wasn't them. George was edging for the door. He had told all enquirers he was a Roman Emperor. He had not mentioned arriving early to anyone. Escape was possible – or it would have been if the scruffy disc jockey had not started searching the room with a spotlight. It fell his way just as he was about to make the final dash.

'There he is!' he shouted. And the game was up. There was more laughing than clapping as the crowds parted to let George, trying to look dignified in his knotted sheets, pass through to where his hostess stood waiting.

'The sweetest ghost I've ever seen,' she said into the microphone. 'Well done, and here's your prize.' She kissed him on both cheeks and then formally presented an enormous pineapple. The crowd roared its appreciation and George, twisting his face into a smile of sorts, wished he was dead.

'Speech! Speech!' they bellowed.

'Thank you very much, Lady Beauchamp,' he said, and would perhaps have been wise to stop there. But he could not resist adding: 'Though I would just like to say that I'm not a ghost, I'm a Roman Emperor,' which of course brought the house down. It was shortly after this that Veronica tried to rescue him from his misery by asking him to dance. He shuffled opposite her for several songs, holding the sheets out of the way of his jigging feet. The exercise seemed to cheer him up enormously and in the end it was Veronica who suggested they stop for a breather.

Now she was lying in bed beside her husband, trying to penetrate his black mood, for which she felt partly responsible.

'Did you enjoy the party?' she tried, reaching out to hold his hand.

'Yes, it was all right.' He let his hand lie limply in hers.

'Much better than I expected anyway,' she said. 'Are you OK, darling?'

'Yes, I'm fine. Very tired that's all.'

Veronica withdrew her hand and turned her back on him with a big sigh. She had tried to make up at least. What more did he expect of her?

8

The Dinner-Date

The dreaded day finally arrived. There it was written in pencil – (a sure sign that she had meant to cancel it) – in her little leather executive diary: 'George Smithers the Black Duck 8pm.' So much for finding out his number and getting out of it. Katherine saw no alternative but to go. That morning she packed a small holdall with the necessary equipment for the evening, since she would be changing for it in the ladies' at work. A dress that didn't crease, patterned with swirls of grey and pink (attractive but sensible); a pair of grey silk stockings (she had preferred stockings to tights ever since Julian); grey leather shoes without too much heel and a matching evening bag.

Organizing her costume and make-up, dawdling over the sea-blue or the amethyst eye colours was fun – about the only part of the exercise that would be, she thought miserably. But even when Katherine ached inside from a combination of loneliness and too many black olives, she was able to look and be a part. She approached her date with George Smithers as she would a difficult business meeting. It was just a question of putting on a decent show and getting through it unscathed. She promised herself that this really would be the last encounter with anyone from that set of people, and that as a reward for her efforts she would go somewhere like Sicily for a week as soon as she could get away from work. Holidaying on her own was something Katherine had come to enjoy. The sense of liberation that always comes from setting foot on foreign soil increased tenfold, she discovered, if one travelled alone. She went for the best package deals: the most luxurious hotels, sea-views, all mod cons in the rooms, pools as well as beaches, lots of health and beauty facilities. With such thoughts in mind, she bribed herself to keep her appointment with George.

George arrived half an hour early for their rendezvous. He sat in the car for a bit, emptied the ashtray, stuffed full of peppermint papers and cigarette ends, into the gutter and checked his appearance in the rear-view mirror. The glass was cracked so his face looked as though someone had cut it in two and put the halves back together wrongly. He was extremely nervous. This time, he told himself, he really wanted things to work out. No stupid faux pas, no rushing her. He would play the perfect knight; he would sweep her off her feet with his charm and kindness . . . He got out of the car to wait on the pavement, even though there was a good twenty minutes to go. Pacing up and down outside the entrance to the Black Duck, he thought back to the Beauchamps' party and hoped that reports of it had not yet filtered her way. He had resolved to tell her all about it himself, to make her laugh at his descriptions of his costume and how he won the booby prize. She was bound to hear anyway, so it seemed the best course.

By five minutes to eight George's nervous state had begun to affect his bladder. He hopped from one foot to the other for a while, whistling 'Land of Hope and Glory', willing Katherine to appear round the corner. But by two minutes to eight, holding himself in one minute more was simply no longer feasible. Moments after he had dashed into the restaurant, a taxi pulled up outside. Katherine stepped out daintily and positioned herself with her back to the door of the restaurant in order to await her escort. It was extremely annoying that he should be late. (Punctuality, in her world, was vital.)

George, in his hurry to get back into the street, hurtled straight into her. It wasn't the best of introductions for an evening which both parties, in their different ways, had been approaching with considerable apprehension. Fortunately it was only George who actually fell over. As he picked himself up, with both of them stammering apologies and explanations, Katherine thought to herself that he was even worse than she remembered and not remotely attractive. Poor George would have been inclined to agree with her. His face was friendly, but flat, like a plate. It sat on top of a body that distributed its weight without any rhyme, reason or symmetry. He didn't eat or drink excessively, but whatever passed his lips seemed to settle for good in and around his stomach. His hips were slim, his legs positively match-like, but protruding over the top of them was an annoying pot of a belly. Above the belly, things narrowed down again. He had once devoted several months to doing weights and circuits in an expensive sports club with the aim of redistributing some of this body-fat. After a while small bulges of muscle began to pop up in his arms and legs and his stomach grew slightly firmer. But with clothes on, these changes – the fruits of so much hard, sweaty slog – were barely perceptible. So he gave it up.

George also had a bit of a thing about his hair. Although not quite thirty, fate had cruelly elected him as one of those unfortunates who start moulting early in life. The situation had not yet become desperate, but the top was definitely thinning and the sides retreating. As a result he washed it less often, and always gingerly and gently, so as to prevent as many precious strands as possible from deserting their follicles for the plug-hole. Slowly, inexorably, however, a small desert-island of hair was forming on the top of his forehead, gradually being cut off from the main growth area by a channel of baldness. The moment when the channel finally formed, when the silly crop at the front really was isolated on all sides, was an event about which George had nightmares. He had a vague feeling that so long as he could be married by the time this breakaway occurred, he would somehow be all right. In the meantime he concealed the problem as best he could with some smart, tough combing backwards and upwards. With his tumble to the ground however, things went somewhat awry. So he's going bald, thought Katherine, who had a cruel eye for detail.

Meanwhile, George thought she looked more lovely than ever and dared to tell her so. She smiled sweetly and thanked him, inwardly wondering if she couldn't fake a fainting fit in order to curtail the hours of torture that lay ahead.

They were shown to a small table in a dark corner of the room, where George caused chaos by trying to help the waiter pull Katherine's chair out for her. When they finally sat down and tried to talk he clumsily proceeded to turn every subject into an opportunity either to pay her a compliment or to suggest that they meet again. But the food was excellent and Katherine found herself in the mood for eating. She chewed slowly, allowing the company and conversation to take up the merest surface of her concentration. Until George, made bold by wine – (Katherine had barely touched hers) – dared to bring up the subject of the Beauchamps' fancy-dress party. She didn't respond to his description of events quite as he had intended.

'Oh dear, poor you, how dreadful. I mean how terribly embarrassing. I would have died.' She spoke the truth.

Nothing terrified her more than the thought of being caught with her outer defences down, trapped in a situation over which she had no control.

'Oh, no, it was hilarious actually. I made some sort of silly speech just to get a few more laughs and then led them all off in the dancing. A superb evening. Super fun.'

'Well, so long as you enjoyed it, that's the main thing.'

He was not sure he had convinced her. 'Rather. Everyone had the time of their lives – Julian and people. You'd have known half the guests there I'm sure. A shame you had to refuse it really.'

'Julian and people?' Katherine couldn't keep back a flicker of curiosity. After all there was still a whole course and coffee to go. They might as well talk about something which she at least found mildly interesting.

'Oh, the usual crowd, you know.'

'I thought they'd all broken up a bit these days, gone their separate ways, got married, that sort of thing; though of course I hardly know any of them really.'

'Well, some of them have I suppose. Though the only one I know well who's got married is Julian and that was some time ago now and it doesn't seem to have made him any less friendly towards the group. In fact it seems to have made him more friendly to some . . .' George might have stopped there if he had not happened to glance upwards and see the first expression of genuine interest on the face of his companion. It was nice to have her listening properly at last. As for Katherine, she said nothing, knowing silence to be one of the best tactics in forcing people to speak, very often about things they would otherwise keep to themselves.

'Well of course I know it's none of my business, but I think Jules is going a bit far this time. I mean you know what he's like; always been a bit of a one for the ladies . . . oh God, sorry.' George had suddenly remembered the identity of one of Julian's girlfriends.

'Don't be silly, that was yonks ago,' she patted his arm, took a swig of her wine and invited him to continue.

'It's just that he and Gloria – you know Gloria Croft? – well I think there's something going on, which is a bit rich. I mean he's only been married a year or something. Seems a bit tough on Veronica if you ask me. I like Veronica, she's always terribly nice to everybody.' He went quiet, thinking back with pleasure to their long dance together at the fancy-dress party. He decided to tell Katherine about it, but she interrupted.

'Yes, yes, Veronica is frightfully nice.' She was anxious to get back to the more intriguing aspects of George's opinions. 'You're probably just imagining things, you know,' she murmured, willing him to expand on his theories a little more.

'Oh, no I'm not.' There was conviction in his voice. Katherine, for reasons she did not pause to question, felt excited. Again, she opted for silence as a mode of encouragement.

'I mean, I thought I was at first – imagining things, I mean,' went on George obligingly, 'when they were just teasing each other sort of thing. But Gloria's like that with everybody, always very jolly and poking fun at everyone. So I thought that was all it was.'

'I'm sure that's all it was,' said Katherine, inwardly convinced otherwise.

'No, no. You see I went to get Gloria some champagne and when I came back, a little while later I admit, but there was such a crush round the bar . . . well when I came back they were gone. So I had a quick scout round for them – I mean, after all I had these drinks for them you see.'

'Quite,' she agreed, now at her most charming, her most poised and interested self.

'And that's when I caught sight of them – pure chance really as there were so many people all dressed up and it was pretty dark – but I'm sure it was them because of his white tights and all those oranges she had on – she was Nell Gwyn you see and he was . . .'

'Yes, but where did you catch sight of them?' she pressed.

George leant forward across the table, glanced over his shoulder for eavesdroppers and lowered his voice. 'To begin with they were just dancing, ordinarily you know, across the far side of the ballroom. I raised the glasses I was holding at them to try and catch their attention. But they obviously didn't see me, because suddenly, right in the middle of the song, he took her hand and led her round the side of the disco to behind the furthest of the big curtains. I didn't see any more after that, but, well it doesn't take that much imagination . . .'

'Quite,' said Katherine again, 'not much imagination at all. Were they there long?'

'Oh, ages. At least I waited a few minutes – I couldn't really believe it – but when they didn't come out I gave up. A bit later I saw them though; all talking together with Veronica and Sids as if nothing had happened. A bit of a cheek if you think about it.'

'It certainly is. It sounds like quite a do this Beauchamp party, I really should have gone after all. Or perhaps it just takes excellent powers of perception to notice all the details of what's going on.'

It took George a few seconds to realize that she was paying him a compliment.

'Oh, I say, no. I just see – I mean saw – what anyone would have seen. It was nothing,' he added, as if referring to some feat of great value.

'George Smithers, you obviously have an eye for observation, why not admit it?' she flattered. 'Ever thought about writing stories? That's all it takes I'm sure, noticing things about other people and getting them down on paper.'

George laughed, his face flushed with pride and pleasure.

They went on to eat their way through several piles of fluffy cream floating in fruit and liqueur sauces, talking now – (or so it seemed to George) – as if they had known each other all their lives. He could not believe how well things were working out.

When the bill came the blobs of cream turned out to be very expensive ones and Katherine's small bottle of fizzy water cost almost as much as the wine. But George did not care. The evening had been an unmitigated success. He had been a hit. She had promised to meet him again. The only disappointment was that she refused his offer of a lift home, insisting on catching a cab instead. But before getting into it she kissed his cheek – quite near the lips – and said she looked forward to seeing him again soon. George was so delighted he thought his chest would explode. He ran to his car and drove home very fast, singing loudly as he screeched round the corners.

9

Married Life Part Two

Julian and Veronica were sitting at breakfast by the french windows in their kitchen, looking out over a cross-section of their underclothes swinging round on the clothes-dryer outside. It was a sunny, cold Saturday; one of those bright autumn days made for country walks and great gulps of fresh air.

'You need some more underpants,' she said absently.

'No, I don't.' He stared defensively at the array of faded underwear in the garden.

'Yes, you do, they're all grey and full of holes.'

'I like them that way.'

'Don't be ridiculous, you can't possibly like them that way. I shall get you some more for Christmas.'

'I can't wait.' He shook open the newspaper.

'Julian . . .'

He took a deep breath, knowing the tone of voice to prelude a major analysis or discussion of some kind.

'. . . we have to work out why things aren't going well between us and put them right.' She could have been telling him to pass the toast, her voice was so flat and matter-of-fact.

'Which aspect of our multifarious problems would you like to discuss? There's so much to choose from . . . let me see now,' he raised his fingers to begin counting: 'There's sex, there's arguing, there's . . .'

'Julian, please . . . if you take that attitude we're never going to get anywhere.'

'I'm sorry, Veronica, but I can't quite view ourselves – as you seem to – in terms of something resembling a difficult maths problem: a little hard thinking and one of us might come up with a solution.'

'Don't you want a solution, then?'

He paused before replying; a historic pause, like that first hesitation before answering the eternal 'do you love me?' That tiny split second of silence scared his wife more than anything. 'Yes, yes, of course I do. It all seems rather difficult, that's all.'

'But why is it so difficult? That's what I can't understand. It should all be so simple. We like each other a lot, we enjoy doing things together – or at least we used to – and we're both intelligent, sensible people. Yet we seem to make things complicated for each other.' Veronica was actually enjoying their conversation. It was such a relief, after weeks of raging silences and sporadic attempts at communicating, to be at least talking about the situation. It filled her with a new hope, a new fiercely idealistic love for him – for both of them, for what they were trying to do. Tears pricked her eyes.

'I think we should go away, have some time together for a bit. What about Herefordshire this weekend? We could throw a couple of toothbrushes into a bag and go now . . .'

'Hang on a minute. I mean let's think about this a second.' Julian wasn't enjoying the conversation nearly as much as his wife. He was fully aware that he had been unpleasant to her in recent weeks, but he felt unpleasant and above all he felt confused. On the Thursday night following the Beauchamps' party weakness of the flesh had overcome all his resolutions. Before he knew it, he had found himself on Gloria's doorstep clutching a bottle of wine. Once its contents had eased their embarrassment, they undressed each other and went to bed. The decision to catch a cab to her flat had been egged on by the feeble hope that finishing off what had started at the party, would satisfy the urge and the curiosity for ever. But like an insect-bite which, when scratched only feels ticklier than ever, he found himself going back for more and more. Julian couldn't help feeling a bit guilty, but at the same time he didn't really blame himself. It was so understandable – to him at least – why he was doing what he was doing. Gloria made no demands on him. Sex with her was fun; not all serious and emotional as it was at home. In between bouts in the bedroom they talked about anything that came into their heads. Nothing clever, nothing fancy; just a chat about this and that if they felt like it. If they didn't feel like it they put the telly on, or read the papers or Julian simply left. There was nothing at stake, so nothing they did could threaten or offend the other. With Veronica, making love – especially recently because it was such an unusual occurrence – triggered a torrent of enquiries, of commentary, of entreaties for reassurance and understanding. In bed or out of it she was constantly trying to milk his mind of its thoughts and reactions. He felt sometimes as if she would like to suck him dry, to wring out every last drop of his inner being for herself. Julian valued his private space, the quiet areas of his mind that were for him alone. He could never throw himself open as she did, tumbling out all her feelings and inviting all of his to join with them for a good thrash around together. He shuddered at the thought of it.

'No, I don't think going away anywhere is going to solve anything.'

'But we need some time to ourselves, to sort things out, to talk.'

'Veronica, I know you find this hard to understand, but this fixation of yours about talking through everything just is not my style. It may help you but it doesn't help me. In fact it drives me barmy.'

She looked at him, appalled. 'And how, may I ask, can we even begin to help matters unless we are prepared to be completely open with each other?'

'I need you to back off a little, Veronica,' he said quietly. 'I can't put it better than that. I need to feel for a while that you don't expect anything of me, that you're not making demands on me.' He was being as honest as he knew how.

'But I don't make demands on you,' she whined. She really didn't understand.

'You do. You expect things of me all the time. Not concrete things, but . . . I can't explain it.' She didn't say anything. 'Do you understand?'

'No Julian, to be quite honest I don't. I tell you I make a hell of a sight fewer demands on you than most wives I know.'

'I'm not talking about you expecting me to do things. It's the way you watch and wait and analyse me all the time. I feel as if you're trying to crawl inside me sometimes . . .'

Veronica was shocked by the revulsion in his voice. 'But I'm only trying to understand you . . .'

'Well, don't. OK? Let's just have a few weeks when you don't try to understand me, when we just let things be. Let's just co-exist for a while, take things as they come and see how it goes. OK?'

'If that's really what you want . . .'

'Yes, that is really what I want.'

'Then I will try,' she said earnestly. 'And I promise not to buy you any new underpants.'

* * *

'Veronica's gone home for a few days,' said George, filling Katherine's glass with white wine.

'Really?' She offered George a basket of freshly baked rolls and helped herself to the smallest, brownest, nuttiest-looking one.

They were sitting high up in a glass-roofed restaurant, with the night lights of London spread out around them. All about their table and along the walls curled the long green fingers of tropical plants.

'Such an original place, George, I don't know how you find them.' They had slipped into a routine of meeting for dinner once every two or three weeks, and each time George made it his business to take her somewhere new and exciting. Since such places generally charged for their originality, this practice had already resulted in two letters from his bank manager. Or rather, the first had been from a computer, telling him in formal, impersonal terms that his current account was overdrawn by more than was permitted and instructing him to rectify the problem. Short of getting a sudden, unprecedented pay rise in the middle of the month, George did not see what he could possibly be expected to do about the situation. His only other account was a deposit one at the same bank, which he had opened with five pounds and many good intentions several years before. The interest crept up by a couple of pence every few months, but that was all.

The second letter had been more personal but more threatening. After worrying on his own for a bit, George had consulted Ted and Sids who assured him that all he had to do was meet his manager and ask for a higher overdraft allowance. In the meantime, they said, he should sit tight and keep paying the minimum sums required by his credit-card people. It all seemed such a matter of routine procedure for them, that George seriously wondered what he had been so worried about. But to buy a little more time and because underneath he was still a bit scared, he did not ring up his bank manager, but wrote to him instead, asking if they could meet to discuss his finances. That was a couple of days ago and since he still hadn't heard anything, he was beginning to convince himself that things couldn't be that serious after all. At least there had seemed no point in disappointing Katherine by abandoning his plans to try out the 'Auberge du Ciel', which was said to be the haunt of lots of famous pop stars. George hadn't told her about this aspect of its reputation, hoping to surprise her when they found someone like Mick Jagger sitting at the next table. (Mick Jagger representing the sum total of George's familiarity with the world of pop music. He wouldn't have recognized any of the lead singers of the day if they had been sitting two inches from his nose.) But as it happened they weren't. The 'Auberge du Ciel' was practically empty when they arrived, and remained so. Only the masses of green foliage prevented their conversation from echoing its way across the room to where scores of bored-looking waiters hung around waiting for the few guests to make their choices and eat their food.

'Nice to have so many waiters to rush round for us eh?' he commented, very glad that he had kept the stuff about pop stars to himself.

'Definitely,' she said. The place gave her the creeps. Not just because of the jungle-creepers strangling and twining their way around the walls, but because it had an air of decay about it, of having seen better days. Which it had – much better days. George's source, a work colleague, hadn't mentioned that it had been a good five years since he last went there. Not being the most perceptive of creatures,

George was actually quite impressed with the decor and the menu. Just as high prices told him that the food must be good, lots of pot plants meant the place must have style. He lacked the confidence to look, to really look, with his own eyes and his own opinion, to perceive the truth that lay beyond these things.

'So she's left him then.' Katherine had saved this comment until their main course arrived. It had taken no mean degree of will-power to hold out for so long.

George did possess enough wit to recognize that an important reason for their continuing to meet was so that he could supply her with information about Julian and Veronica. Sometimes she made a pretence of wanting to hear about Teddy and Sids as well, but he wasn't so dumb that he did not see where her true curiosity lay. When he thought about it, this did bother him – not because he found it sinister, but because it made him jealous. But on the other hand she was always so grateful for every snippet of information and then attentive and kind afterwards that it seemed silly to mind.

So he knew at once to whom Katherine was referring when she said 'so she's left him then'. In fact he had been waiting for it; waiting for his cue to pipe up with all the details that he had been able to muster since their last meeting.

'Yes, she's gone home – to her parents' place in Herefordshire.'

'Does that mean she knows?'

'About Julian and Gloria?'

'No, about Julian and the milk-woman, who else?'

Katherine was actually expressing real impatience, but George laughed. 'You say the funniest things, you know . . . I think that's partly why I like being with you so much.' He reached for her hand, nearly knocking over her wine glass. She caught it just in time.

'George honestly . . . not when we're eating.' Part of the ritual of their evenings together was that after the food and the release of information, Katherine would tacitly reward him by allowing her hand to be held while they drank their coffee and waited for the bill. The goodnight kiss before she got in the taxi was part of the same unacknowledged deal. If things had gone particularly well, she even let him kiss her on the lips. But though on several occasions he opened his mouth, hers remained firmly shut. All his timid tongue ever encountered was a firm wall of teeth and lips, and that only for the briefest of seconds before she pulled away.

'Sorry about that.' He dabbed at his mouth with his napkin, more to clear the sweat of embarrassment than because he thought there were any bits of food or sauce to be wiped away.

'That's all right, Georgie. You were just about to tell me if Veronica knew about Julian and Gloria . . .'

'No – at least the word is that she doesn't.' (The 'word', as ever, being the joint opinion of Sids and Teddy.)

'So I suppose the general strain of it – of having such a secret – must be telling on the marriage. I mean he can't be showing as much interest in her, if you know what I mean, as before. She must be able to tell there's a difference. She must suspect something at least.' Katherine was thinking that he could not be making love to her as often.

'Katherine, do you mind if I ask you something?' he ventured.

'I shouldn't think so. Go ahead and I'll tell you if I mind or not.'

'Well it's just that I sometimes wonder if you're not still just a little bit fond of Julian Blake – I mean just a little bit, you know . . .'

She laughed immediately; a soft, natural laugh.

'Oh George, you are sweet. But the answer is no, definitely not. I feel an interest, yes – or a concern rather. But it's just the sort of concern anyone might feel at watching people they know and like hurt each other. That's all it is. I feel sorry for them you see.' She spoke so sincerely, with such compassion in her voice that George would have been convinced even if she had been speaking in Russian. He believed her instantly and absolutely and felt very glad that he had finally dared to put the question that had been burning a hole in his heart for so many weeks. How kind of her to care, he thought.

'I mean, what poor Veronica must be going through . . . to drop her job like that and rush home means she must be very unhappy.'

'Well I'm not sure if it's quite that drastic. I don't know exactly how long she's going to be away for; but I didn't get the impression she'd resigned or anything, so I suppose she must be planning to come back sometime.'

'Yes, I suppose she must. And meanwhile loverboy can have a riproaring time without the worry of getting home for the night. Very nice, I must say.'

'Yes, but I like Gloria,' said George.

'You like everybody, George, that's your trouble.' It was an accusation, not a compliment.

'I don't, I don't at all. For instance I loathe . . . I loathe my bank manager for a start off.'

Katherine laughed again and took hold of his hand. 'You're priceless, Georgie, did you know that? Priceless.'

If George had had a tail he would have wagged it. As it was he held her small fingers, with their impeccably painted nails, lovingly, gently, stroking them as if he never wanted to let go.

'I'll give you a call about another meal shall I then? I'll call you next week shall I?'

'Yes, call me next week and we'll arrange a time. I'm looking forward to it already, George, I really am.'

*   *   *

Veronica had no idea that her husband's way of keeping fit on Thursday nights had slipped from a sporting to a sexual nature. The only people in on the secret whom she ever ran into were Julian's closest friends; and an unwritten rule amongst them was never to sneak on each other's indiscretions. After a rugby tour in France when Teddy had ended up doing a strip-tease and Julian had kissed the pouting lips of a slim dark French girl, the reports they took home were of the blandest kind. When Veronica enquired what the partying – she knew enough to know there would have been parties – had been like, both their faces set into studies of disinterest. Julian said the booze supply had been scanty and Ted spoke of the company and events as if a ladies' coffee morning would have been more dynamic.

In fact Veronica did not suspect her husband of infidelity for a second. They had been communicating with such difficulty for so long that there was no change in the pattern of his behaviour that she could have been expected to detect. Sex had gone from at least every other night (before they were married), to being so infrequent that she could seldom remember the last time. But that too had started quite soon after the honeymoon and had never been something that made her think he was having an affair. The truth was Veronica did not mind too much about the sex side of things; she rather suspected she should mind more. But each night, when they pulled their deluxe duvet up to their ears, she was so sleepy that it was a positive relief when he made no advances on her. She didn't mind making love, once things got going, but it was always rather an effort to start with. She had also got herself in a bit of a fix by exaggerating, from very early on, the extent of her arousal. The small groans she now emitted were more to satisfy his expectations than to express her true reactions. Once started, such pretences, annoyingly, have to be kept up. The main reason that sex was important to her was as an indication, a barometric reading, of the state of things between them. She liked making love because it invariably meant they were feeling relaxed and happy with each other. Not because she was of the multiple-orgasm school.

She decided to go home because she really felt she needed to get out of London for a bit. It would be a good opportunity to think about things, to catch up on some sleep – she always seemed to be tired – and to give Julian a breathing space too. When he said that she was always pestering him for reactions and commentaries on his thoughts and feelings she knew he was right. She knew too, when she sat down and thought about it, that this must be rather infuriating and that it was no wonder that Julian had begged her just to let things rest for a while. But stopping herself from doing it was a different matter. When he was quiet for so long; when he did not look at her or touch her for days; when the only noises he made were intermittent sighs, she could not resist asking what the matter was. Sometimes she would leave the room in order to force herself to let him alone. But such resolutions never lasted very long and before the evening was out she would be digging for some sort of response or explanation for his mood. When the sullen silence persisted she sometimes found herself turning nasty in a desperate bid to provoke some sort of reaction – anything was better than being ignored.

Julian had been rather sweet about her going away, the most concerned she had seen him for months. Although it was only for an extended weekend, he reacted to her departure as if it were on a much grander scale, telling her to phone every day and offering to drive her to the station. She assured him that she would call, that she could manage alone and that they would both feel a lot better for a complete break.

Deciding to take off on her own was in itself a confidence-building exercise. On the train she had a fantasy about leaving Julian, starting her own publishing company and becoming one of those glamorous, husbandless, childless, rich career women who were always popping up in magazine and newspaper articles, but seldom in real life.

Outside, the colours of late autumn were in full bloom; rusty reds and sunflower yellows glowed in the evening sunshine, basking in its warm light. As the train sped deeper into the country Veronica could feel herself beginning to unwind.

Her mother seemed very pleased to have someone to talk to and spent the evening moaning about how inconsiderate her father was. (He had gone shooting in Spain for the week.) Coming out in sympathy with her mother's righteous indignation against husbands, Veronica, in spite of her original intentions, fought the temptation to telephone Julian to say she had arrived safely and that everything was all right. Mrs Kembleton, who had spent many months apart from her husband during the course of their marriage, when they pursued their respective hobbies of shopping and travelling and shooting and fishing, thought nothing much of her daughter coming home alone for four days. It was only by staying apart that she and Ashley Kembleton had managed to remain together so long. Besides, Aunt Claudia, Ashley's elder sister, was due for the weekend. It was a blessing that Veronica would be around to help entertain her.

10 ∫

The Tennis Match

Veronica was not the only one to be enjoying the final shudders of a late summer. The inmates of the second-floor flat at number 68 Thurloe Road also chose to take advantage of it by having a last thrash around with their tennis rackets. This uncharacteristic display of energy on a Saturday morning had stemmed from a heated discussion between Peter and Ted the night before as to who had won their last match. Each had vivid memories of a crashing victory over the other. By the time the King's Head (a horrible pub useful only for its proximity to their flat) called last orders, they had each thrown down the gauntlet for a deciding game the next day. George, *in absentia* due to a dining engagement with Katherine, was elected to play the role of impartial umpire.

Since most people had decided that the year's pathetic ration of summer had already been dealt out, there was no trouble in getting on to one of the municipal courts in Regent's Park. Teddy had insisted they play there because he knew of an excellent pub near Primrose Hill where the loser would be obliged to stand them all several rounds of drinks.

What Peter Sidcup lacked in terms of natural athleticism he more than made up for with cunning. Ted, the sweat pouring off him in rivers, tore around the court, putting all his heart and every ounce of energy into winning each point. Opposite him, the cool figure of his friend in long white flannels hardly seemed to move at all. Each time Ted managed a shot that required some real running in order to return it, Peter made split-second decisions – based on the conservation of his energy, the current score and the likelihood of Ted flagging – as to whether it was worth the effort of chasing the ball. He sacrificed many points in this way, especially during the first set. But after a few games, when Ted's shirt was clinging to him and there was barely a speck of moisture on Peter's forehead, things were already looking very much in the latter's favour. It was only after the end of the first set, which he won 6–4, that Peter took off his pullover. His most powerful weapon, against which his tired friend rapidly became completely helpless, was an artfully sliced drop-shot. No matter how much pace Ted put on the ball, his opponent could make it plop back, so that it dropped only inches from the net. If Ted made a lunge for it, either in anticipation or to try and return it, Peter sailed a lob over his head. If, by a miracle of will-power, Ted was able to run back fast enough to get to the lob, the effort left him too shattered to do anything about the next shot. Although Ted was actually the better tennis player, he was neither fit enough nor artful enough to secure a victory.

Meanwhile George sat like some puppet-king on a rickety umpire's chair overlooking the proceedings. He was more interested in his newspaper than the game – pages of it kept blowing onto the court during crucial points – and proved singularly inept at keeping the score. Anger at George's incompetence was the one thing that united the two players. For the second set they unanimously voted to dismiss George from his duties. But this turned out to be even worse, since he then felt at liberty to yell out comments of encouragement, criticism and sympathy from his flaky green throne.

'Don't know how you missed that one, old chap,' he called down to Ted on several occasions, 'you could see he was going to lob the thing.'

'Thank you, George, and fuck off,' wheezed Ted, when he was unable to hide his fury any longer. George rolled his eyes and sucked his cheeks in at Peter, nodding disapprovingly in Ted's direction. Peter, to his credit, ignored this attempt at a silent show of complicity against his opponent and instead growled at George to get on with what was left of his newspaper. George sulked until the end of the second set when they decided to call it quits. The original challenge had been for five sets, but Peter won the second one more easily than the first and Ted was beginning to feel ill. In accordance with their upbringing, they shook hands at the net and said 'well played' a couple of times. Then a stony silence descended during which Peter tried not to look pleased and Ted told himself to be a good sport. George was despatched to look for missing balls.

When they got to the pub, Ted, being of a naturally pleasant disposition, got out his wallet with good grace.

'The old ticker's just not what it was,' he commented, after pouring the first half of his pint down his throat without pausing for breath.

'You talk like a geriatric these days, Ted,' said Peter, 'getting really quite morose you are. Look at George and take heart.' He slapped George on the back.

'What do you mean?'

'Nothing, nothing, I did not mean a thing. We're all in the prime of life, the peak of health and with the rosiest of futures before us. Cheers.'

'Cheers,' said George, but suspiciously, because he knew

he had been the butt of some joke which, as usual, he had missed.

'And how's Katherine?' asked Ted kindly.

George blushed and grinned. 'Just great, thanks, Ted. Just great.'

'Yes, I think you have cause to feel rather proud of yourself on that score,' put in Peter, 'I would never have thought it possible. Truly I wouldn't.'

George kept his eyes on his beer because he had rather exaggerated the physical side of the relationship. 'I guess it takes all sorts . . .' he said into his beer mug.

'My sentiments exactly,' continued Peter. 'The next thing to do is marry her and then try out this latest rage for extra-marital affairs.'

'Oh, no, when I marry that will be that.'

'Really? How conventional of you, George.'

'I don't know,' said Ted, 'I think it's rather refreshing.'

'I sense a little disapproval from Mr Charleston here as regards a certain mutual friend. Can this be possible?'

'Oh, dry up for a bit, Sids, can't you?'

'Our friend – hitherto uncriticizable in your eyes if I recall – is only exercising a healthy appetite for . . . let us say . . . variety.'

George, his ears pricking up as they always did when the conversation came round to the subject of Julian and Veronica, sat very quietly hoping they would continue.

'I'm not saying I approve, mind you. On the contrary, as it happens,' went on Peter. 'But I think Veronica is more than capable of looking out for herself – and Gloria too for that matter, though I'm not so sure on that one.'

'Yes, I know, I know,' interrupted Ted, 'it's not them dammit, it's . . .'

'Really?' Sids raised one eyebrow and sipped his whisky chaser. 'By simple deduction then, it would appear that your concern is for your friend . . .' Then his tone of voice softened: 'Teddy, old man, if only you could accept that Julian is not one of those whom one should waste time worrying about. No one is more concerned or better able to please himself than Mr Julian Blake . . .'

'Never mind, let's just leave the subject shall we? It's all pretty boring anyway. Boring and predictable.' With visible effort, Ted brightened and turned his attention back to George. 'So it's wedding bells on the horizon then eh?'

'Oh no Ted, nothing like that . . . At least not yet anyway.' But George deliberately put on a secretive look, so as to plant the idea that his and Katherine's intimacy had indeed reached the threshold of such a wonderful possibility.

11

Mr Fish

The interview between George and his bank manager had finally taken place. Or rather with the deputy assistant manager, since it turned out that the manager himself was too busy to keep the appointment. This annoyed George a lot, especially as it took them half an hour to work out whom he could see. Eventually he was shown into a stuffy little room with no windows and barely any furniture. It reminded him of the interrogation scene in a bad thriller he had seen on TV the night before.

A stocky, balding man with beady-button eyes led the way, clutching a slim brown folder with a big label on it saying G. Smithers.

'Sorry about the room, they're doing up the place so we're a bit short on space. Harold Fish – pleased to do business with you.' Mr Fish spoke in a jolly, squeaky voice which made George feel uncomfortable.

After these preliminaries Mr Fish cleared his throat and assured his visitor that there were many ways out of his financial difficulties. First, he recommended that he open a loan account, but only for the amount by which he was overdrawn already. This did not provoke a very enthusiastic response so he moved quickly on to suggest something George had not heard of before, called a Save and Pay account. This sounded much more promising. It was a facility, chirruped Mr Fish, that was the very latest addition to the bank's new account reform programme, and had been developed with people like George specifically in mind. But George's hopes and his face fell when all it turned out to mean was that he should transfer a certain sum each month into this account for the sole purpose of paying bills. Although no financial wizard, he knew that if he worked out his average monthly outgoings and transferred an appropriate sum to pay them, he would practically have an overdraft before he started. It also became clear during the course of their discussions that Mr Fish saw no possibility of increasing George's current overdraft allowance.

'Well, thank you, Mr Fish, but I think I'll leave it then.' George pushed back his chair to get up and go.

'I beg your pardon, Mr Smithers?'

'Well, none of these things are really what I'm looking for, you see. None of them really suits my needs. So I thought I'd leave it.'

'I'm not sure you quite understand, Mr Smithers.' The voice had gone up a pitch and warbled more than ever. 'We have to reach a solution now. I have explained the options open to you and now you must decide which you are to choose.'

'But, for heaven's sake, it's not as if I owe a fortune or anything. I mean it's only six hundred pounds, and I get paid at the end of this week.'

'But unless your pattern of spending changes radically, Mr Smithers, in a few weeks' time we shall find ourselves in a similar situation, only a little worse, shan't we? I strongly recommend both a Pay and Save and a Loan Account. Otherwise I'm afraid things could get quite unpleasant.'

George was trapped. A good half an hour later they had worked out his average outgoings and deducted them from his salary, to arrive at the monthly standing order for a shiny new Pay and Save Account. Mr Fish went at his pocket calculator like a man needing a fix. Then more had to be subtracted for instalments to pay off his Loan Account. At the final reckoning – Mr Fish's fingers flashed mesmerizingly across the panel of his calculator – George had £5.20 a week, at the most, with which to splash out on luxuries.

'I think we might have to cut down on some of our credit card expenses too, if we are to make sure we have sorted things out successfully, eh?'

George said nothing. He felt as though he had signed away the rights to his life. But there seemed no way out. Even the minimum payments on his two credit-cards were getting rather high.

It was as a direct consequence of this that the next time he met Katherine it was for a drink only, in a noisy pub in Covent Garden. On the phone he had told her that he had some difficult news to confess. She had been terrified that he was going to say he loved her. So when he blurted out, red-eared with embarrassment and humiliation, that he couldn't afford any more dinners for the time being, she was very relieved.

'Oh, George, is that all? I mean, I am sorry, but I thought it was something much more serious.'

'How could anything be more serious? I can't do anything, not a thing. I don't know how I'm going to bear it.' He hung his head and looked so miserable that she actually began to feel quite sorry for him.

'Come on now, Georgie, it's not that bad.' She patted his hand. 'What about a pay rise or something?'

'I've had mine for this year already.'

'Oh dear.' Katherine couldn't think of anything else to say.

'I shall miss our dinners so much . . .'

She had a sudden panic that he was going to cry. 'George, now seriously, I won't have this. Come on, let's go and have a meal on me – it's high time I paid.'

'No, Katherine, I couldn't . . .' He was torn between delight at the offer and horror at the idea of being paid for by a woman. It wasn't just out of chivalry that he had reservations. Treating her to meals was his only way of showing his feelings, of giving her something that she would accept. It also made him feel a little more masterful to be the one footing the bill. But after a few protestations he gave in. 'Just this once,' he told her.

Katherine linked her arm through his and led him off to a wine bar round the corner. His not having much cash certainly wouldn't mean they had to stop having their nice chats together, she promised. George, the lovely Katherine on his arm, had positively glowed with happiness and pride. It must mean she likes me really quite a lot, he thought.

Katherine had taken to jotting down notes after their meetings. She drew diagrams too, of matchstick figures joined together by arrows and hearts and crosses. The dinner in Covent Garden had resulted in some of her most dramatic scribbles yet: the matchstick figure under the letter 'V' had a big bubble of a stomach on it, in which sat a crude rendition of a baby. Angry black lines connected this figure to two more pin-men on the other side of the page, who were encircled in a large heart under the initials 'J' and 'G'.

A week later Katherine pulled out the black notebook from her bedside table for the umpteenth time and went over all the lines of the drawings again, this time in red ink. Then she drew a large question mark underneath. After all, she reasoned, George had not been entirely sure. Silly old indecisive George, backtracking from his suggestion as soon as he had made it. She wondered if she could bear the tedium of meeting him again. So much blurb about Ted and

Sids and his job, coupled with endless, dreadful hints about how much he liked her. It was all she could do sometimes not to scream at his pancake face to shut up. But inside she knew full well that she would indeed agree to meet George again and that she would even pay for another dinner, and another. For he was her window, her TV screen into the intriguing, stormy life of Julian Blake. Like an addict of a soap opera she had come to thrive on the instalments of the drama he relayed to her. Each morsel of gossip only made her hungry for more.

Having once known Julian so well, so intimately, lay at the heart of Katherine's fascination; as if that gave her the right to know what he was getting up to. She felt too an increasing pity and sense of identification with the women involved. So under-nourished and suppressed was her own emotional life, that it had begun to feed, parasitically, off the joys and sorrows of other people. As the weeks went by, the vicarious pleasure – and pain – she derived from George's reports assumed an increasing importance in her life. Nearly all her spare time she now spent thumbing through her notes, doodling in the margins, going over her drawings again and again.

12

A Weekend Away

The trouble with using George Smithers as a periscope into the lives of the Blakes was that he was liable to get things wrong. This was not just because he lacked any real powers of perception. It was also because, recognizing Katherine's interest in the matter and wanting only to please her, he tried a little too hard to spot developments in the situation. Consequently, he read truths where there were none and failed to notice them when they threw themselves at his feet.

Between them, with George's information and Katherine's hungry imagination, they moulded the image of a wife suffering terribly from misfortune and mistreatment. The pregnancy angle added the final tragic touch to their picture of her misery.

True, the situation with all its deceits and misunderstandings contained most of the seeds required for such a modern domestic tragedy. But there were two important factors that their prying minds did not take into account. Firstly, Veronica was never designed to play the role of tragic heroine; she was too pragmatic, too much of an expert at externalizing her feelings, being rational, seeing the bright side and generally finding a way through. If she was pregnant, she certainly did not know it yet. And even if she was, and even if Julian then openly ran off with another woman, she was the sort of girl who would cope somehow. At the back of her mind she knew this – that she would always manage and be all right, whatever happened. And the sense of this power, the inner knowledge that she was a survivor, only made her stronger.

The second vital cog in the wheel of events, which neither George nor Katherine could possibly have foreseen, was the presence in Herefordshire that weekend of Aunt Claudia. For many years Veronica had thought her aunt completely odious – about as boring and unfriendly as adults could be. Until her fifteenth Christmas, when for some reason, the tables turned: Aunt Claudia was suddenly the only adult worth talking to while all the others seemed patronizing and insincere.

Claudia Jezebel Kembleton came from a mould of tall, strong, rather gawky women who seem to have gone out of production in more recent generations. In spite of being several years younger than her brother (Ashley was now fifty-eight and Claudia fifty-three), the two of them had always been very close. This was the more surprising since Claudia had received the classic second-hand treatment of the not-particularly-wanted daughter, while her brother had fallen easily into the role of the accomplished, good-looking, respectable only son. After acquiring a reasonable degree and a cricket blue, Ashley Kembleton had completed the necessary equipment for his life by landing the wealthy blonde Lavinia Hampton-Marsh and setting up home in a fifteenth-century manor house on the family land in Herefordshire. From there he proceeded to do all the hunting and fishing expected of him while at the same time making successful moves on the stock market so as to increase the already considerable family fortune. A son, very much in his likeness, already stood waiting in the wings, ready to step in and continue these activities into the next century.

Where Veronica had been a little spoilt, her Aunt Claudia, in an identical position some thirty years before, had been ignored. Her mother died when she was still quite small and Mr Kembleton senior quickly found a petulant, neurotic replacement who had indulged the adorable Ashley and been infuriated by his wilful, gangly younger sister. As a result, the moment she was able to, Claudia left the family home and devoted her life to being a rebel, albeit a genteel one. After travelling for many months around Europe, she went to live in Paris, finding a niche for herself amongst a group of artists who drank a lot of red wine and believed in the liberation of women. During this time she tried to establish herself as a theatre critic, but ended up paying her bills by teaching English. After several years of struggling, bohemian style, to make ends meet, she wrote a book on French theatres which was snapped up by a reputable English publisher. The book quickly became a coffee-table classic of its day and Claudia was encouraged to compile other similar studies on different types of European theatres. She readily obliged and was amazed to find that among some circles she was referred to as an expert on the subject. None of the books were ever quite as good or sold as well as the first, but they provided a reasonable income and kept her busy. Aunt Claudia made whirlwind visits to Herefordshire when she could, but it was usually only at Christmas time. The rest of the year she spent flying between her flats in Paris and London, giving talks on theatres and women's rights and developing a taste for expensive French wines.

Mrs Kembleton was pruning roses and her daughter having tea when Claudia arrived.

'Hello, Veronica, how nice to see you. It makes up for the appalling manners of your father . . . I've seen Lavinia in the garden and she told me he's in Spain. Fancy not telling me about his silly shooting trip. We only spoke a month or so ago and he said it would be fine . . . Not that I've got anything against your mother, but you know how it is . . . But how are you, my dear?'

'Fine, fine.'

'Well, you don't look fine. You look terrible.'

'Thanks a lot – that really makes me feel great . . .' Veronica was not in the mood for her aunt's brand of hearty honesty.

'Now, now, I didn't mean to offend. It's all relative you know, since you happen to be a rather fine-looking woman. Not a bit like your toothy old aunt here.' She started to laugh, but stopped abruptly. 'You just look tired that's all – tired and a little sad. But you've got that protective leave-me-alone look on your face, so I'm going to wash some of the London grime off my face and leave you to it. I'll see you at dinner.' She patted Veronica on the head and left the sofa to go upstairs. At the sitting-room door she paused and turned. 'But if you do want to talk, don't for heaven's sake be coy about it.'

Veronica muttered a thanks and busied herself with clearing away the tea things. She knew that she wanted to talk to someone, but wasn't sure if Aunt Claudia really fitted the bill. They normally discussed books and plays and gossip about the publishing world. Since her aunt was so solidly single, the type of emotional crisis which she now found herself confronting was not an obvious subject on which to open up. But the alternatives were her mother (out of the question) and her girlfriends; but this trouble with Julian felt altogether too major to be thrown at the mercy of her usual ring of confidantes. Besides which, it was a little embarrassing to admit to one's friends only a year and a half after the wedding quite how badly things were going.

Throughout dinner, amidst the low hum of polite conversation and the gentle clatter of cutlery on china, Veronica wondered whether to confide in her aunt. There was no question of doing so that night because her mother had invited Dr Middleton and Reverend Morley to 'add some masculine flavour to their meal' (as she said to each one when she welcomed them at the door with her tinkling laugh and her polished smile).

After dinner, when all Veronica wanted to do was go to bed, she had to sit up and watch the doctor and the vicar consume the best part of a bottle of port. Having been sociable up until this point, she now went deliberately silent as a way of stating her disgust: both of their male dinner guests made a living out of prescribing abstinence as the way towards physical and spiritual health. Yet beside her, the doctor, whose nose was even bigger and redder than she remembered, wheezed on a fat cigar, while his holy companion slurped port and rustled his way through Lavinia's box of after-dinner mints as if he hadn't eaten all day. But Veronica's silence was wasted. No one seemed to notice. Or if they did they didn't care. Lavinia was in full flight. After no less than five glasses of wine her laugh tinkled more like a bell than ever, and her eyes danced from one guest to the other. She adored being listened to, especially by men. And whatever the two gentlemen may have thought beneath their smiling faces, they were humouring her perfectly.

As for Aunt Claudia, she had brought a full glass of red wine through with her from the dining-room, and, whenever she could get a word in edgeways, was interrogating the doctor in her usual earnest fashion about some highly infectious tropical disease of which Veronica had never heard, and on which Dr Middleton seemed decidedly ill-informed as well.

Finally, well after midnight, the vicar heaved his enormous frame from the deep embrace of the most comfortable of the armchairs, shedding sweet-papers like confetti from amongst the ample folds of his cassock, and announced that he had to go. The doctor was polite enough to follow suit.

'They remind me of Tweedledum and Tweedledee those two,' said Claudia after the door had shut.

'But they're so sweet the two of them,' said Lavinia. 'Old-fashioned maybe, but terribly, terribly sweet.'

Veronica decided to keep her opinions to herself and went straight upstairs to the welcome quietness of her own bed. She lay awake for a long time, listening to the whispers of the dry leaves in the orchard below her window, wondering what to do. The weekend had by now taken on the aspect of one of those momentous turning-points in a life; Veronica knew she was toying with decisions which would affect her entire future.

She had left London with the sole intention of giving them both a break before returning to try again. But now she was not so sure. With a flip of her stomach she realized that for the second evening in a row she had not phoned Julian. Not on purpose this time, but simply because she had forgotten all about it. In the meantime the germ of an idea which had begun as a daydream on the train, was slowly taking shape. Why not step out of this marriage, which seemed to do nothing but make her tired and upset, and make a go of it on her own? She had always been so conventional, she scolded herself, so unquestioning about what she wanted for her own happiness. Why on earth should she battle on with the constraints and the compromises of marriage, belittling herself in the process? Why not make the world her oyster instead, just as Aunt Claudia had done?

*   *   *

At breakfast the next morning Veronica said shyly: 'I was thinking of taking the dogs out before lunch – do you feel like coming too?'

'No, thank you darling, I've got a million and one things to see to this morning.'

'I meant Aunt Claudia actually; I mean, I knew you would be far too busy.'

Aunt Claudia was already smiling. 'Yes, yes of course, an excellent idea, I could do with some exercise.'

By the time they were ready to go out, dark clouds had been pulled like curtains across the sky and it was already starting to drizzle.

'A walk in the rain, even better,' said her aunt cheerily, as they rummaged around to find her some wellington boots and a mackintosh.

'You're quite mad, both of you,' said Lavinia, which made them even more determined to go.

The dogs didn't mind, and raced on ahead, excited by the tingle of rain on their backs and all the smells rising from the damp earth. They set off up a mud track at the back of the house and were immediately glad of their gum-boots. The path was overgrown with bracken and brambles, forcing them to walk shoulder to shoulder. Aunt Claudia had brought one of old Mr Kembleton's walking sticks which she wielded like some Arthurian sword, hacking at the thickest bunches of wet greenery and the prickliest of the brambles.

'I've two complaints against your dogs,' she gasped at length. 'They're too energetic and they've got ridiculous names – whoever heard of a labrador being called Flopsie for goodness' sake? And as for the setter, my heart goes out to her, even though she's a temperamental old bitch . . .' All Aunt Claudia was really trying to do with these comments was to break the silence, and she succeeded. Veronica laughed and called out to the dogs who had disappeared into the acres of thickets on either side of them.

'Flopsie! Prissy! Here, girls, come here!' Her voice was powerless against the pelting rain and the whip of the wind.

Or perhaps the dogs just pretended not to hear her; only the occasional wagging tail appearing over the tops of the bracken showed that they were still in the area.

'You know why they've got such stupid names, don't you? You must have heard the story a million times . . .' She had to shout to make herself heard.

'No, I haven't actually.'

'Really? Well it's just that Mum lost the battle to get the pekineses she wanted, so she got her own back by insisting that Dad had to accept whatever silly names she gave his gun dogs. He thought it all rather a laugh at the time and now we've just got used to it. Mum always chooses the names. The last labrador was called Popsicle, remember?'

'So she was, wretched beast.'

At that moment they rounded a bend in the path to find themselves confronted by a fierce little stream.

'My goodness, the bridge has been washed away – there's usually a bridge.' The labrador had already paddled her way across, her thumping tail splashing the water, while the setter was holding back, less certain of making the crossing.

'We really ought to turn back you know – I mean our wellies just aren't up to it.'

'Oh, come on now, in for a penny . . .' And Aunt Claudia, who had on a pair of mauve ankle-length wellingtons that Lavinia used for gardening, struck out into the stream, wading furiously. By the time she got to the other side her boots were full of water. Balancing precariously on each foot in turn, she emptied them out, laughing and calling to her niece not to be a sissy. Veronica, whose boots were a more practical length, did not get nearly as wet.

'Typical you, Aunt Claudia, you never shrink from anything, do you?'

'And what's that supposed to mean exactly? I'm the biggest coward I know. Hey look, a spot of sun.' Sure enough, the storm finally seemed to be passing; the clouds had thinned, toning down their black anger to a docile grey and allowing tiny cracks of blue to peek through. Aunt Claudia threw back the hood of her mackintosh and shook her wet hair. Her gentle 1920s-style bob had gone very curly in the rain, giving her a jaunty, boyish look.

'I mean that you've spent your whole life having the guts to do exactly what you want and not worrying about what's expected of you all the time,' said Veronica, squeezing out her pony-tail as if it were a wet cloth.

'Some people would call that being selfish.'

'Well they're just envious then. If we keep going up here we get to that clump of trees on the hill that you can see from the garden, then we can cut down to the road and go back that way.' She added: 'I wish I had the courage to do what you've done.'

'Well, my dear, I am flattered I must say. And what, may I ask, has brought all this on? You've always struck me as a lady who knows her own mind perfectly – and acts accordingly. You've nothing to be jealous of as far as my meagre life is concerned I can assure you.'

Now that the rain had stopped and the wind died down it was easier to talk. The only interruption was the dripping foliage and the occasional bark of excitement from the dogs.

'To be quite honest, Aunt Claudia, I've just about decided to go it alone, as you did. My job earns me quite enough to set myself up in a flat; I'm doing pretty well at it and know enough people to start my own freelance editing company or something in a few years – or perhaps just get right to the top of Arlingtons – they're so small that it would be quite possible . . .'

'Whoa there, hang on a minute. All this sounds great apart from the bit at the beginning about getting a flat on your own . . .'

'Yes, well I was coming back to that . . . you see I've decided that getting married was perhaps a mistake. It's not so much Julian himself that's the problem . . . it's just that I think I was wrong to opt for marriage itself, as a way of life I mean. It takes so much energy and in the end it's all a big compromise anyway, so I don't really see the point. It's not as if I'm dying to have babies or anything either. And anyway, if I did, I could go to a sperm bank or something and have my womb impregnated with the genes of some superman I'd selected from a catalogue . . .'

'Veronica, stop.'

Surprised at her aunt's tone of voice, she did stop – walking that is – and turned to look at her. 'I'm telling you all this – I've not breathed a word to anyone else – because I know you're about the one person who will understand, who won't give me some clichéd rubbish about commitments and stuff . . .'

'Well, then, I'm afraid I'm going to disappoint you, my dear. How about perching our wet rear-ends on this rather convenient tree-trunk for a few minutes?' The dogs, apparently exhausted from all their racing around the undergrowth, flopped down beside them, panting heavily, the steam rising from their pink tongues and sodden coats.

'I don't know where to begin, Veronica, except to say that I think the life you are suggesting for yourself would be unwise.'

'But how on earth can you say that? I mean, look at you.'

'I am looking at me – and that's why I'm telling you this.'

Suddenly her aunt looked old and tired and very wet.

'I'm quite strong on the outside you see, Veronica, but underneath it's rather a different story. Now I don't want what I'm going to say to start making you feel sorry for your old aunt or anything ridiculous like that. Nor do I want you to go sharing this information with anyone else, though I know of course you wouldn't dream of such a thing.'

Veronica waited to hear what her Aunt Claudia was going to say with a mixture of astonishment and apprehension. This was the last thing she had been expecting.

'To put it bluntly, Veronica, I would not recommend my life, past or present, to anyone. I've managed quite well at times, but at other times not so well. To be honest, I have made some downright stupid decisions. I have not the faintest intention of giving you all the grisly details, but . . . but . . . the person I fooled myself into thinking I wanted was married and unpleasant and the person I should have settled down with got bored of asking me and finally went off with somebody else.'

'But what about all your feminism and things?' Veronica could not stop herself interrupting now.

'Veronica, being feminist does not preclude the possibility of being happily married. I used to think it did. I used to think it was clever to be on my own, to be completely independent and all that sort of thing. Well, it is, but it can also be bloody lonely. And the older you get the more lonely it can get.'

'Oh,' was all Veronica could think of to say.

'You know, one of the most important things for us human beings is the search for permanence. I suppose it comes from being scared about dying or something. So we all grind along looking for ways to carve our names on the wall, be remembered, make something that lasts, you know. Well, it seems to me that being married, having a family is one of the best ways of doing just that. It's a very creative thing I think, being married – and not just because children tend to appear as a result of it. It can be managed just as well without the marriage certificate of course, if one is clever enough to spot the right person. People don't bat an eyelid these days, unlike when I was your age.' She looked wistfully up the path ahead of them. 'Creating a bond of understanding between two people must be the most satisfying thing humans can hope for. I've done it of course, but only fleetingly.' She shook her shoulders, as if throwing off an unpleasant thought. 'My God, look at what you've done to me, I'm getting quite gloomy.' She patted Flopsie's wet head. 'Well, what have you got to say to that, my dear?'

'I'm a little surprised, I suppose. You always seemed so . . . so *together*. I never thought . . . but why do you never say any of these things in public?'

'Oh, it's far too late for that. One gets committed to a persona you know. It's much easier to charge along as I am, as I always have been, than to start baring my soul and openly regretting some of the decisions I've made. And I've had more than my fair share of good luck; I thoroughly enjoy my modest fame and my comfortable income. But you can have those things as well as a husband you know. Much more fun to conceive in bed, I should imagine, than going to a sperm bank – though I've never done either – I mean of course I've been to bed . . .' Her aunt actually blushed and Veronica laughed.

'But I thought you hated children . . .'

'I did for practically all of the time that I was still capable of having them.' She gave a sharp laugh. 'And then when I changed my mind, there was no one to have them with. And I was too boringly traditional to think that bringing up a child was something a woman should do entirely on her own, unless she could possibly help it. But look, enough of all this chat about me and my mistakes. The important thing is that you don't make the same ones.' She turned and gave her niece one of her frank stares. Looking into her grey eyes, Veronica wondered that she had never noticed the sadness lurking there.

'If you've made a mistake with the man himself, that's another matter of course. If it is Julian, then by all means pull out. If it is marriage *per se*, then hang in there for a bit longer and see if you can make it work well. See if you can make it work for both of you, so you both get the most out of yourselves as well as out of each other. You see, I'm pretty romantic at heart – perhaps it's just because I've never been married and had my illusions shattered.' She cleared her throat and stood up from the tree-trunk. 'Well, that's my advice for what it's worth. Feel free to ignore it of course. Gosh, aren't you hungry? I'm ravenous.' She waved her stick like a battle-banner. 'Forward! To lunch!' she cried and strode off up towards the road that would lead them home.

* * *

It rained in London too that weekend. As if sweating out all the uncharacteristic heat of the day before, the sky oozed and drizzled in an ugly grey way throughout Sunday.

Julian had not been enjoying his time to himself nearly as much as he had expected to. The rugby season had come to an end the weekend before, so he had been looking forward to a couple of days doing useful things on his own. Instead he whiled away Saturday morning lying in bed reading the papers, listening to the radio and feeling rather slobbish. When he finally got up he found that there wasn't any milk left. By the time he got to the corner shop Mr Jones was just pulling down the shutters. Julian jumped up and down waving his arms and tapping frantically on the window. But Mr Jones, showing his yellow teeth in a mean grin, pointed at the 'Closed' sign and promptly disappeared behind the lowering blind. Since the prospect of a five-minute drive to the supermarket seemed like too much effort, Julian sauntered back home and made do with five slices of toast and black coffee. This start to the day put him in a bad mood. It wasn't just that he didn't get the breakfast he wanted. It was because, at the back of his mind, he knew that Veronica would have made sure there was enough milk for breakfast. Failing that, she would certainly have known what time Mr Jones shut up shop on a Saturday and got there in time.

He spent the afternoon watching sport on TV and trying not to wait for the phone to ring. Veronica, he was certain, had deliberately made a point of not calling him the night before. He had been half-expecting something like this, some sort of game to try and punish him for not being the sort of husband she wanted. They were always playing games with each other anyway, trying out different moods to see what sort of reaction they could provoke; feigning indifference, sulking, being over-talkative or sullenly silent. He wondered if many other married couples behaved in the same way, or whether it was just a sign of incompatibility.

As Saturday afternoon became Saturday evening and nobody called, Julian began to feel neglected, then annoyed. This hardened his resolve not to phone Veronica first. He'd given up his Saturday night he told himself, as first the six o'clock, then the nine o'clock and then the late News passed before his square eyes. Here he was, staying in especially in case she phoned, when he could have been out enjoying himself.

In fact Julian had not given up anything very much. As soon as he knew that Veronica was going to be away for a long weekend, he had deliberately made no fixed arrangements, so as to be free to see Gloria. But Gloria, who was used to being left to entertain herself at the weekends, had some family commitment, a grandmother's birthday or something, which meant she wasn't available until Sunday. She too had said she would try to call and arrange a meeting, if she got back to London in time. Yet not a word from her either. When the television started making a noise resembling the death-throes of a seal, Julian finally gave up his vigil and stomped upstairs to bed. But he was too angry and too hungry – all he had eaten that day was bread and jam and a Mars bar – to go straight off to sleep. It took a good two hours of reading to get his eyelids to feel heavy enough to close into something that would, eventually, become a fitful slumber.

Sunday, with all its grey rain, looked in danger of being even more depressing. He could not believe that Veronica still had not called. After a decent bowl of cereal – Mr Jones threw open his doors for a brief couple of hours on Sunday mornings – and a browse through the papers, he picked up the phone to call Herefordshire. But his finger found its way to dialling Gloria's number instead.

'Oh, Julian, it's you,' she said, 'I was going to give you a buzz this afternoon.'

'Not interrupting anything am I?' he said sarcastically.

'Well, you sound in a good mood, I must say. Of course, you're not interrupting anything, silly. I got back very late from the country last night' – (most of Gloria's family lived in Surrey) – 'and have been catching up on a bit of sleep, that's all.'

'What about if I came over sometime today?'

'Like when exactly?'

'Well . . . what about now? I'm at a bit of a loose end actually.'

'I'd never have guessed. I suppose that as well as being "at a loose end" as you so romantically put it, you do have some vague desire to see me?'

'Now you're being silly. Of course I want to see you. I always want to see you . . .'

'Don't get carried away with emotion, darling, it doesn't suit you. Come over now then, though I might be in the bath when you arrive.'

'I don't think I'd mind that very much . . .'

'I didn't think you would. See you soon.'

Gloria put the phone down and did a quick tour of the flat, picking up dirty coffee mugs, emptying ashtrays and stacking magazines and letters into piles. The tidying up was more out of habit than from any serious concern about whether her lover thought her slovenly. In fact, she decided huffily, as she punched a few cushions into shape, her lover thought about her – as a living, breathing human being – very little indeed. It was all her own fault, she knew that well enough. She had walked into the affair entirely of her own accord; it had been lust not love; it had been for kicks, because she was bored and because she had always fancied Julian but never before dared to do anything about it.

The unnerving part of the business was that this particular fling was not following the usual pattern of her affairs. It had begun, like all the others, with the excitement of the challenge, the successful catch and all the thrills of novelty. But that slow, deadening boredom, which eventually got so deadening that she brought the thing to an end, was simply refusing to materialize. There was something about Julian himself, an elusive quality which she found intriguing. He had told her lots of confidences about his past love-life, some of them truly astonishing, but an inner part of him always held itself in reserve, no matter how coaxing she was. Deep inside the man lay a hard inner core that prevented him from ever caring fully for or giving himself wholly to another person. In short there was a fundamental aloofness about him which she found very attractive. Presuming he was also like that with Veronica even induced a certain sense of empathy with her rival.

She truly wished she could get tired of him – it would make matters so much simpler. But, instead, she was finding that each time they met she had to work harder than ever at keeping up her usual flippant banter and pretending there was nothing more at stake than whether he wanted to eat before or after they went to bed. Increasingly a whiney, annoying tone was creeping into her voice when she spoke to him; the tone of a little girl who wants to be told over and over that she's clever and pretty; the tone of someone who can't get enough of a good thing. It worried her. She was still in control, but only just. Once she would have loved a weekend in the country with her family. But this time she had been itching to get back to London. The only reason she had not called him as soon as she woke up that morning was because she wanted time to make herself look her best for when they did meet.

Although Gloria did not realize it, it was not so much Julian's magnetism that was to blame for her new-found sensitivity. It was simply that she had long since outgrown the man-hunting game, but had not yet found an alternative. She was ready for some real romance – for love indeed – but, as always when one is primed to greet these emotions, they tend to prove most elusive. By the time she lowered herself into a thick white fuzz of sweet-smelling bubble bath that Sunday morning she had come to the conclusion that it was time to pull out. She was too much of a realist to fool herself into thinking there was hope of any other solution to her predicament. Even if Julian left Veronica for good, she knew that she, Gloria, would be nothing more than a phase he passed through en route to something else.

She put on a bathrobe and some slippers – to hide the dreaded lumps on her feet – and let him in. (He hadn't noticed her bunions yet and she didn't want him to.)

'Hmmmmmm – nice to see you, nice to kiss you,' he said, holding her close.

'Yes, well, always glad to be of service, you know.' She laughed quickly to show that this was not meant to mean anything he should worry about. 'And it's quite nice to see you too, I suppose. Cup of tea?'

'Well, I was wondering if we couldn't first . . .'

'No, we couldn't.' It would be so much harder if they went

to bed. 'I'm going to put some clothes on. Help yourself to whatever.' She pulled away and strolled into her bedroom as if she had not a care in the world.

When she emerged, in jeans and a sweater, Julian was sitting with a cup of coffee looking through one of her magazines.

'They're all the same these things, I don't know why you bother to buy them. Once you've read one you've read the lot. There's a coffee for you.'

'Because they're reassuring and because I like reading articles on diets and orgasms. And the fashion pages can be quite good.' She wished she could think of something funny to say, but her mind seemed to have dried up of ideas suddenly.

'Like old friends are they?' he said, pulling her into the crook of his arm.

'Something like that.' She sighed. It was all going to be even more difficult than she had feared. Sitting curled up against him on the sofa felt so cosy.

'Talking of old friends, do you think Ted is all right?'

'Teddy?' Julian was surprised. 'Of course he's all right – Ted's always all right. Why do you ask?'

'Well, you know we were quite good friends – I mean, I got to know him a bit. Well, I've told you that already haven't I?'

Julian nodded, not really interested. He was more concerned about whether he could persuade her to peel off her clothes.

'He doesn't seem to want to see me any more. At first I thought he was genuinely busy, but it's been going on so long now, that I'm sure it's more than that. He really doesn't want to see me. Don't you think that's peculiar?'

'Very,' said Julian, starting to stroke her left ear.

'And there was always something sad about him – I don't know, I can't explain it very well . . . but there was always something at the bottom – the way his eyes looked sometimes – that made me feel terribly sorry for him. Do you know what I mean?'

'Hmmm,' said Julian, nuzzling the top of her head.

'Is it this secret woman he's got? Is it that?'

'You seem awfully interested in Ted all of a sudden,' he murmured, kissing her eyes.

'No, no . . . I just like him. I want to know how I've offended him.' She pulled back and looked Julian in the eyes. 'Seriously, what do you think it is?'

'Nothing, absolutely nothing. Ted can be a moody bastard and all he's really in love with is the bottle. So can we leave the subject and concentrate on each other instead?'

Not many minutes later Gloria's defences had fallen. She forgot about Ted and she forgot about her promises to herself as regards Julian. They could wait till the next time after all.

* * *

Veronica knew she couldn't change overnight. But her talk with Aunt Claudia did make a big difference to her attitude towards her marriage. It made her re-realize that there were lots of reasons why it was worth trying to make the thing work. It forced her to remind herself that although she was a very capable business woman, there was a whole other side to her that looked for satisfaction in traditional, sexist things like having a man and building a home and family. Aunt Claudia, with her curt sympathy and advice, helped her to see that if she played her cards right she could develop both sides of herself – the independent and the dependent, cosier bits.

She spent Sunday afternoon dreaming over the papers and making intermittent attempts to phone Julian. Since the number was constantly engaged, she came to the conclusion that it was either out of order or that the receiver had not been replaced properly. She thought about using this as an excuse for pretending that she had tried to phone on the previous two nights – as she had promised she would – but decided against it. Dawdling over the papers, thinking about things, it came to her that perhaps she had been expecting her husband to behave too much like one of her girlfriends in terms of how they spoke to each other and shared their feelings. In her customary analytical way, she forced herself to think it all through thoroughly, right from the beginning. She made herself remember all the numerous occasions when the way she had needled him to open up and confide his thoughts had only succeeded in making her frustrated and him annoyed. She saw now that all she had done was to make him retreat further from her than ever.

With the generosity of spirit that comes easily at a distance, she concluded that Julian had been absolutely right. She pushed too hard and she pushed all the time. By Sunday evening she had created an entirely self-critical portrait of their marriage, with the blame for their problems resting squarely on her shoulders – more squarely than Julian would ever have placed it. But Veronica, like lots of women, had a tendency to take the emotional responsibility for everything and to cast herself in the role of well-intentioned martyr.

Fortunately, by the time she got through to Julian (who had taken the phone off the hook so as to cover himself during his visit to Gloria), some of her ardour for being the sole guilty party had worn off. Their conversation went very well. Julian (who had the grace to feel a little guilty himself when she explained the problems she had had with the phone) was pleasantly surprised by his wife's mood and tone of voice. He had been expecting sulks and wheedling for reassurance. Instead she sounded sure and happy and rather refreshed. So much so that he even felt a pang at how much she appeared to be enjoying herself without him. But he had the grace to squash that feeling too. He hadn't exactly been pining.

'I'm going to stay on till tomorrow afternoon as I said I would. Since I've got the day off it seems silly to spend it in London – though I feel quite ready to come back. I'll try and get home for supper.'

'Fine. Perhaps we could go out for a meal or something,' he suggested, in a sudden panic that she would expect him to put something in the oven.

'That's a lovely idea. I'll make sure I'm back by eight then. I feel great you know – so much better than when I came away, you can't imagine.' She wanted to tell him all about what she had been thinking; how she believed they could make their marriage work; how she realized that she needed him to be happy as much as he needed it; how it was all her fault that everything had been so vile. But wisely, she held back. To start talking like that would only get her back into the vein from which she was determined to extract herself. And anyway it would not sound right – it would all sound corny and insincere and he would only think she was angling for some sort of emotional response.

'Well, you do sound as if you feel great I must say. What have you been up to?'

'Taking lots of fresh country air that's all and getting drenched with Aunt Claudia. It peed down all day and we walked the dogs.'

'Yes, it rained a lot here too.'

'Perhaps that's what affected the telephone.'

'Yes, perhaps.'

'I've promised to drive Aunt Claudia to the station so I must whizz. I'll see you tomorrow about eight. Bye then.'

As Julian put the phone down he marvelled for the umpteenth time at the unpredictability of women: he would never have expected Veronica to be so transformed by a mere forty-eight hours out of his company. She sounded happier than he could remember in a long time. He toyed again with the self-pitying idea that it was his absence that had cheered her up so much, but soon abandoned it. She seemed keen enough to come back after all. To his surprise, he felt quite relieved at the idea.

His afternoon with Gloria had also reinforced his certainty that he would never fully understand women's moods – how they got in or out of them and why. First of all she had shown this sudden concern as to whether Teddy was all right or not. So what if Ted hadn't been able to meet her for dinner for a few weeks? He hadn't seen that much of him either. He couldn't see what the fuss was all about. Then, after they had been to bed, she had gone all quiet and strange and refused to tell him what the matter was. She had done that a couple of times recently, but never quite as bad. It reminded him, unnervingly, of the games he and Veronica had been playing with each other over the last eighteen months.

So Julian was discovering what he should perhaps have been intelligent enough to guess in the first place: that the complications of feelings, demands, needs, commitments – and all those other age-old concepts – do tend to assert themselves when two people start spending time together. It can take a while and they may lie disguised as other things – but not for ever. Eventually the traditional battle-grounds of give and take, reward and punishment, victory and defeat get marked out and used. He had always told Gloria honestly that all he wanted was a simple, just-for-fun, no-strings-attached extra-marital affair. And that is just what she said she wanted as well. They had never even broached subjects like love, or him leaving Veronica or anything like that. But, as Gloria at least was finding, feelings are not very good at being boxed and labelled. They tend to spill out in the end, messing up their surroundings and causing unwelcome complications.

13

Katherine and Gloria

Katherine had taken a presentation home to work on for the following day. She had already crunched all the numbers and worked out the sales, stock and share figures for each area, so it was just a question of stringing the facts together with a few salient points. The only difficulty was a political one. The figures were bad. But the product (a perfumed mouth-wash that actually tasted quite pleasant) had been the brain-child of the MD, Mr Fairclough. And it was to Mr Fairclough that she was making her presentation.

Even so, it was the sort of work that she usually found easy once she got started. In her large neat loops and with her thick-nibbed fountain pen, she would write herself a complete script of what she wanted to say. From this full version she would then extract key phrases and words to be typed on to charts for use on an overhead projector. It was a ritual she had gone through literally hundreds of times before. There were some people who could ad lib all the time; but Katherine had quickly recognized that this did not suit her temperament. She needed to have a full written speech in her head beforehand – just as she needed the costume and make-up to go with it. The speech-learning part had got much easier over the years. The products and their performances changed, but the same theories were always being applied in the hybrid language of commercial business-jargon. It was almost a question of altering the numbers and the adjectives to suit the product.

She had got as far as writing: 'WHOOSH': 'A PRODUCT ASSESSMENT' at the top of a large piece of white paper. And underneath that – since she wanted to begin with something positive – a sub-heading: 'BRAND PERSONALITY' followed by the words: 'Confident, aspirational, modern'. Seated at her shiny red desk, with its matching shiny red chair and desk lamp, her large tortoise-shell executive glasses perched on the end of her nose, her face an immaculate symphony of Beige Baby and Peach Blossom tones, Katherine could herself have been taken as a representative of all these qualities. What better model could there be of the cool, glamorous, successful businesswoman of the eighties, working late in her own smart little home?

Although small, Katherine's flat was divided into clearly defined areas, each with their own specific function. She was currently seated in the 'study', which was separated from the 'sitting-room' by a formica shelving-unit that housed her music-centre, her telephone, two dangly green pot-plants and a small collection of books and magazines. On the other side of this the sitting-area comprised a chubby sofa and two bean-bags, each covered with a careful arrangement of cushions, all in various shades of lilac, pink and mauve, to match the flowers on the wallpaper. There were two small pine coffee-tables: one in the corner with a white television and video on it and one in the centre of the room with a vase of dried flowers and a tile saying 'Home Sweet Home' decorating its surface. The dried flowers were a fuzz of soft pinks and matched the decor perfectly. The red desk set had worried Katherine at first because of it clashing with the colour scheme. But she had got round the problem by re-painting that tiny section of the room white and by positioning the bookcase so that the red plastic was only visible if you looked sideways on your way through into the kitchen.

The surface of the desk, like the rest of the flat, was completely tidy. The pad was positioned exactly in the centre; on the right sat a pen-stand containing two biros and two sharp pencils; to the left and up a bit was the Anglepoise lamp. Everything else was neatly stowed away in the drawers. The light threw Katherine's head and shoulders into relief as a large silhouette on the wall beside her. With her head resting on her left hand and her eyes cast down at the almost blank page, she looked like some poet waiting for inspiration.

Katherine's imagination was indeed working furiously, but neither on things poetic nor on the subject of mouth-washes. The focus of her thoughts, a focus that was causing much pen-sucking and the regular emission of long, heavy sighs – was Veronica Kembleton. She fought the temptation to fetch her notebook and retrace the drawing of the pregnant matchstick figure. It made her want to cry just thinking about it. She could not explain her feelings to herself any better than she had to George. She did feel concern – for Veronica at least – and, having been loved and wronged by the same man, she felt a right to feel such concern. But added to that was the more mysterious, irrepressible sense that she had somehow been meant to see all this, to be made aware of the state of the Blakes' marriage and to learn something from it. She never once let it cross her mind that she was prying or that she was wrongfully exploiting the sensitive George. In her eyes she was merely an objective bystander, put in the way of information, the rights and wrongs of which she was far better placed to judge than any of those involved.

The presentation did eventually get written that night.

But it took all her considerable powers of self-discipline to wrest her mind from its exercises in compassion and moral indignation, and to force it to fill the blank page. In the end the script was shorter than usual and rather more frank than she had intended. But it would have to do. Since it was well past midnight when she finished, she decided to leave the charts till the morning (her secretary always arrived after her anyway).

She had already turned the light out when a niggly, needling thought poked its way into her obsessive mind. She was going to get six, instead of her usual eight hours' sleep. Was it therefore worth putting on another layer of her eyecream? Funny little sleep lines appeared otherwise, lines which she presumed would one day turn into fully-fledged wrinkles. Any other woman, no matter how vain, would have let the matter drop. But Katherine could not. She dragged herself out of bed and over to her dressing-table. She was sitting there, gently massaging the soft skin above and below her eyelids, when the telephone went. Her first, sinking thought was that it was George. But then she realized it was too late for him since, in spite of all his silliness, he was quite hung up on being gentlemanly. Ringing her at 1.15 am was just not his style. Whoever it was, she had no intention of answering it.

She got back under her tangerine-and-cream-coloured duvet and buried her head between the starched white sheet and pillows. But the phone – she had one beside her bed as well – kept on ringing. It could of course be a wrong number. This seemed the most likely possibility since it was absurd that anyone she knew should be calling her at such an hour. The odd thing was that the caller just let it ring and ring. Most people would have given up much sooner. By now the ringing was getting very annoying indeed. If it was someone who knew her, they definitely had every intention of waking her up. She decided to count ten more rings and then pick the thing up and quickly slam it down again. She was by this stage extremely angry. Apart from it being an unsociable hour, she did not like receiving unexpected phone-calls; they disturbed her routine and grated on her nerves.

The ten rings passed. She gave it five more and then picked up the receiver. If the cable had not caught round the edge of her digital alarm clock and knocked over her glass of water, she would have succeeded in her plan to hang up immediately. But the few seconds' distraction and delay caused by the accident, meant that she could not fail to hear the distraught voice of her mother: 'Dear God, what have you been doing, Katherine?'

'What do you think I've been doing?' she retorted. 'What does anyone do at 1.15 on a Thursday night? I've been sleeping – or rather trying to.'

'Katherine darling, I'm sorry, but listen. I . . . I'm afraid I've got some bad news, some very very bad news . . .'

My father's died, she thought at once; and decided in the same instant that although this made her sad, it was not shattering; it was not something she could not bear.

But it wasn't her father it was Tommy, her brother.

'He . . . I don't know how to . . . dead,' her mother could barely speak she was sobbing so much. '. . . his own life . . . he took his own life.'

'Where?' said Katherine, because she could think of nothing else to say.

'Brazil.' It was barely a whisper. Then Katherine's father came on the line.

'Your mother's very . . . we all are.'

'How?'

'He . . . he . . . he jumped . . . jumped from a building.' Her father's voice had gone thick and husky.

'I'll come home tomorrow. I have a presentation . . . I'll catch the afternoon train. I'll call from Victoria.'

She quietly replaced the receiver and went back to her dressing-table, where she spent five minutes rubbing even more cream round her eyes. She rubbed with the tips of her fingers, slowly, rhythmically, with her eyes shut.

A tuneless humming noise filled the room. It took her several minutes to realize that it came from the back of her own throat. It was a whiny, hollow, empty sound that rose directly from the black emptiness inside her. She was more scared at the humming than sad at Tommy's death. Because she had no control over it. The strange, inhuman noise suddenly stopped, as it had started, of its own accord. It was as if a monster, till now buried deep within her, was introducing itself. The thought preoccupied her. Perhaps Tommy had had one too. Perhaps Tommy's monster had made him jump. She wondered what hers would make her do now that it had woken up.

* * *

'Brilliant, Katherine – absolutely brilliant. How you handled Fairclough was a bloody miracle. All that stuff about brand-compassion, brand-fatigue . . . I loved it. Didn't understand a bloody word of it mind you . . .'

'Dick, I wonder, would you mind if I went home and took a long weekend off?'

Dick Gordon, Katherine's boss, could not help being surprised at the request. She was the one member of his team who had all her days off, all her holidays worked out and cleared with her colleagues months in advance.

'No, of course I don't mind. Go ahead, my dear. There's nothing wrong I hope . . .?'

'Well yes, something has happened . . .'

'Nothing serious I hope . . .' said Dick, not really paying very much attention.

'Well, yes, actually . . . you see . . . it's my brother – he's committed suicide . . . he was in South America.'

'Oh, Katherine I'm . . .'

'So I'd like to go at lunch-time if that's all right.'

'Yes, yes, yes, of course. I'm so sorry, Katherine . . .'

'I'm not sure how many days I'll be away next week . . .'

'Don't even think about it, don't worry, take as much time as you need – just give us a call when you're ready.' He put out his hand to pat her on the shoulder, but she stiffened immediately and he quickly withdrew it, feeling awkward and useless. She had worked for him for five years and he still barely knew the girl.

'I'll see you anon then.' She turned to leave his office where they had been having a post-mortem on the Whoosh meeting.

'If there's anything I can do just let me know . . . I mean don't hesitate.'

'Thank you very much, Dick.'

As if there is anything you could possibly do, he thought scornfully to himself. Looking through the glass walls of their open-plan offices, he saw Katherine's smart, erect figure disappearing down the corridor. They couldn't have been very close, Katherine and her brother, he decided. Otherwise she would never have been so calm about the whole thing. Fancy her doing the Whoosh presentation with that on her mind. What else had lain hidden behind that perfectly painted face, he wondered.

Although still early on Friday afternoon, Victoria station was full of commuters trying to get a head-start on the weekend rush to leave the city. Straining to read the notice-board of departures without her glasses, Katherine nearly tripped over the legs of some scruffy travellers who had collapsed, plainly exhausted, against their ruck-sacks. They all had unkempt straw-blond hair and brown faces. One with a gold stud in his left ear and sky-blue eyes reminded her of Tommy . . . She moved quickly on, stepping over their suntanned limbs, to get nearer the board. She was going to have to hurry to catch the three o'clock. Having fought her way back to the queues for tickets she stared enviously and impatiently as the two lines either side of hers moved briskly forward. Her own turned out to be a sluggish line of cheque-writers and people who did not speak English. She was left with one and a half minutes in which to run for the platform. The station was undergoing repairs; endless chalked notices directed her round a labyrinth of bollards and poles till she thought she would scream. As her watch pipped the hour she tore down the platform and threw herself on to the train. Fortunately there was still a lot of room and she had no trouble securing a set of four seats to herself in a no-smoking carriage.

It was only as she sank gratefully into her seat that she realized for the first time that she had brought no luggage with her. Not a comb, not a toothbrush – nothing. For Katherine, whose life was a perfectly constructed jigsaw of routines and matching patterns of behaviour and dress, forgetting such a basic necessity was unthinkable. In fact it was terrifying. The thought of being without her Carmen rollers, her special creams and make-ups was bad enough. But what really scared her was the act of forgetting itself, the loss of control.

Her first instinct was to get off the train and race back to her flat. A quick explanatory phone-call home and she could be back at the station within a couple of hours. Grabbing her brown snakeskin briefcase she stepped into the aisle to make for the nearest door. But she stepped back again almost as quickly. Coming down towards her, clearly looking for somewhere to sit, was Gloria Croft. Katherine had no hope of getting to the door without bumping straight into her. It was very possible that Gloria had seen her already, their eyes having caught for the merest fraction of a second before Katherine had thrown herself back into her seat.

Heart thumping and hands trembling, she slung her coat across the empty places opposite, swung her briefcase on to the seat beside her and quickly clicked open its smart gold locks. Pulling out her presentation, she began to study it closely, keeping her head half-turned towards the window.

A few seconds later, she became aware of a person stopping and looking in her direction. Flexing her eyebrows and crinkling her forehead at the words in front of her, she pretended to be lost in the deepest, most complicated of thoughts. Out of the corner of her eye she caught sight of a pale, slim hand, with chipped pink nail-varnish, pushing her coat towards the window-seat. Then a pair of dark-stockinged legs in uncomfortable-looking high heels came into view. The person sat down and one of the legs crossed over the other.

'It's Katherine, isn't it?' said Gloria quietly.

Katherine pretended not to hear. She was wondering whether she could still scoop up her things and make a dash for it. But as she thought this, the train lurched forward. She frowned even harder at the papers on her lap. Her fingers were leaving unpleasant sweat-marks down the sides of the clean white pages, she noticed.

'Katherine Vermont, isn't it?' tried Gloria again.

Katherine had to look up. Gloria had forgotten how good-looking she was – such a fine slim face, big brown eyes and immaculately shaped blonde hair framing the whole picture. They were far too familiar with each other's faces to pretend they did not recognize each other, although they had never had a proper conversation before.

Gloria, having spotted Katherine's abortive attempt to escape (and not recognizing it as such), decided on impulse to join her. She was feeling lonely. Anything was better than a train journey spent sitting with nothing but her own thoughts for company. The rush to get to the station and secure a ticket had left not one spare moment for buying a magazine or a bar of chocolate to help while away the time.

'I had a real rush to catch the train,' she said.

'Yes, so did I.' Katherine put her papers down on her lap and stared out of the window. The train, having jerked forward a few hundred yards, like a car badly in need of choke, had now stopped completely.

'Bloody British Rail,' said Gloria.

'I know,' replied Katherine, thinking that if the train had left when it should have done, she would not be in the loathsome position of having to make small talk with Gloria Croft. Her mind was such a jumble of worries – about the monster, about Tommy, forgetting to pack, what to do in general – that the last thing she felt capable of was being chatty. Added to that, the thought of Julian Blake was somehow more repellent than ever. And Gloria, as his lover, made Katherine feel physically nearer to him than she had for years; the sense of it repulsed her. This woman had touched him, all of him, perhaps only yesterday. Julian's smell – it had been so distinctive – seemed to pervade the carriage. Katherine got up, opened the window and took some big gulps of air. She could feel a reservoir of hatred for the man filling her brain, flooding her consciousness until her head ached with the sheer weight of it. Julian and Tommy, she was thinking; they were such good friends – we all were. We were happy then. But it all got ruined; it all got ruined when Julian pulled away, when he left me and Tommy in the lurch. That man has actually ruined our lives, she thought. Strange that the idea had not presented itself so clearly before.

'Are you going home?'

'Yes.'

'So am I. I live near Gatwick – well, near Crawley really. What about you?'

'Oh, I live further on down the same line.'

Gloria hardly noticed her companion's reticence, so involved was she in her own desire, her own welling need, to talk to someone, anyone, so long as it was a woman.

'Is this your coat?' Katherine nodded. 'Do you mind if I put it up here so that I can sit by the window?'

'No, no, of course not – I'm so sorry.' She fought the impulse to be rude.

'I've had enough of London, I can tell you,' went on Gloria, when she had re-arranged herself so that her knees crossed a mere inch or so from Katherine's blue silk stockings. 'In fact I'm going home to get away from it all for a bit. Let my mother cook me lots of cakes and serve me heaps too much – all that sort of thing. Let myself be spoilt for a while. I've had such a rotten week.'

'Really?' murmured Katherine. She was hoping that now they were on the move, the smell of Julian would leave the carriage, that it would be pulled out of the open window and lost amongst the suburbs of London.

But Gloria felt encouraged to go on. She had reached that stage, more common to women than men, when some of her feelings had to spill out. She was so full of unhappiness and resentment that nothing could have stopped her, not even the frigid, prickly responses of Katherine Vermont at her most unsociable. Katherine was not a close enough friend to be dangerous; nor was she a friend of Veronica's. She knew too that Julian had no residue of feeling for the girl with whom he'd lost his virginity. In fact, the knowledge that Julian had once done the same thing to Katherine – that she was, in effect, a fellow sufferer, encouraged Gloria to open up.

'I don't know if you know,' she began, speaking quickly,

in a rush to pour it all out, '– though you probably do, I mean everybody does – but I've been seeing Julian Blake quite a lot recently.' The relief of talking about it was enormous. 'I know it was frightfully wrong and all that – I mean with him being married – but it just sort of happened. And . . . well . . . things can't have been exactly great for him to have been looking can they? I mean I hardly had to offer him much encouragement . . . he was definitely looking for something – or someone – and I suppose I just happened to be around.' A lump of self-pity started to block her throat. She swallowed hard. 'But I just want to tell you that it's all history now. You can tell anyone that bothers to ask that Mr Blake has put himself back on the tracks and told his lover' – she enunciated the word aggressively – 'kindly to go back to where she came from. I just crawled out of the woodwork you see. And now I'm simply expected to crawl back into it again.' The tears actually started to brim over at this point and she began rummaging in her handbag for a tissue.

'Here,' offered Katherine, 'take this.' She held out a small white hanky with trimmings of pink lace and the initials KV stitched in one corner.

'Oh no, I couldn't, I'd make it all mucky, I've got a wretched tissue somewhere.'

'Don't be silly, it's only a hanky.'

Gloria gave in and blew her nose loudly. 'Thanks. What a sight I must look.' She did indeed look somewhat dishevelled. Her make-up had smudged round her eyes and her nose was all red from being blown so hard. 'Still, I'm only going home so I suppose it hardly matters.'

'So, it's all over then,' prompted Katherine, 'between you and Julian, I mean?'

'You could put it that way, yes.' She made an attempt at a bitter laugh, but had to blow her nose again.

'He can be very cruel, Julian,' went on Katherine, now

speaking in a low strange voice that made Gloria look up.

'Of course, you've been out with him yourself, haven't you – ages ago?'

Katherine nodded and looked out of the window. Her face assumed the pose of one barely able to recall such a distant memory.

'You were a bit cut up about it, weren't you? At least that's what Julian said.' Gloria was one of those people who often spoke without pausing to consider the effect of her words on her listener.

'So he talked about me, did he?'

'Oh, you know – I mean, yes, he did, a bit – but just as one does talk about these things a little bit.' Gloria blundered on, in truth a little scared by the dead, cold look – she presumed it was from hurt pride, but wasn't sure – in Katherine's eyes. 'Don't you talk about past lovers with current ones? I thought everybody did. All part of the whole bloody silly ritual of hitting the sack; before the "you still respect me don't you" – you know the sort of thing.' Gloria was still too close to the business of being rejected for her cynicism to sound very convincing. But she was trying to be jolly partly in self-defence and partly to perk Katherine up a bit; the notion that she had been a subject for discussion seemed to have touched a nerve. The entire balance of their conversation changed in consequence; instead of Gloria angling for sympathy, she now wanted very much to make up to the girl opposite for having said something thoughtless. Obviously the affair with Julian had left a rather more lasting effect than anyone could have imagined. But Katherine was so good looking and so confident, that Gloria, even as she thought this, found it hard to believe. Still wanting somehow to atone for her bungle, she decided to reveal something – a jewel of a secret – which she had fully intended to take with her to the grave. Because both of them had been close to Julian Blake and then hurt by him, it seemed fitting to share with Katherine an intimate detail about his life. Like a parting gift, in token of their having passed through the same areas of pleasure and pain.

'It wasn't just female lovers he talked about either.'

It took a while for this to sink in. When it did Katherine's eyes opened very wide.

'You can't be serious?' She giggled.

Something about Katherine's response caused Gloria to pull back a little bit – to pull back closer to the full extent of her knowledge on the subject, which wasn't very much.

'Well, when I say "lovers" I really mean "lover". There was only ever one I think – though as you can imagine, he didn't exactly open up on the subject.' The two of them were now leaning closer together, conspiratorially. With every jog of the train their knees touched. Temporarily at least, all barriers were down.

'When?' A small, delicious shiver crept down Katherine's spine.

'At university. With his friend Teddy – you know Teddy?'

Katherine nodded.

'It was during their first term I think. It didn't last long – brief but passionate, you know. And if there was one, there's no reason to suppose there weren't more.'

'Quite.'

Gloria's authority on this subject, which she made sound so definitive, was in fact based on one drunken confessional session very early on in her affair with Julian. They had teasingly started to play the truth-game, with a rule that a glass of wine had to be drunk between questions. Gloria had asked him, amidst much ear-nibbling and nose-rubbing, if he had ever had an affair with a man, without the slightest expectation that the answer would be yes. But the way he suddenly got so abrupt and defensive told her at once that she had stumbled on a truth. Unable to suppress her curiosity – who would have guessed such a thing of Julian Blake? – she had needled him for more details. Only by sheer persistence and a display of not being shocked – (when she couldn't help being a little bit) – did she wheedle out of him the name of the other person and when it had happened. As to how it had started and finished or why, she had got absolutely nowhere.

'It was just something that happened; it was over before it began,' Julian said over and over again. 'It meant nothing then or now. Just forget it.' He then made love to her in a way that made her wish such revelations could be made more often, and which left her in no doubt as to where his sexual preferences now lay.

The subject was never raised again, though Gloria did wonder about it sometimes. There was something different between vaguely knowing various gays – which she did – and being so intimately acquainted with a man who had slept with another man whom she also knew quite well. It also made her wonder what had gone through Teddy's mind about the episode. In all their long chats, he had never dropped the slightest hint, not even when he was very drunk indeed. She would have liked to see what she could coax out of him on the subject; but since he suddenly stopped having time for their pizzas and wine evenings, she never got the chance. Gradually other, more important things, like feeling lonely, wanting to be loved and trying to wean herself off Julian, fell into the limelight of her mind instead. Like him, she came to regard it as 'just something that happened', similar to all those experimental sessions she had heard went on after lights-out at prep schools between boys who turned into the most staunchly heterosexual of men.

Finding herself playing the part of rejected lover – and in the company of one similarly afflicted – revealing this secret about Julian seemed a perfectly excusable thing to do. It made her feel as though he hadn't got away scot-free after all. Katherine's reactions were also very gratifying, since they comprised all the incredulity and interest which the revelation of such a confidence warranted. As the train approached Gatwick Airport, Gloria felt something close to a sense of achievement. She stood up, stretched and pulled down her battered leather hold-all from the luggage rack. Peering at a very dim reflection of herself in the dirty window, she prodded at her hair and pinched her cheeks.

'No need to give Mum too much of a shock, is there?' She smiled at Katherine. 'By the way, what brings you home so early on a Friday afternoon, I forgot to ask? Not another broken heart I hope?' She actually laughed.

'In a manner of speaking.'

'I beg your pardon?' The train was stopping and Gloria was already half-way towards the exit door, not really listening properly.

'My brother's broken his heart – and every bone in his body besides.'

'I'm sorry, Katherine. I don't think I follow you and I'm going to have to rush. Nice to have met you. Bye.' Tottering on her high heels, she bundled herself off the train. Just before slamming the door shut she called: 'I hope your brother gets better, or whatever.'

Gloria had practically reached the ticket barrier and was just out of earshot when Katherine stuck her head out of the train window and yelled: 'He can't get better, he's dead.' Gloria stopped and looked back.

'He's dead, dead, dead. He killed himself. He threw himself off a bloody roof.' She was shouting hysterically now. Gloria dropped her bag, horrified at the sight of Katherine's pale, screaming face squashed between the small sliding windows, her clean blonde curls blowing against the grimy panes. As she made a move to come forward, the train began to pull out of the station, the noise of its engine making Katherine's words even more unintelligible.

After Katherine had shouted at Gloria about Tommy being dead, she felt a little shaky and decided to go to the toilet to fix her face. The train, forging its way downwards through the home counties, threw her from side to side, making her stagger like a drunk. Someone had written 'Fuck off Pig-Head' in bright red lipstick across the mirror in the loo. She tried to wipe it off, first with some toilet roll and then with some tissues from her handbag. The tissues, being more absorbent, were quite effective, but she only had a couple and so wasn't able to do the job properly. She stared at herself through the blood-red smears and wondered at how pale she looked. Her eyes seemed very big suddenly, and very dark against the horrible whiteness of her skin. She stood on tiptoe to get her lips into a part of the mirror where she could see them clearly. They looked drab and sad. Another layer of something was definitely called for. The train joggled violently as she tried to put her lipstick on. She seemed to have lost all control over the movement of her hand. She managed as best she could – so what, if the lines were a little crooked for a change? As an afterthought she dabbed big red splodges of lipstick on her cheeks as well, to fix the ghostliness of her face. Getting what glimpses she could of her reflection, something, she knew, was still not right, not right at all; but what it was exactly she could not decide. All her thought processes had gone into slow motion. She pulled at her hair a bit and chewed her lips till they bled, to make them redder still. It was the eyes she decided at length; that was what was wrong. Something had to be done about the eyes – they were altogether too black-looking and gaping, like two dark holes. Not like eyes at all, in fact. The train had pulled into another station, so the jigging of her muscles should have stopped. But her hands and arms continued to shake obstinately, as if they had somehow adopted the jerky movements of the carriage. In spite of this hindrance, she managed to extract a small compact of white powder from her handbag – a dusty substance that she normally used in minute quantities below her eyes to make them look brighter and to hide any dark shadows. Now she dabbed liberal amounts along the top and bottom of her eyelids, smudging the eye-shadow she already had on right up to her eyebrows. Dissatisfied with the result, but still unable to work out why exactly, she gave up and reeled back in the direction of her seat. On the way she suddenly felt very tired and sat down in the first empty space she saw.

The man opposite her stared and stared, fascinated by the clown face of the young woman. Katherine, being good looking, was more than used to getting second glances. But this man really didn't seem able to take his eyes off her. Trying to keep her gaze focused away from his, out of the window, she consoled herself with vicious thoughts: 'Disgusting things, men. Only ever have one thing on their minds; one simple, stupid, disgusting thing. Like Julian, like this man, like the whole bloody lot of them.' She burned with fury on behalf of all womankind for their miserable predicament of being allied to a species of perverts and sadists. She thought of Veronica, blown up with child, while Julian romped in bed with Gloria. She thought of Gloria, with her gulping throat and red nose. Then she thought of Tommy whom Julian had betrayed as well. He'd left him just as he'd left her, just as he'd left everyone. And now look what had happened. Tears of rage and indignation were streaming down her painted cheeks.

The monster was now sitting on the shoulder of the man opposite, grinning at her in triumph at having escaped. The man himself, apparently oblivious to the creature, was instead staring in such a way that any second she expected him to proposition her.

By the time the train pulled into her station every sorrow,

every injustice she could think of seemed to lead straight back to Julian Blake. If ever there was a root of evil, she decided, he was it. Something had to be done – not just for her, but for all the people he had hurt or destroyed. Wild ideas raced around her mind in search of some weapon she could use against him. Aside from outright murder – which would be difficult – there didn't seem much. Then she remembered Gloria, or rather Gloria's gem of a secret. It wasn't much but it was better than nothing. Anything was better than nothing. Once Katherine had thought of what she could do she felt much better. Her hands even stopped shaking – a fact which she celebrated by blowing her nose. Since she had given her hanky to Gloria she had to use one of the dirty tissues and consequently got red lipstick all over her nose as well. As she got up to leave the train, she felt so much recovered that she dared to say to the man opposite what she had been bottling up ever since she sat down.

'Fuck off, Pig-head,' she hissed, pushing past his knees.

14

The Tadfield Dinner

Peter and Teddy were playing tiddly-winks. The area of play was the coffee-table in the sitting-room, covered with its usual array of overflowing ashtrays and half-empty coffee cups, each lined to various degrees with interesting layers of white and green scum. George for once occupied the sofa – (there being an unwritten rule that this was for Peter to recline on during the day and Teddy to sleep on at night) – where he lay studying wads of literature about savings accounts and low-interest loans. Seated on the floor at either end of the oblong coffee-table were Peter and Teddy. In front of both their noses was a line of wine glasses, like a set of goal posts, each full of various shades of wine. The object of their game was to take it in turns to fire a tiddly-winks counter down the table, with the specific intention of landing it in one of the opponent's full wine glasses. Three consecutive shots were allowed; the clutter on the table served as legitimate obstacles and if touched constituted the penalty of a free shot to the opposition. If the goal was achieved within the statutory allowance of three shots, the wine could be drunk. Indeed it had to be drunk immediately. If not, that counter, wherever it lay on the table, was an open target for the opposition to hit and claim for himself.

The game had been going on for some time and both competitors were well into the respective frames of mind that accompanied their ventures into the fields of over-indulgence. Teddy got blander and smiled a lot; while Peter got more acerbic and argumentative.

'Bloody hell, Charleston, you have the luck of the devil,' he roared, as yet another of Teddy's counters plopped successfully into a glass of wine.

'Pure skill, my dear chap, pure skill,' replied Teddy happily, as he poured the smooth contents of the glass down his throat. 'Mmmmm, and a nice one too that. The St Emilion, was it?'

'You may pull it off with tiddly-winks, but with wines you always have been and always will be an unschooled amateur. Some, as they say, have "it" and others don't. Your palate I fear falls into the latter category . . .'

'Get on with it, Sids, I'm getting thirsty. And you must be positively parched, you poor old thing . . .'

'Fire!' shouted Peter, squeezing down on a tiddly-winks counter as hard as he could. It took off at great speed and landed squarely in George's full cup of coffee.

'I say, good shot, old chap. But you've lost it, of course.'

'Not at all. What if I down the contents of the mug – surely then fair play would mean me having a second bash.' Peter started to fish around in George's coffee with a biro.

'What the hell are you doing?' cried George, so engrossed in his brochures that it had taken him several seconds to realize that his beverage had become absorbed into the sphere of action. He tried to grab the mug from Peter, but was too slow.

'Come on now, chaps, give it back. I've only just made the bloody thing.' George was feeling particularly hard-done-by since his new economy measures meant that when his flatmates had started putting together a kitty for a trip to the off-licence, he had had to decline. They had returned in high spirits, with several bottles of good wine and the ridiculous idea of challenging each other to a tiddly-winks championship.

'Give it back,' he whined.

'Much as I would like to oblige, honour forbids me – my own honour, that is.' Peter held up the coffee cup like some holy chalice. 'Don't you see, Smithers, that this coffee-mug stands between me and possible victory – sweet victory over a drunken scoundrel who can't even tell the difference between a Neuf-du-Pape and a St Emilion? I appeal to you, Mr Smithers, in the name of all that is honourable, all that we cherish, all that we believe . . .'

'Oh, for Christ's sake have the bloody thing,' interrupted George, now truly irritated. 'I'm going to bed.' He scooped up his papers and marched huffily out of the room to coos of mock apology from Peter.

'Poor George,' said Teddy, still smiling. 'He says he's going to have to borrow money from his old man – not much fun at all, that.'

'Poor George indeed, Edward. And that is precisely how he should have been christened: "Poor George". Because he is one of those unfortunate individuals in front of whose name one always feels inclined to place the adjective "poor".' As he spoke, Peter carried on poking round inside the cup and at last managed, by drinking some coffee and resorting to his fingers instead of the biro, to produce the counter. '*Voilà mon brave*!' he cried, when at last he met with success. 'And now to war.'

At this strategically important moment the telephone rang. After barely the first ring George came flying out of the bedroom in his shirt and underpants and made a lunge for it.

'It's Batman himself,' murmured Peter, as he carefully took aim – curling his tongue over his top lip in the effort of concentration – and fired a neat shot that landed directly in front of one of the fullest, reddest glasses of wine. 'How's zat! The claret too!'

'You haven't got it yet,' said Teddy, with one eye on George. It evidently wasn't Katherine, because his face had fallen and he was saying that he would hand over the phone. Looking miserable he passed the receiver over to Ted. 'I don't know where she's got to – it's been ages . . .'

'Who is it then?' whispered Teddy, with his hand over the mouthpiece.

'Oh, it's only Julian,' George sighed and sloped off back to his bedroom.

'Jules. To what do I owe the honour?'

'Hi Ted, how's it going?' came the familiar voice of his friend.

'Fine – excellent in fact. Since I am beating our mutual rival at an astonishingly complicated' – he had severe trouble getting his mouth around the syllables – 'game of tiddly-winks. Great game. Forgotten what a good game it was. Used to play at Evesham – do you remember?'

'Sure do,' replied Julian in as jolly a way as he could, but sensing immediately that Ted, thanks to the booze, was on a very different wave-length to him.

'Look I won't keep you from what must be . . . Crikey what was that?' Peter had let out a shriek of victory as his counter splashed successfully into the glass of claret.

'Nothing at all,' said Teddy with a giggle, 'just my opponent getting mildly excited over what must be one of the pettiest victories in the history of the game . . .'

'Look, Ted,' put in Julian, a little desperately, since the conversation was getting nowhere. 'I've only one quick question, nothing to tax the old brain too much.'

'Fire away,' slurred Teddy, thinking this rather a clever

analogy with the action of the tiddly-winks game but, fortunately for Julian, not able to get a message from his head to his voice to articulate the thought.

'The club dinner – Saturday. It's definitely no birds, isn't it?'

'Jesus, have you gone soft in the head or what? Of course it's no birds, it's always no . . .'

'Yes, yes all right, keep your cool. There was talk from Chalkie that this year's dinner might include wives and girlfriends, that's all – but never mind, sorry I asked.' He would have added that he couldn't agree more – about keeping women out – but Veronica was sitting on his lap twiddling his hair in a rather pleasant way; and since it was at her instigation that he had agreed to double-check on whether the annual dinner was stag or not, he kept his silence – in spite of Teddy's continued cursing at the very idea.

'So, I take it you're going?'

'Rather . . . Shit . . . Look old man, I've got to sign off and deal with an aggressive counter-attack – I say that's rather good, "counter-attack", don't you think?'

'Ingenious. Sorry to have interrupted and all that, but I just wanted to make sure you were on for the dinner. See you then.'

Julian was about to put the phone down, when Teddy added: 'And I nominated Sids as guest speaker, so you'll have the good fortune to see him too – that is, if he's up to it after the thrashing he's getting tonight . . .'

'Wonderful – I can hardly wait.' Julian put the phone down with the mixed feelings of one who knows he's being left out of the fun, but not at all sure that he wanted to be involved in it anyway.

'Bloody Blake,' said Peter a little later, when they had decided it was easier to drink the wine without having to fire plastic counters into it first.

'Not the same with him now, is it?' agreed Teddy.

'You miss him don't you, Ted?'

'Like hell,' replied Teddy sarcastically, promptly disappearing into the lavatory – a glass in one hand and a bottle in the other.

Peter sat and thought about Julian Blake for a while. He was becoming increasingly convinced that the man wasn't worth the bother. Larking around at university had been one thing – part of another world altogether; a world in which they had all been irresponsible, when none of their various misdoings had been serious enough to warrant judgement or blame. Even then Peter had taken the precaution of warning his sister Mary off Julian. During her first term at art college, she came up to Oxford a lot to spend many pleasant weekends with the three of them – Peter, Julian and Teddy. Julian Blake was trouble, he cautioned, after he thought he'd spotted her looking at him in a certain way. Mary had the grace to be touched rather than annoyed by her brother's interfering concern. She felt nothing at all, she assured him, even though it wasn't quite true. Then, fortunately, she fell in love with a man doing a thesis on Baroque Art and started spending all her spare time in London.

It was Peter Sidcup's weakness for wine that had drawn him into friendship with Julian and Teddy. They had met at a Wine Society dinner and discovered a sense of humour in common as well as a disdain for the intellectual snobbery of many of their fellow-students. Of the three, Julian and Teddy, whose colleges were next door and who had known each other for years, spent much more time together. From the beginning it suited Peter to be more on the edge of the friendship, to fall back on the easy fun it provided when he felt in need of it. He was a man who valued his own company and privacy enormously. Sometimes he would sink from sight for days; resurfacing cool and refreshed from communing with his own thoughts and a few good books. Peter was more the intellectual, genuinely interested in his work, while Julian and Teddy played at it, just as they played at rugby. They often teased him for his aloofness and studiousness, but his intelligence made him witty and pleasantly self-assured which was why the friendship held. He lived exactly as he wanted, being one of those rare, contented individuals who can afford the luxury of not caring too much about the opinions of others. Sometimes this made him obtuse to other people's feelings, but it guaranteed his honesty, emotional and otherwise. Much of Peter's inner security came from his family. He did not talk about them much – he did not have to; his devotion to his younger sister was obvious and the harmony of his home life shone through the photo on his mantelpiece and his ability to be happy.

After a couple of years sorting himself out in London, Peter was now realizing that he had long since passed through the phase of having friends like Julian. The man's blatant selfishness and apparent lack of compassion for anyone's feelings except his own was simply getting to be too much. Peter was no moral prig and knew full well that he himself could be arrogant and self-willed, but never, he hoped, in the mindless, bulldozing way that Julian managed.

Mary had summed it up perfectly in a recent letter from Paris where she was on a prolonged visit to the Baroque Art student who had secured a year's teaching post at the Lycée: 'Don't take offence,' she had written, 'but I must confess – from this safe distance – that of all your friends I find Julian the hardest to stomach. Teddy is a dear and poor George is really very sweet. But Julian is so pleased with himself it makes me sick. Veronica's fortunately the sort that can cope with it, but I couldn't for a second. He was all right at college – just a bit pig-headed, but then you all were. And me too, I shouldn't wonder. Since then he's got positively smarmy. As I say, don't take offence. I've been wanting to tell you for ages. I do like all your other friends a lot.'

Peter valued his sister's opinion far too much to be offended, especially since it coincided with the way his own thoughts were turning. Julian should never have got married. And having done so, he was wrong to expect his friends to help him deceive his wife. Peter may have been cynical about many things in life, but marriage was not one of them. A good marriage was something in which he believed. Perhaps, because he was the product of one.

*   *   *

Life in the Blake household was now running quite smoothly. It bore little relation to how either of them had envisaged their married life would be, but it was a *modus vivendi* which they both found quite comfortable. Julian did not enquire too closely about what had happened on Veronica's weekend home, but he was sensitive enough to spot immediately that some attitude in her had shifted, very much for the better in his opinion. He no longer felt as though he was coming home each evening for an extended session of psychological analysis and was consequently much more inclined to be open and pleasant. Indeed Veronica seemed so relaxed that he sometimes dared to think that she showed insufficient interest in him and would sulk a little. But such sulks were infinitely preferable to the black moods of before: they did not go on as long and after a while he would confess what was bothering him, which usually led to enjoyable little reconciliation scenes, very often in the bedroom.

He had no regrets at all about giving up Gloria. Things had not only been getting far too domesticated, but recently a terrible hang-dog look had started appearing on her face when she wasn't on her guard. Julian liked Gloria for her cheek, her sexiness and her independence – qualities to which the hang-dog expression bore no relation whatsoever. Judging that it was just a question of time before this new element in her attitude became the focus for discussion – what it meant and why it was there – he decided to get out fast. Added to that, the change in Veronica clouded his sense of moral justification for being unfaithful to her.

When he made his farewell speech to Gloria she put on such an excellent show of nonchalance that he wondered at first if he had not imagined the hang-dog look all along. She told him to stay for a drink anyway and rushed off to get a corkscrew as if they were celebrating an anniversary. But then she gave the game away by pouring wine down her throat faster than he had ever seen before and by lighting cigarettes when she already had one smoking in the ashtray. This behaviour, coupled with lots of tight little grins and an excessive use of the word 'marvellous', told him that his first judgement had been entirely correct. As naturally as he could, he got through the large glass of wine she had insisted on pouring him before announcing that he really ought to be going. Hustling him busily to the door, she refused to be kissed and waved him off with a corny quip along the lines of: 'See you around, heart-breaker.' The moment the door was shut he was sure he heard something approaching a gasp of pain coming from behind it. He hesitated for a second – but only a second – before hurrying down the stairs, grateful to have got off so lightly. During the next few days tiny stabs of guilt did have the grace to prick his conscience, but they met with solid resistance from the voice of reason – (a voice which helped Julian out on practical and emotional issues alike). He had always been completely honest with her; he had never promised or proffered love; it had always been only for fun; she knew that as well as he, so he could not be held responsible if she had started to feel something more.

Veronica felt a bit like an actress who, having tried to ad

lib her way through a part, is suddenly handed a script. She marvelled at how difficult things seemed when they weren't going well and how easy they seemed now that they were. Aunt Claudia's advice had been the key to it all – had set her going down the right track – but since then she had discovered many other ways of oiling the wheels of her marriage. For a start, she shed some of the ideological conviction that two people joined together by matrimony should constantly bare every corner of their souls to each other. Being realistic, Julian was not much interested in all the tiny pulses of her thoughts and feelings and never would be. So she began keeping them more to herself and discovered that such emotional privacy could be enjoyable in itself. This made it easier to leave Julian to his own thoughts as well. She stopped worrying all the time about how things were going and found that this had the immediate effect of making them go better. The two of them still had their various huffs and puffs at each other, but it was all quite mild, not nearly as fundamental as their previous disagreements. Best of all, this slight withdrawal of her attentions made Julian want them more. She had forgotten how much pleasure there was in being wanted.

By Veronica's original standards of behaviour she was now much less emotionally honest with her husband. But she had come to the conclusion that marriage, rather than being some form of romantic bonding, was actually much more of a pragmatic thing. In making it work she saw now that acting out parts, assuming certain roles – albeit at the cost of absolute honesty – was essential for keeping things going well. She discovered how to be quite manipulative in this respect. For example, if she wanted Julian to put his arms around her and murmur tenderly that he loved her, the last thing she now did was to reveal this desire by throwing herself at him and covering him with kisses. Such behaviour was guaranteed to send him straight to the television or a newspaper. Instead, a display on her part of independence, bordering on indifference, worked wonders. Curious at her reticence, he would be the one to approach her for some emotional reassurance. Sometimes there was a sulk or two to weather in the process, but they generally got there in the end. Far from worrying about what she might earlier on in her life have labelled as insincerity – or untruthfulness, even – Veronica was happy to discover that marriage gave such scope for creativity. It wasn't, as she had always assumed, about constructing a single, joint operation – unifying two harmonious souls into one, and all that. It was a much more complex business of creating three operations: hers, Julian's, and a third that came into being through the friction, contact, harmonies or whatever of the first two. All in all, she was finding it a rather exciting process, especially in the area of experimenting with what she could make happen and what she couldn't.

On a whistle-stop visit of Claudia's to London she had the opportunity to tell her aunt of her new-found domestic happiness. Claudia's agent had cancelled a meeting at the last minute and on impulse she called her niece to see if she could sneak out of the office for an indulgent tea at the Ritz. Veronica, normally very conscientious about office hours, surprised herself by agreeing. Part of the reason she did so was because she wanted to explain how well under control her private life now was.

'It's all one big game I've realized,' she confided happily, spreading lavish amounts of jam and cream on her scone. 'Slipping into different roles, adopting a different persona – all those little ploys to get what you want out of each other – that's the way marriage works.'

Aunt Claudia hesitated before responding. So this was how her advice had been put into practice. 'You don't make it sound very romantic, I must say.'

'It isn't,' replied Veronica flatly.

'Oh, but there should be room for romance, Veronica. I never meant that there shouldn't be room for romance.'

'It was trying to keep the "romance" alive that made things start to crumble.' She licked the jam and cream off each finger in turn. 'I was always trying to get him to bare his soul to me – going for spiritual union, togetherness and all that.' She laughed scornfully. 'Which of course only succeeded in driving him away. No, it's got to be much more business-like than that if things are to have any hope of ticking along smoothly.' Now that she was so sure she understood the subject, she spoke with great confidence. After all, her aunt had never been married.

Claudia was disappointed at Veronica's clinical approach to the most important relationship in her life. Her recommendation to make a go of it had always been on the basis that she loved Julian. In Claudia's book, loving – truly loving – a man precluded playing calculating games with him in order to keep life sweet. She turned the conversation back to publishing as quickly as she could; an area in which she could admire rather than despise her niece's pragmatism. She realized sadly that Veronica would never suffer for love, as she had done. Then she wondered if that was not an inner strength in the girl and tried to scold herself for being negative. But it didn't work. Suffering for love was important she decided, although she struggled to put her finger on quite why exactly.

'What time does it start?'

'We're due to eat at eight thirty so I was thinking of getting there at eight – perhaps a bit before, even.'

'It should be fun.'

'Yes, yes it should. Sorry you're not coming too, but you know . . .'

'Don't be silly. I suspect secretly, deep down you're rather glad,' she grinned to show this did not bother her at all, 'and

I think I'm rather glad for that matter. It was very good of you to ask – I didn't for a minute expect them to say yes. You'd all feel constrained if women were there. Anyway I'm shattered. A telly dinner, a hot bath and an early night are all I want in the world.'

'I'll try not to be too late back.'

'Don't worry, I'll be in bed before you've got through the speeches I should think. Here, do you want me to do that?' Veronica had an impressive knack with tying real bow-ties.

Julian stood happily in his socks and shirt-tails, letting his wife fuss over him. He really was looking forward to the rugby dinner. It was a long time since he had let go a bit with some solid drinking. He wondered, as he stood there, sticking his chin in the air to make Veronica's task a little easier, why, knowing that he was going to have a tremendous headache the next morning did not and would not deter him from overdoing it.

'There – all done.'

'Thank you, darling.' He kissed her on the nose. She lay on the bed and watched him finish his toilet for the evening. Black tie suited him very well.

'Very dashing, I must say. Don't talk to any tall dark handsome ladies will you?'

'Wouldn't dream of it,' he said easily, thinking that anyway Gloria had been auburn and on the short side.

'Any idea where Deirdre hides my handkerchiefs these days?' Julian had an uncanny knack of forgetting where even the most obvious things lived – whether it was the sugar or his underwear.

'Top left-hand drawer?'

'So they do,' he said, in a tone of genuine surprise, as if it was the first time his handkerchiefs had ever resided in such a place. Veronica, who had stopped allowing herself to be irritated by such things, started flipping through the

TV pages of the evening newspaper in order to plan when to have her bath and cook her omelette.

'Right, that's it. I'd better be off. The traffic can be awful on the south circular at this time of night . . .'

'Go on then.' She was kind enough to refrain from pointing out that even with appalling traffic he would be at the club house well before eight o'clock. 'Don't forget to tip-toe when you get back.' (This being the nicest way she could think of telling him not to wake her when he stumbled in drunk at two in the morning.)

'I'll be as quiet as a mouse, my darling. Have a nice evening.' He kissed her fondly on the lips, strolled out to the car and roared off down the road, the revs of the engine giving away his real, suppressed enthusiasm.

* * *

Charles White, known as Chalkie to his friends, got more than usually drunk at the dinner that night. It was his last official function as Captain of the Club, a job which had turned out to be far too political to be enjoyable. Being the first to arrive, he had started his celebrations very early on. Several frothy pints of bitter and a couple of double whisky chasers – accompanied by the grand total of two and a half crisps to do the job of soaking it all up – had already passed his lips by the time they went through to eat.

'Let the dinner begin,' he roared, banging the gavel according to the tradition of Tadfield Club. Although their numbers were relatively few and they floundered very much in the lower echelons of the London league, the club had once been famous for producing national players and still derived pride and pleasure from this fact (amongst themselves anyway). Musty photographs of teams kneeling before trophies – from the days when they still won trophies – lined the walls of the bar and dining-room.

'A toast to our founder,' shouted Chalkie after only a few minutes, when most had hardly registered the arrival of their grey prawn cocktails. Making various toasts throughout the dinner was all part of the ritual, as indeed was the extraordinarily poor quality of the food. But it was not usual to begin the toasting so early on.

'Steady on, old chap,' said Teddy, who was sitting to one side of him, 'some of us have got a bit of catching up to do.' He drained his wine glass to show commitment to the cause and speared a rubbery prawn.

'I see Gladys has excelled herself again. Nice that some people can always be relied upon to live up to their reputation.' Gladys had looked after the kitchens of the club house for as long as anyone could remember. She never showed the slightest interest in the game, nor in whether the food and drink she was called to serve was in celebration of victory or in consolation at defeat. All comments she made about anything – whether it was the weather, the price of fish or the political demise of the country – were voiced in loud monotones of the deepest pessimism. Her ideological touchstone, the name to which she referred all her opinions was Harold. Presumed to be 'Mr Gladys', Harold was a figure who attracted much sympathy in the club, although no one had ever set eyes on him. Their sympathy grew not just from Gladys's finesse in the field of culinary art and from her penchant for expressing thoughts loudly and violently. She also happened to be built like one of the large deep freezes in which she stored her packets of bullety prawns. In fact, as had been mentioned on more than one occasion, Gladys would have been of invaluable assistance in the middle of the scrum-line.

'A toast to Gladys and all who sail in her!' bellowed Chalkie, raising his glass unnecessarily high above his head. On cue for her moment, Gladys stood, arms akimbo, in the doorway that led through from the dining-room to the kitchen. She scowled at them all and shook her head in disapproval, actions which, over the years, the club members had come to interpret as a sign that she was really enjoying herself.

'So, glad it's all over are you?' enquired Teddy when Chalkie had sat down again.

'Too bloody right I am.'

'You certainly seem to have made yourself popular, I must say.' Teddy bent his head towards the captain's ear. 'Gandell and Hemmings are off to Culbridge, have you heard?' (Culbridge being their nearest rival as a club.)

'Of course I'd bloody well heard. Stupid buggers. Like bloody kids the lot of them.'

'I don't know though, Chalkie – whether you were right to leave them out of the St Albans game . . . I think they had a point being pissed off with you at that.'

'Oh you do, do you?' The captain ran his hand through his prematurely grey hair in a nervous gesture that had got much more frequent over the last year. He looked at Teddy down his nose, which was wide and crooked from having been crushed so many times in Tadfield's honour.

'It's all very well being clever after the event, smart-ass. I'd like to see how you'd have captained the side. All your favourite little buddies would have gone into the first XI no doubt – like beauty-boy Julian over there, who has been turning up for about one practice in a million.'

One of the announcements Chalkie had to make was that this was to be his last season. It had not been an easy decision. Audrey's whining about being left to entertain the twins on her own every weekend had played a part. But even more persuasive had been the near-riots prompted by practically every tactical change he had tried to implement during the preceding nine months. The whole business had thoroughly soured his attitude to the club, the players and the game. He was thirty-two and had originally intended to keep going for at least another couple of years. It was a bloody shame the way in which the whole thing was going to come to an end.

Peter Sidcup did not enjoy the dinner at all. He had expected as much. Drinking a lot was something he did fairly frequently, but always, he liked to think, with a certain amount of style. Dining with a lot of beery, out-of-condition rugger-thugs was about the most unstylish way of getting drunk that he could think of. He was there purely as a favour to Teddy, who, typically, had left the organizing of the guest-speaker until it was too late to ask anyone appropriate. Knowing even before he gave in to Ted's pleas, that a less suitable person to make a guest speech at the Tadfield rugby dinner would be hard to find – (he had little interest in the game and barely knew any of the club members) – Peter had resorted to the only sure means of getting through it: several excruciatingly rude jokes. Since he was not in a position to make digs at any of the players and since he had gathered from Teddy and Julian that it had not been the happiest year in the club's history, this route had seemed the only viable one to take.

Peter had an acidic, clipped way of talking which made people listen. He delivered the jokes in his usual dry, deadpan way which meant there were a couple of seconds before the lewd pennies dropped and his audience roared their applause. But roar they did, far too pleased with the punchlines and the effect of the alcohol to worry that their guest-speaker had no central theme or message for them all. Peter's agreement to go through this exercise in public-speaking had not been without its conditions. Firstly, Ted was to buy him a bottle of malt whisky of his choice (he was still making up his mind as to which one); and secondly, he was to be allowed to speak first, so as to have done with it and be able to sink into an alcoholic daze for the rest of the evening without it mattering.

Peter's speech, in terms of its delivery, was actually the finest of the lot. After him, a red-haired freckly young lad who was sitting on one side of the captain stood up and spoke at great length about various tackles and tries that he had 'been privileged to witness'. He seemed fond of the phrase and used it many times. To Peter's ears each detailed description of action on the pitch sounded like a repetition of the last. He yawned several times in succession and thought about going. But the metallic after-taste of the cheap red wine had assaulted and furred his tongue so much that it seemed worth trying to wash some of it away with a quick slug or two of port. He eyed the decanter making its slow progress round to his end of the table. It had got stuck beside the freckly-faced speaker, who was now gesticulating so violently, that all the many vessels containing liquid within his range looked in severe danger of being swept to the floor.

'Right, my turn, Crotty,' cut in Chalkie suddenly, tipping some port into the boy's glass and yanking him down into his seat. Peter breathed a sigh of relief as the decanter continued its slow journey towards his end of the table.

Chalkie stood up and banged the gavel so hard that all the glasses and crockery rattled. 'Sorry to interrupt and all that!' he shouted, not sounding sorry at all. 'Drink up, man, and don't look so bloody miserable'. He patted the ginger-haired boy hard on the back just as he was putting his glass to his lips.

'But I've got a few things to say, you see, and I'm rather bored of waiting to say them.' He stared defiantly at his audience, who merely blinked back at him, clearly unimpressed.

Chalkie shook his handful of papers and began. First, he told them he was going to hang up his boots. This brought a few murmurs, but nothing like the reaction he had been expecting, or hoping for. Then he proceeded to tell them in no uncertain terms what an unpleasant task it was trying to captain a side of 'such uncommitted, squabbling woofters'. This too caused far less of a stir than he had intended. Quite what he was expecting, Chalkie himself would have found it hard to say. But he thought his words would have some impact – provoke a bread roll or two at least. These were his last moments of public importance in the club; he wanted them to be marked in some way; he wanted to be remembered for something. His speech, which had seemed so biting when he was sober, now sounded as pathetic as the men he was criticizing. Nobody was sitting bolt upright, nobody was looking angry or shocked. Indeed they were all looking dangerously close to being bored. It was for this reason that Chalkie decided to make use of the lunatic letter which Gladys had put into his hands when he arrived earlier in the evening. He had been in a rush at the time to check through his speech and to get the first couple of pints down. So he had only glanced once at it, hardly had time to take it in at all in fact. It was from some crackpot making allegations against Julian Blake – tedious, sentimental stuff about not sticking to his commitments. All very odd really. He had meant to tell Julian about it before dinner, but what with one pint and the next, and putting the finishing touches to his speech, he had forgotten all about it.

Now the thought of the letter hit him, inspirationally, as one way of at least screwing a few laughs out of the bleary, gaping faces of his colleagues. Since Julian was no close friend of his and since his absence rate so far that season had broken new records, Chalkie felt no qualms about the idea of embarrassing him in public. Indeed the idea grew more attractive by the second.

'And now I've really got some scandal for you lot . . . hot off the press, we have here . . .' he rummaged for the letter, 'an anonymous complaint about one of our members. From the nature of the grievances I'd say our complainant was female.' He cleared his throat and began to read the letter in his highest most ridiculous falsetto. This sparked several guffaws immediately.

'. . . lack of emotional stability that has severely damaged the lives of several people,' piped Chalkie, his voice going up even higher as he warmed to the challenge. He was on to the second page and they were still roaring with laughter. All except Julian, who was looking puzzled, and Peter, who was looking serious, as if he sensed some approaching disaster. Chalkie had by now reached the last paragraph, which he had not even skimmed through before. As he started to read it now for the first time, he thought that perhaps it was going a bit far, but it was much too late to stop.

'. . . Julian Blake's desire to hurt women must come from one thing only – that he doesn't really like women at all. Because it's not women that attract him, it's men. Men like Teddy Charleston. They were gay-boys together at university and all the world should know it. They're living a lie and they shouldn't get away with it . . .' At this point Chalkie's hitherto robust falsetto fizzled into silence, joining the quietness of the whole assembled company. Feeling giddy, he slumped back down into his chair. For several long seconds, all eyes moved expectantly from Julian to Teddy.

Given their respective theatrical histories, it should perhaps have been Teddy who leapt to his feet to save the situation. But it was Julian. He jumped up on to the table and put on his most simpering pose: batting his eyelashes, puckering his lips, one hand held limply in front of him while the other dabbed at the corner of his eyes with a napkin, he minced down the table, daintily picking his way through the debris of dirty plates, glasses and cutlery. The tension broke and there was a relieved outburst of clapping and laughter even before he spoke.

'Well, little ol' me jus' wants to know one tiny thing,' he squeaked, in his best Southern drawl. 'If I'se so much lak a lady, how cum A'm havin me a little ol' beby-child in jus' six months' time? How cum I'se a goin to be a fader?' Once this information had sunk in, there was a collective gasp of astonishment followed by a hearty round of applause. Julian bowed extravagantly to all sides of the table, using his napkin to make a flurry and then stepped back over to his seat. Standing on his chair he raised his glass and pronounced:

'Please join me, gentlemen, in toasting the health of my child and the sickness of all those who make a living out of slander!' They all dutifully drank and the dinner hobbled on to its natural end.

*   *   *

'Good dinner?' Veronica's voice was slurry from sleep. She squinted at her digital alarm clock. Only quarter to one. She decided not to be angry with him for waking her up.

'Not brilliant, actually.'

'Oh, really?' She couldn't make up her mind whether to open her eyes properly and resign herself to really waking up or whether to keep them half-closed and try and maintain her semi-sleepy feeling. Julian was changing with the door open and the landing light on, but the effect was still quite dazzling.

'You can put the main light on if you like,' she said at length, having decided that the sleepy feeling was only a figment of her imagination.

'No, I'm through now anyway.' He slung the pile of clothes he had taken off over the banisters, put the light out and felt his way into the bedroom and over towards the bed.

'Well, I'm sorry the dinner wasn't that good. What was it, bad food or what?'

'The food was bad for sure. That's nothing new. No, it just . . .'

'It just what?' Veronica realized that his sulky tone was

not from drinking too much, as she had first presumed, but because he was genuinely depressed. 'It just what?' she repeated.

'It just got a little out of control, that's all.'

'Well, I wouldn't have thought that was anything new either . . .'

'I told them all about you being pregnant,' he blurted out, not knowing how else to tell her.

'You what?' Veronica sat up in bed. 'Jesus Christ, Julian. I've only missed one period – I haven't even had a test – what the hell made you do that? Even if I am, it's not safe to go advertising it to the world for at least three months . . . What on earth got into you?'

He looked away from her into the area of blackness which he knew housed their wardrobe. If he really concentrated he could just make out its outline. He wondered how much he should tell her.

'It's so unlike you,' she said, a little more gently now, 'to do something like that. Was it boasting or what? Please tell me, I just don't understand.'

'No, it wasn't boasting. And I know about the three months business. So I said you only had six months to go.'

Veronica flopped back against her pillows, unable to think of anything to say; sheer amazement now outweighing all her anger.

If there had been any way in the world that Julian could have engineered things so that Veronica never heard about the letter or how he had responded to it, he would not have uttered one word about the events of the evening. Indeed, he would have paid all the money he possessed, together with a hefty loan and a double mortgage, if it could have sealed the lips of every one of those attending the Tadfield Rugby Club dinner. But some things were simply impossible. Veronica would hear about it all right. Which was why, somehow, he had to tell her about it first.

'There is a reason why I did it, Veronica,' he said, after a long, weighty silence.

'I'd be glad to hear it.'

They were lying stretched out on their backs, side by side, like stone figures on an ancient tomb. They even had their hands folded on their stomachs.

'It will sound so damned silly, that's the trouble . . . I mean it is silly, the whole wretched business . . . but at the time . . . well at the time, I suppose I panicked a bit.'

'For goodness' sake, Julian, I don't have the faintest idea what you're talking about.' He sounded so serious, that she was now beginning to be worried. 'Just tell me what's going on.'

'Nothing is going on at all,' he said quickly, realizing that by delaying his explanation he was only making matters worse. 'It's utterly stupid and very simple. Chalkie – you know the captain – somehow got hold of a stupid letter – made it up himself I shouldn't wonder – saying all sorts of unpleasant things about me, which he read out in his speech.'

'What sort of things?'

'Well, lots of ridiculous things about me not being committed and stuff but also . . .' he paused for breath, 'claiming that I was gay.'

Veronica actually burst out laughing. 'Oh, my God, I don't believe it! How stupid. How incredibly childish can you get . . .'

'No, but that was not quite all. The letter also claimed that Teddy and I had an affair at college. Utterly ridiculous of course.' He didn't look at her even though it was dark. 'Anyway, I don't know what got into me . . . but they all seemed to be taking it so seriously that I suddenly had this crazy idea of jumping on the table and telling them all you were pregnant, to prove . . . well, to prove they were wrong for thinking what they were thinking.'

Veronica hesitated for quite a while before saying anything; not because she wanted to impress him with a meaningful silence, but because she had so many things she wanted to say she did not know which one to begin with. In some peculiar way she felt rather touched at Julian's defence of his heterosexuality, as if it had been done partly to protect her and their marriage. She was also curious, both as to the origins of the letter and whether there might be an element of truth in the accusation. But she didn't want to make him more miserable than he clearly was already.

'It does sound as if you over-reacted rather. I mean, sometimes an over-reaction makes it look as though you've got something to hide . . .'

'You don't understand; they were taking the wretched business so seriously. I had to do something . . .'

'And – now don't get angry – I have to ask – was there anything, anything at all, between you and Teddy?'

'Jesus Christ. Now I'm having to convince my own wife.'

'All right. Sorry. Sorry I asked. Forget it.'

'Why can't a couple of blokes be good friends without people making nasty accusations. It makes me sick.'

Something about the way Julian was speaking, the vehemence of his anger, allowed a sneaky little doubt to enter the back of Veronica's mind. She thought about Julian and Teddy having an affair. She tried to imagine them in bed together. She tried to conjure up some jealousy at the very idea of it. But it was useless, she couldn't make the notion seem real. It was absurd, the whole thing.

'I don't see what the big deal is,' she said truthfully. 'I don't think I would even mind if something had happened between you two.' She turned towards him and put her hand on his chest. His skin felt clammy; she could feel his heart beating very fast. He seemed scared. A strong desire to comfort him overtook her. 'Julian, darling, it doesn't matter. None of it matters. I probably am pregnant; and if I'm not we can just say we were mistaken. It's not so unusual to mistake missed periods for pregnancies. And as for you and Teddy . . . it's all so silly. So what? So what if you had? I bet half the guys round the table have played around with other blokes at some stage – even if it was just . . .'

'Veronica, just leave it will you? I've told you what happened; now you know everything. So let's just forget it for a while and get some sleep.'

'But what about the letter? To me that's the only worrying thing. Who the hell wrote it, and why? That's what's really nasty in this whole stupid business – that someone should dislike you enough to do such a thing. Who could it possibly be I wonder?'

He had been wondering how long it would take her to get back to the letter.

'Like I said, it was probably Chalkie, playing a practical joke, getting his own back for all the practices I've missed.'

'But you've hardly missed any. You've attended every week so far this season.'

Julian's heart thumped. How bloody careless. Of course she thought he had been diligent over attending practices; it had been his night for Gloria.

'The odd match, yes – you've skipped on a couple when we've been going away for a weekend, but practices . . . no, I don't think you missed a single one. How strange . . .'

'Well, I don't know,' he interrupted quickly, 'the guy never liked me very much anyway.' And this seemed to satisfy her, for the time being at least.

In fact Chalkie had shuffled up to Julian after the party had adjourned to the bar to make something of an apology.

'Sorry, old chap. Didn't know it got quite so hot. Here, you have it. Meant to give it to you before dinner actually, but it slipped my mind. Then it just seemed like a good idea to read out a few snippets . . . looks like someone's really got it in for you, eh? Not to mention old Ted over there.'

He indicated the chair in which Teddy was slumped, with a bottle of whisky under his arm and a large tumbler in each hand. Julian had accepted the letter as dismissively as he could, telling Chalkie that none of it bothered him in the slightest.

'Oh, and congratulations by the way . . .'

'Er, thanks.' He strolled into the gents, locked himself in the toilet furthest from the entrance and sat down to study the thing properly. It was written in block capitals. He read over everything that Chalkie had broadcast at the dinner-table. Clearly the rantings of someone whose only real grievance was a broken heart. (Never having had his own heart broken, Julian had no notion how severe the suffering of such a grievance might be.) But even before he opened the letter, he had already decided on the identity of its author. It had to be Gloria. She was the only one with enough motive to hurt him. What's more, she was the only one whom he had ever been crazy enough, during one of their silly games when they had both had far too much to drink, to hint that there had once been something between him and Teddy. She had struck him as so unshockable, so discreet and such a good listener, that at the time it had not seemed such a terrible thing to do. It was the next morning that the memory of his half-confession came back at him like a stab in the gut. He thought back carefully over what he had actually said, consoling himself with how vague he had been. He hadn't really spelt anything out, not in so many words. Gloria had never referred to it again either, which served to reassure him as to how little he had given away. As the weeks passed, time helped close the memory as it does a wound. In fact, before the appearance of the letter, Julian had almost succeeded in convincing himself that he had told Gloria nothing at all.

* * *

'Where is the letter?'

He thought Veronica had fallen asleep. 'I burnt it.'

'What else did it say?'

'Oh, just lots of nasty things about me, my character, that sort of thing.'

'How horrid.' She snuggled up into the crook of his arm.

'Sorry about the pregnancy thing. I shouldn't have done it. I don't know what got into me really. So silly.'

'Never mind. You know, I rather think I am.'

'You are what?'

'Pregnant, stupid.'

'How can you tell?'

'Hm? I don't know.' She yawned luxuriously and stretched. 'I just feel different, that's all.'

Early the next morning Julian was woken up by the sounds of Veronica retching in the bathroom. A few moments after the chain had flushed, she appeared in the doorway of the bedroom looking pale.

'My God, so it's true,' he said. 'But that's wonderful. And I don't just mean because of . . .'

'No, I know. It's amazing. I must have a test. Julian, what will we do with a baby? I just can't believe it. I don't know what to think.' She threw herself on to the bed.

'Steady on there, take it easy.' They hugged each other close and he stroked her hair. If there is a God, he thought, then I owe him one.

15

Lighting The Fuse

'What on earth's got into Ted recently?' George's question was directed at Sids, who, from his usual supine pose on the sofa, was working his way systematically through *The Times* crossword. Following his customary methodology for the exercise, he had completed all the across clues and was just starting on the ones going down.

'Simply because a chap does not share your natural ebullience during every second of his life, Smithers, does not mean that something has "got into him", as you so graphically put it.'

George had just returned from two weeks at his parents' house in Brentford. This late 'summer holiday' had been prompted by two, not entirely unconnected, things: firstly, that he could not afford to take a holiday anywhere other than with his parents; and secondly, the need for just such a length of time in order to wage a campaign for an injection of cash – or even a loan – from his father. In spite of a good deal of pre-planning as to how and when to make his move, things had not gone too well – or at least they had not turned out remotely as George had been expecting.

Problems between George and his father went back a long way. Being an only child, there had always been pressure on him to take over the family business. But managing a company that made electrical lift-fittings was not a career-path that George had ever found very appealing. With a determination that surprised even him, he had held out against both his parents' wishes, struggled through law exams and made his way to London. His mother had long since forgiven him for choosing this option, but his father found it more difficult. If the conversation kept to sport and cars, they were all right. But the moment money (Henry Smithers liked to expound on the unsung fortune to be made out of electrical components), or any related subjects came up, all lines of communication between father and son were immediately pulled tight with tension and resentment. Asking for financial help was never easy. In the end George made a complete bosh of it. Forgetting all resolutions for tactful, gentle approaches to the subject, he let slip about his state of penury during the first of their disagreements. This had the dire effect of setting his father absolutely against the idea; and – worse still – of giving him extra fuel for all the arguments that flared up during the course of the next ten days.

In the end, surprisingly, it had been George's mother who saved the day. On the last morning of his stay she slipped into his bedroom with a cup of tea and a cheque for six hundred pounds. George, who had only ever associated his mother with filling his stomach and a silent acquiescence to every word uttered by his father, was astounded. Especially as the account was in her maiden name, which he hardly knew. Mrs Smithers explained to her son in hurried, breathy whispers, that her father had opened this account for her with a lump sum of money on her sixteenth birthday, that she had just let it sit there, had never had to touch it, had never bothered to tell Henry about it, had been keeping it for a day when it was really needed, and now that day had come, and he wasn't to breathe a word to his father. A big wet kiss and she was gone, slipping back into her cooking, her crochet and her quietness.

Six hundred pounds was not a fortune, but it was a big help. He decided not to mention it to Mr Fish, but to put it in his post office account and use it, sparingly, for enjoying himself. Such an act of kindness by his mother also touched his (not always very sensitive) soul very deeply. It made him think of her differently. It made him wonder, for a few moments at least, what lay behind her steamy puddings, her balls of wool and her silence.

George had returned to London slightly humbled but with renewed vigour. He was disappointed to find that the various elements of his life in town did not respond in kind. For a start, Katherine seemed to have disappeared. He had been ringing her flat constantly since his return, at all hours of the day and night, with no success. Added to that, a black cloud appeared to have descended over his flatmates since his departure. In fact George had the vague feeling that a mysterious but fundamental change had taken place during his sojourn in Essex.

His question to Peter Sidcup was one of several attempts to get to the bottom of what had gone wrong.

'Come on, Sids – crashing out with a bottle in my bedroom all the bloody time. You must admit that he's very out of sorts. Ever since I got back he's been like it.'

'Perhaps there is some connection between the two events. Had you thought of that, Smithers?'

'What do you mean?'

'Think about it for a few hours and see what you come up with.'

George thought. 'Oh I say . . . I hardly think so. You're not serious are you, Sids? It can't really . . .'

'No, Smithers, I'm not serious.' Peter sighed. A certain

depression was making him more acerbic than usual. George, with his denseness, was unfair cannon-fodder, he knew. 'How about demonstrating your culinary skills with a frying-pan and a packet of bacon, old chap?' he suggested, as kindly as he could, a few moments later. George's bacon-butties tended to be nine-tenths grease and one-tenth buttie. Peter, who laid claim to a delicate stomach and tended to eat out or not at all, had to be positively ravenous to get through one. But Teddy wolfed them down and it was mainly with Ted in mind that Peter had made the suggestion. Smells of frying bacon wafting under the door of George's bedroom, where Ted had spent the majority of all evenings since the Tadfield dinner watching his mini-portable television and drinking whisky, might just tempt him out. But even when the smells of pork fat had reached nauseous levels as far as Peter was concerned, the bedroom door remained closed.

'I'll take Ted one,' said Peter after a half-hearted bite at his own.

'Good idea,' gobbled George, his mouth full and grease trickling in thick rivulets down his chin.

Peter knocked a couple of times, but the only answer he got was the hum of voices talking on the television. So he went in anyway. Ted was lying propped up against George's one rubbery pillow, staring blankly at the TV screen. The bottle of whisky which had been two-thirds full when he went in, now lay empty on the floor beside the bed.

'Here you are, old man, some dinner for you. Though why you should be waited on hand and foot, I can't think.' He sat down on the end of the bed and put the plate beside Teddy.

'Jolly decent, old chap,' said Teddy, slurring his words terribly and ignoring the offering. Still looking at the screen, he waved his hand dismissively at Peter. 'Not hungry.'

'Can't say I blame you, they are somewhat revolting.'

Peter lit one of his slim cheroots and gave some thought to what he should say next.

'We could go for an Italian round the corner you know. George's bacon sandwiches are not the only cuisine available in London.' Teddy still said nothing.

'Edward, I'm offering to buy you dinner. You could at least make a show of interest, or disinterest, or something. For God's sake, man, you can't spend the rest of your life moping because of some stupid bloody incident which everyone has forgotten about already . . .'

'I don't know what the fuck you're talking about and I don't want to know. Fuck off and leave me alone. Take George out to the bloody Eytie if you're so desperate for company.'

Peter, whose lips were naturally thin, pursed them to a bloodless slit of a line. He wanted to help Teddy, but the latter made it impossible. 'Suit yourself, Charleston,' he said quietly, leaving the room and shutting the door soundlessly behind him.

George had fallen asleep, mouth wide open and legs splayed out, in front of the television. Peter, disappointed in both his flatmates, rescued his *Times* and retired to the sanctity of his own room, where he began studying the property pages.

* * *

Getting pregnant was something Veronica had discussed on numerous occasions with her career-oriented girlfriends. It was always viewed by them all as a problem: when to let it happen, how to fit it in, what amount of time to take off work, whether to bother at all. Now that some were married, and most were much nearer thirty than twenty, a few on the periphery of her circle had taken the plunge and had babies. They were regarded by Veronica and her closest allies with equal quantities of horror and fascination. How could she leave her job at such a critical time? How could she bear to get so fat and to spend her days and nights changing nappies? How could she cope with such a commitment?

With her natural penchant for being very organized, Veronica had worked it all out in advance. Once she was head of her section (the educational section) of the publishing company – a rise which she estimated would take another five years – she planned to take a few months off to have a child. By then she would be thirty-two. With all the statistics on older mothers being more likely to have mongols and miscarriages, she did not want to leave the business much later than that. If her promotions were slow in coming, she would perhaps have to think again. And that was as far as she had got. Until her doctor recommended she take a break from the pill and spend a few months with another form of contraception. She had taken up his suggestion of using the cap, but without much relish. Traipsing to the loo on the rare occasions that Julian got the urge and messing around with creams that made the wretched thing slip out of her hands and shoot across the bathroom like some rubber rocket, did not do much for her libido. She would return to the bedroom distraught and bad tempered, sometimes to find that Julian had fallen asleep waiting for her. After a few of these episodes she took to putting the thing in automatically before going to bed and gave up on the creams altogether. That was how the unscheduled pregnancy came about.

It all happened so quickly, from suspecting to having it confirmed, that there was no time to dread the results. On the day she was sick, she rushed off to see her doctor during her lunch-hour. He called her at home later that day to say that the result was positive and to offer his warmest congratulations. Since she had felt a bit queasy all morning, she mumbled something to her boss about food-poisoning and took the afternoon off. The call from Doctor Morris came before Julian got in from work. She put the receiver down and waited to see how she really felt about it, half-expecting panic or fury to descend now that she knew it was true. But the happiness wouldn't go away.

Julian could not believe the effect on his wife of something which he would have expected to make her angry and upset. Best of all was the way the excitement at the news completely over-shadowed the nightmare of the Tadfield dinner incident. She really did not seem to mind at all. The evening after the doctor phoned he came home with an enormous bunch of yellow and pink carnations and a small velvet box.

'This is to say sorry and congratulations all at the same time.'

'There's nothing to be sorry for, darling.' She kissed him tenderly. 'You were just a bit prophetic, that's all. It doesn't matter a bit.'

'Hang on, before you open it,' he put his hands over the little box, 'I want to say something else.'

'Well, be quick about it, I don't think I can wait much longer.'

He turned from her and made a big show of taking off his jacket and tie while he talked.

'It's just about the other business, you know, the accusation . . .'

'Darling, you don't have to . . .' she couldn't bear to see him squirming. She wanted him strong, protective, secure always.

'No, I must, because people will probably say something – make a dig or something – at some stage and so I want to get things clear.' He put his hands in his pockets, jingled his change and looked at the floor. He had been thinking of little else all day: whether to tell her that he had gone through a tiny, silly ridiculous phase with Ted; a phase which had meant nothing to him and which had finished almost as soon as it had begun. There were no conceivable witnesses to what had actually taken place and he was absolutely convinced that nothing like that would ever be repeated in his life. Ted, he was sure, would never breathe a word. In the end it was this conviction, that the case against him could not be proven, which made Julian err on the side of dishonesty when the moment came.

'Ted and I go back a long way. We were at prep school together – well, you know that. We've always been excellent friends and we've gone through phases, like most friends, of being quite close and then quite far apart. And that's it . . . I mean, that's all there is to it. We lived in each other's pockets at college – we did everything together, but . . . I mean it never . . . there was never anything else.' His eyes met hers. 'Honestly darling, there was nothing.' The believing, forgiving expression on her face made the lying easy. 'I just needed to tell you that. I just need you to believe in me, even if no one else does.'

'Of course I believe in you,' said Veronica throwing her arms around him and making one of the most serious mistakes of her life. Because she did believe him, utterly.

The little box contained a pair of pearl drop-earrings. When Veronica had put them on she decided that she felt well enough to be taken out to dinner. In the restaurant she refrained from drinking and found herself overtaken by an urge for radishes. They confided both the problem and its likely cause to the waiter who was delighted to keep a steady supply beside her throughout the meal. Veronica ate three courses, popping quantities of radishes into her mouth between each one.

* * *

'. . . I couldn't say this to one of my friends because they just wouldn't understand,' called Veronica from the kitchen to the sitting-room (where Julian was secretly wishing she would stop talking long enough for him to put the telly on without it looking like a rebuff), 'but I really feel wonderful about getting pregnant. I mean the one thing that I always thought I would mind about – my job – just doesn't seem to be bothering me at all. In fact I'm even finding it rather difficult to concentrate at work. It's like, well, I suppose everything has just been put in perspective suddenly. I mean you can't get more important than the creation of human life, can you? It seems to be sort of dwarfing everything else . . .' Since there had been no sounds of concurrence from the sitting-room for a while, she popped her head round the door for reassurance: 'You do see what I mean, don't you?'

Julian swung his head round and up so quickly from the newspaper that he cricked his neck. 'Absolutely.'

Veronica paused in the doorway, preoccupied with her own train of thought. 'I'm not saying I want to give up work for ever or anything.' She absently licked the wooden spoon with which she had been stirring a saucepan of bolognaise sauce. 'It's just that some of that urgency I used to feel about getting to the top seems to have disappeared overnight. Perhaps it won't last. Perhaps this is all just first-reaction euphoria. A fat tummy, swollen ankles and piles will soon set me to rights, I'm sure.' But she referred to these side-effects of child-bearing fondly, as things to be looked forward to more than dreaded.

'Piles?' Julian experienced one of the many twinges of gratitude that the pregnant condition was the preserve of women.

'Yup, I was reading about it today,' she called from the kitchen, the wooden spoon now back in the bolognaise. 'It's very common apparently. It's not sub-conscious fears of losing the baby by going to the loo or anything, it's . . .'

Further amplification on the subject was prevented by

the telephone. Veronica, since she was within arm's reach, picked up the receiver with one hand, while continuing to stir with the other.

'Hello? . . . Hello? . . . Hang on, who is this?'

'Who is it?' shouted Julian, making it even harder for her to hear.

'Who's speaking, please? Oh, it's you. You sounded jolly odd for a moment . . . Yes, just a tick and I'll get him. It's Ted,' she said, handing the receiver to Julian, who had come into the kitchen to find out who it was.

But on hearing it was his friend, Julian shook his head and waved his arms, mouthing like some deaf person trying to speak: 'I don't want to talk to him, I'm not here.'

'Why ever not?' she whispered furiously. 'Of course you must speak to him. I said you were here anyway. Come on, don't be silly.'

Reluctantly and a little roughly, Julian took the receiver. He cleared his throat before speaking. 'Ted, old man, to what do I owe the pleasure?' He put his arm round Veronica and dipped his finger in the bolognaise to show her that he knew he was being silly before and to try and stop her from mentioning it later.

'Tonight, old chap?' he made a face at her and did a thumbs down sign. "Fraid not. Dinner's already on the boil so to speak. What about next week some time? A lunch, maybe? I quite want to be home in the evenings at the moment as you can probably imagine.' He gave Veronica's shoulders a squeeze. There was a long silence, followed by what sounded like a dry sob. Julian was a little appalled, not having cried himself since he was thirteen. Tears at home had never been allowed: 'They're not part of a grown man's make-up and I won't have it,' his father used to roar.

'I say, Ted, pull yourself together, old man.' He made a despairing face at Veronica.

'Please, Jules, please. It's very . . . I mean, I'm very . . .'

'Yes, you certainly are.'

'I need to see you, Jules.'

Julian took the phone to the other end of the kitchen. 'Nonsense. Don't talk rot. Certainly not tonight. Another time as I said. Do try and get a grip on yourself . . . Hello? Hello? Ted, are you still there or have you fallen asleep? Look, as I said . . . Jesus Christ,' he held the receiver out and looked at it in amazement. 'He hung up. Can you beat that? The stupid bugger hung up.'

'Perhaps he got cut off. Why not call him back and see?'

'I'm damned if I will. He bloody well hung up, I'm sure of it.'

'I thought he sounded a bit strange, I must say.'

'Drunk,' said Julian, stomping back into the sitting-room.

'Well, it's hardly something to get in a complete tizz about, is it?' she said when they sat down to eat and she realized that he had let the phone-call put him in a bad mood. 'Like you said, he was just drunk, that's all.'

'I know, I know. I just find it extremely irritating. How absurd to expect me to drop everything and rush out to have dinner with him just because he feels a bit low. As if I didn't have a life of my own to lead . . . I've told him, he's really going to have to watch the booze – it's making a complete idiot out of him.'

'I suppose he must have been as angry as you were about the Tadfield thing,' said Veronica absently, her mind more on how unappetizing her plate of spaghetti bolognaise looked.

'Oh, Ted didn't mind – saw the funny side – you know Ted . . . darling, is anything the matter?' The colour had drained visibly from Veronica's face and she was holding her stomach.

'No, I just . . .' She kicked back her chair and made a dash for the downstairs loo, reaching it in the nick of time. For the rest of the evening all thoughts of Ted, the Tadfield dinner and other unpleasantnesses were mercifully forgotten as Julian exaggeratedly fussed around Veronica, puffing cushions and fetching glasses of water. It was only a passing spell of nausea. A little while later, she allowed him to make her a mug of instant soup and some buttered toast, which she ate curled up in his dressing-gown on the sofa.

*   *   *

Most of the time, for most people, life ticks along pretty smoothly. Especially the lives of people like Veronica and Julian Blake, Teddy Charleston, Peter Sidcup, Gloria Croft and the rest of them. They have their ups and downs of course – like George's money problems or Julian's affair. But, usually they manage to sort themselves out, such troubles as they have getting smoothed away by time or luck or both.

But underneath this surface of normality – of people behaving more or less as they are expected to – lies a dangerous sea of private thoughts and undiscovered truths. For very rarely do people express the hidden, truest depths of how they feel. Instead they say what they think they ought to say, act as they think they ought to act, while their real, inner thoughts remain unvoiced. (Those hidden notions and desires can be so extreme, so unacceptable, so tactless or embarrassing – far too shocking to be expressed.) And so an untapped reservoir of human feelings and potential acts remains concealed below the surface, lying dormant until some event forces an eruption. It may only be an infinitesimal thing, the merest pin-prick of a happening, which lights the fuse. But once it is lit, the flame travels fast; and soon enough a whole patch of that underworld, which makes up the inner lives of human beings, is thrown up in a blast of chaos.

In this case, the spark that lit the fuse was Katherine Vermont. Or perhaps it would be fairer to say it was Julian himself, since his earlier behaviour had done much to shape the development of Katherine's strangely intense emotional make-up. Whatever it was, it would all have fizzled out if human nature was not so vulnerable and if there had not been secrets – many, many secrets – to catch light and gather momentum along the way. Katherine's motive (inasmuch as she was mentally capable of such a thing), was to hurt Julian Blake. But her bomb did not explode as she meant it to. Julian suffered from a little shell-shock, a few minor injuries in the fall-out. The main victim was someone whom she barely knew; and someone whom she would have had no inclination to hurt, since he had certainly contributed little towards the breaking of female hearts.

16

The Explosion

It was a tramp who found him, since it happened a little before dawn and the streets were empty. He had fallen so perfectly that at first Tom thought he was just lying on the pavement having a doze. But as he looked more closely he saw that there was a pool of blood by the head and no sign of life in the body. He nudged it gently with his toe to be sure. Although he had long since retired from adhering to social conventions, his first reaction was to tell someone in authority about his find. Death was, after all, quite important. Somebody had to be told. Something had to be done. He felt a little light-headed with the responsibility of it all and with the thrill of seeing a corpse at such close quarters. Rather than make him fear his own end, the sight excited him, made him feel very much alive. After a good inspection from all angles – but without touching it again – he scuttled off to South Kensington police station (where his face was well-known), and got a cup of tea for his pains.

'Your friend is not dead,' said the Inspector quietly, neutrally, in the tone he reserved for such occasions, 'but his injuries are very severe indeed. Would you like to notify his family or would you prefer us to handle it?'

'No.' Peter's voice was at its coldest, its most acidic. 'We will.'

'Oh, I say, Sids . . . I'm not sure that I can . . . that I could . . .'

'I will do it, George.'

The Inspector coughed before continuing with his business; a vile, throaty noise, that suited the ugliness of the morning. 'Now then, as to the cause of the accident.'

George threw a glance at Peter who did nothing to acknowledge it. Instead he stood, staring out of the sitting-room window as if the Inspector's words meant nothing to him at all.

'He clearly fell out of the window. The question is whether the fall was accidental or not.'

'But you can't mean . . .' began George in a voice pitched several notes higher than usual.

'. . . I mean that, judging from the amount of alcohol in his bloodstream, your friend was very drunk indeed. The question therefore remains as to whether he fell accidentally, whether it was attempted suicide or – for I'm afraid we must consider all options, gentlemen – whether he was pushed.'

George wrung his hands. Peter continued to stare out of the window.

The Inspector spent a good forty minutes asking questions, taking statements and looking at the point from which Ted had made his unfortunate exit from the flat. The window was high off the floor and only a couple of feet wide. Along the outside of it was a small ledge, on which the soberest of men would find it difficult to stand for long.

By the time the policemen left, George was in a state of high excitement, brought on largely from fear.

'Jesus bloody Christ,' he wailed, almost before the door

was shut, 'I can't believe it, I just can't believe any of it . . . Christ, it's bad enough that Ted should . . . but now the police think we did it . . . I just can't believe it – that man thinks we tried to . . . to murder . . .'

'Shut up, George, and don't be absurd. He thought nothing of the sort. It was all routine. So stop bawling.' George obediently went quiet while Peter poured them both a large whisky.

They sipped in silence for a few moments, thirsty from shock.

'Do you think he was really trying to kill himself, Sids?' whispered George at length. 'Do you really think that Ted . . .'

'Of course he was trying to kill himself.' Peter drained his glass. 'He's been trying to kill himself for years.'

George, as seemed to happen to him more and more these days, felt there was an enormous aspect to the situation which he did not understand. But before he could ask Peter to illuminate, he left the room.

George remained on the sofa, now gulping his whisky and battling with the impossible idea of Ted – jolly old Ted – throwing himself out of a window deliberately. True, he had seemed a bit down recently, but never once had it struck him as anything like a suicidal sort of depression. He was sure Sids had got it wrong. Teddy had simply had several too many, leaned out of the window for a bit of air and accidentally toppled out. And he would probably be all right. Ted was a survivor – at least that's what Sids always said. The whisky, which had at first been fortifying, was now making him feel weak, close to tears even.

Peter reappeared. 'I've rung the hospital. He's in a coma. And I've spoken to his mother. She's on her way down now and I'm going there myself. I suggest you go into work as normal. Nothing you can do. You'll only feel worse if you sit around.'

The tone of command was reassuring. 'I suppose you're right. Poor Ted.' George got up from the sofa, still in his dressing-gown; but he could not resist going over to the window before leaving the room.

'I'm sure he didn't mean to, Sids. It was just the booze, I'm sure of it.' Peter didn't say anything. But as George shuffled past him to get to the bathroom, he gave him two gentle pats on the shoulder as he went by. For some reason those pats made George want to cry more than ever.

17

Aftermath

Peter called Julian from the hospital to tell him what had happened. It is hard enough knowing how to react to any sort of bad news. But when the person being informed of the disaster feels, secretly, implicated in its cause, then the challenge can be very tough indeed. Julian did not manage his lines very well.

'Oh, my God, how terrible,' he said. 'Will he . . . I mean is this coma-thing likely to be permanent?'

'Put it like this: He'd be better off not coming out of the coma at all.' Peter Sidcup, who guessed more than anyone about the reasons for Ted's unhappiness, did not feel inclined to help Julian very much in coping with the news.

'Jesus, Sids, I don't know what to say. Poor Ted. How awful. That fucking booze – I told him, I tried to warn him . . .'

'Yes, I think the police are going to blame alcohol as well. They'll call it an accident I'm sure of it.'

'But they'd be right – wouldn't they?'

'I don't know, Julian. You tell me.'

'What the hell do you mean?'

'Never mind, never mind.' The strain of the morning was beginning to tell. He was saying things he had no intention of saying. 'Listen, when can you get here?'

'To the hospital?'

'Yes, to the bloody hospital – where do you think – Butlins?' Peter's anger was not just at Julian, it was at himself, at all of them for having been so useless, for not having been able to help, for not really having tried to help, for being selfish, blind . . .

Julian did not want to go to the hospital. He was scared at the thought of seeing Teddy trussed up with wires like some bionic hedgehog. More than that, he was scared at the thought of the still-manageable pangs of guilt growing any stronger.

'I'm very busy . . .'

'Don't tell me you're too bloody busy to spare a few minutes for someone with whom you were once . . .'

'Stop it, Sids. I'm useless at hospitals. Bloody useless. I mean what's the good? The wretched chap's in a coma, he won't know whether I'm there or not . . . and his family – his mother I mean – won't want people like me barging in . . .'

'Very well. A pub then. We must talk, Julian – about the letter.'

'The letter?'

'I suppose it's shock that is making you so obtuse. I hope it is. I am referring to the letter whose contents were shared with us the night of that delightful dinner at Tadfield Rugby Club. I need to find out who wrote it.'

Julian was feeling more frightened by the second. 'I don't know who the bloody hell wrote the fucking letter and I don't see what on earth it has to do with Ted being laid out in a bloody hospital . . .'

'Then you're even dumber than I thought . . . I'm running out of money – that was my last ten pence. The King's Head

– the one near our flat – at seven tonight. Julian? Will you be there? You must be there.' There was just time for a faint, reluctant 'yes,' before the line went dead.

For a few minutes Julian sat trying to let the news sink in. He was terrified that Peter might know about Teddy phoning and begging him to come round. Even though he hadn't mentioned it, Julian had the uncanny feeling that Peter knew everything – not just about the phone-call, but about everything. Feeling really quite panicky for the first time in his life, he called Veronica. Her immediate commonsense practicality washed over him like a cold shower of relief.

'It's terrible, absolutely terrible. But, Julian, don't you go dumping any of the guilt on yourself. I'm going to say that straight away because I can tell already that that's what you've been doing. Friends and relatives always do that when people have accidents. It's stupid. Whether he did it on purpose or whether he slipped, has nothing to do with you. If you had gone out to dinner with him he would have done it afterwards. If it hadn't happened last night it would have happened another night. OK?'

'Are you sure?' He felt quite pathetic.

'Of course I'm sure. You're just torturing yourself for nothing. It's totally pointless – pointless and ridiculous. There was no reason in the world why you should have dropped everything and rushed round to have dinner with him. I mean, he didn't sound that desperate or anything did he?'

'Not really . . .' he lied.

'There you are then. It would not have made a blind bit of difference. So forget it. The main thing is whether he's going to get better or not.'

'From what Sids said it doesn't sound like it.'

'Oh dear. Poor, poor Teddy. What a thing to happen.'

'Sids wanted me to go to the hospital, but I just don't think there's any point.'

'Quite right. You couldn't do anything. And I expect his mother's there, isn't she?' Julian had never loved his wife so much. 'How terrible for her, what with his father being so ill and everything. He doesn't have any brothers and sisters does he?'

'No, no, he doesn't.'

'Darling, I'm so sorry. It's all so awful.'

'I'm meeting Peter after work, so I'll be a bit late.'

'Are you sure that's wise? I mean talking about it isn't going to do any good either.'

'No, I know. But, actually, I think Peter needs some reassurance.' He didn't want to mention the letter.

'Yes, of course. Terrible for Peter – and George too – being just next door when it happened. They must feel guiltier than anyone. I'll see you after your drink then. And don't worry, darling – there was nothing that could have prevented it. It is just one of those ghastly things that happens.'

So Veronica unwittingly helped pad out Julian's armour against confronting the full implications of what had happened and why. She was partly right in what she said. Just as Peter was. Ted had long since placed himself on a course of self-destruction. The role Julian had played in his life – up to and including refusing to have dinner with him on the night he toppled out of the window – could simply be said to have speeded up the process a little. Along with the letter itself, of course.

*　　*　　*

By the time Peter arrived at the King's Head he had recovered some of his composure. An afternoon lie-down – (he hadn't been able to sleep) – followed by a hot shower and another large whisky had worked wonders. It had never been his intention to force any sort of confrontation with Julian over the part he had played in Teddy's life. To him it all seemed pretty obvious. The two close friends had got very close indeed during some stage of their first year at university – in fact shortly before Peter had first run into them. What for Julian had been only a passing phase had for Teddy been a way of life, merely waiting to find expression. None of this would have mattered very much at all, except that Julian remained the only figure in Ted's life in whom it did find expression. So, as Peter had deduced many years before, Ted loved Julian. Only Julian's intense selfishness had prevented him from noticing it. None of these things were important to Peter in themselves. It was only Ted's sadness which had ever prompted him to think about the matter at all. But a man cannot easily say to another man: 'I know you love him and I am sorry that it makes you suffer.' Such things simply could not be mentioned. Such things have to be confined to those undercurrents of true feeling which so seldom find expression.

Peter regretted his childish challenges to Julian on the telephone. Anger, he knew, was not going to help or change anything, least of all Julian. Through the blur of his own sadness and sense of failure, he saw that the letter had been the real trigger; it was the reading of the letter which had opened the floodgates of Teddy's misery. And it was therefore the letter-writer whom Peter really wished to confront. Not because he was foolish enough to want to cause the author any physical harm. But because he wanted to make that person aware of the dire consequences of her petty action. He wanted to tell the lady, whoever she was, that this malicious prank had wrought chaos in the lives of other people. As Veronica had rightly said, they all felt guilty in their own ways. Peter just wanted to make sure that the guilt was spread as widely as it should be, that no one escaped their responsibilities. It also gave him something to do. While Julian could listen to the soothing, rational voice of his wife,

Peter had decided that action, however desperate, was the only thing that was going to make him feel any better.

'Forgive me, Julian, for being a little short on the telephone. The tension I guess . . .'

'How is he?'

'Just the same. Connected to various machines which channel things like air and food in and out of his body. It's gross actually, quite gross. It's not Teddy lying there at all of course. It's something sub-human. They should pull the fucking plug out and have done with it; that's what Ted would want, I'm sure.'

'How's his mother taking it?' Julian did not really want to know the answers to these questions. He was asking them out of a sense of duty, in response to an unwritten set of rules entitled: What to Say in a Crisis. During the day, the pangs of guilt, which had characterized his first reactions, had been superseded by a real, albeit selfish sense of loss. If he had not had sensible, rational questions to cling to he might have cried or been sick into his pint of beer. Where Peter's instinct was to attack the problem, to try as best he could to unravel what had led up to Teddy's death, Julian's was to escape it. He couldn't wait to get home; to bury his head in Veronica's soft swollen breasts and have her tell him that everything was all right. Being so near the flat, being near Peter, was somehow making it all worse. He had deliberately driven the long way round to the pub, so as to avoid going past the window from which Ted fell – or jumped.

'I think his mother might die of shock. I'm being quite serious. She dotes on Ted – only son, husband an invalid, and all that. She has a sister or someone with her. They're just sitting beside the bed watching. I think a small whisky would wash this beer down rather well. What do you say?'

Julian nodded.

'Right, my friend,' he continued, once he had set the drinks down on the table, 'who wrote that letter?'

'What the hell has it got to . . .' started Julian, but Peter's voice cut across his like a whip.

'That letter, Julian, is what set Edward on the road to throwing himself out of the window. Because that letter referred to a homosexual relationship between you two at university. You may have closed your eyes to the fact, but, although your antics dealt with the situation marvellously – congratulations by the way – not all those present were able to react so well.' Peter pressed on, talking quickly and quietly, without concern for his companion's obvious fear as to what he might say next. 'I do not wish to discuss your sexual history. All that is important is that for Ted the shame, the truth, or whatever it was, hurt him too deeply for him to laugh it off as you did. Added to that, it brought home to him the fact that he had not found someone who could return his affections.' Peter paused here, but only for a second. Just long enough to decide against putting Julian through the rigours of confronting the truth about how much Teddy loved him. He was probably suffering somewhere behind that soft, spoilt face.

'From that moment he proceeded to drink to ridiculous excess. Until he had gathered enough courage to throw himself out of a window. Being gay may be all right in some circles, but Tadfield Rugby Club is, I suspect, not one of them. Edward had been lonely in private for most of his life. He could not bear to make that loneliness public – and a cause for mockery to boot. That, for what it is worth, is my reading of the situation. The letter brought matters to a head. It is to the writer of that letter that I wish therefore to speak. I wish to make them aware of the consequences of their foolishness.' Trying to keep control of himself was making him sound pompous, he knew; but he was too cross with Julian to care.

'Gloria. I think it was Gloria. I hinted one night . . . hardly said a thing . . . but she must have put two and two together . . .' Julian kept his eyes averted from Peter's. 'Then . . . resentment I think . . . you know the sort of thing . . . trying to get her own back at me for . . .'

'For loving her and leaving her?' suggested Peter. He felt cruel. The sight of Julian's self-pity, when the suffering of his entire life must have been the merest fraction of what Ted, his supposedly closest friend, had gone through, struck him as laughable.

'You won't . . . you won't say anything to anyone will you, Sids?' Julian fiddled with a beer mat.

'Dear God, Julian . . . does your astonishing propensity to think only of yourself extend to all occasions?' Peter slammed down his beer glass. 'No, don't worry, old chap, I won't say anything to anyone. Not through concern for your welfare, but because such gossiping might cause pain or harm to other people. And I think quite enough damage has been done already. Wouldn't you agree, old boy?'

'What are you going to say to Gloria . . .?' he began. But Peter had already picked up his briefcase and was half-way to the door.

Although Peter had not been kind, Julian still felt relieved. Recent events were making him more fiercely protective than ever of his own happiness – and Veronica's too of course. Peter had been right in that respect: what had happened to Ted was bad enough. There was certainly no reason why his and Veronica's new-found contentment should be allowed to fall victim as well. She believed what he had told her and he wanted to keep it that way. When Peter said he would not tell anyone, Julian trusted him absolutely. Fortunately Peter had always been very solid in that respect. And whatever he said to Gloria, in his current mood, would almost certainly scare her into silence as well.

*　　*　　*

Gloria was not expecting visitors. Nor was the buzz of the electric doorbell a pleasant surprise. One evening in ten she shut herself away for a lengthy and very private session of all the various beauty treatments on which her mind and body had come to rely for their well-being. The processes, although resulting in lots of shiny smooth surfaces designed to enhance her natural assets, were not very alluring in themselves, since they mostly involved the lavish application and subsequent removal of creams.

Once she had enjoyed the rituals, now they only depressed her. As she sat tending to her sore feet, trying to ignore her rumbling stomach, with the lather of the face-pack clinging to her face like bits of cream pie, all she felt was old and lonely. The game was up – it had been for months. She followed her old life-style like a stale actress who has lost all energy and inspiration. So low did she feel that she was seriously considering her mother's suggestion of chucking in London life for good and starting afresh somewhere quiet and provincial; somewhere gentle where she didn't have to act and where no one knew about the multifarious mistakes of her past life. Somewhere where bunions didn't matter.

She was about two-thirds of the way through her half-hearted ablutions when Peter rang the buzzer at the entrance to the block of flats. Mercifully, the de-hairing and feet-soaking rituals had been completed; but the heated rollers were still in and little padded sticks were wedged between each of her toes, spreading them out like a knobbly fan, to facilitate the applying and drying of nail-varnish. At first she ignored it. But her sitting-room lights were clearly visible from the street, so she knew it was hopeless. After about the fifth buzz she hobbled on her heels to the entry-phone.

'Yes, who is it?' she snapped, making the inconvenience of the visit plain in her tone of voice. But Peter was not going to be put off so easily.

'Gloria, it's Peter. I must speak to you at once. It's very urgent. Let me in.'

'For God's sake, can't it wait till tomorrow?'

'I said, it's urgent.'

Annoyed, but seeing no alternative, Gloria resignedly pushed the button to open the downstairs door. Scooping up the array of creams and implements from the sitting-room table she dashed into the bedroom and threw them on the bed. There was just time to whip out the curlers and the toe-pads and discard her bath towel for a dressing-gown, before the ding-dong sounded, announcing Peter's arrival on the third floor.

'This had better be good, Sids,' she said as she opened the door.

Peter Sidcup was not normally given to melodrama. In fact he despised such displays of indulgence in his fellows. But by the time he got to Gloria's flat he felt that he had been holding himself in all day. He had controlled his emotions before policemen, doctors, relatives and friends alike. Now that he had got to the cause – albeit the most superficial of all the causes behind Ted's fall – he felt some release of his feelings would be justified. Some people in such situations become violent, others emotional. Peter simply grew vicious – as verbally vicious as he could be. He waited until the door was safely closed behind him before beginning.

'Destroying marriages was not enough, I take it? You had to try and destroy the man himself with a few smutty stories. Or was it that having failed to break his marriage you had to wreak some pathetic form of revenge by spreading malicious gossip? Yes, that must be it. That's the sort of bitchy tactic I'd expect from you, Gloria, embittered as you are by your own failure to hold down a man for more than five minutes.'

'Peter' – Gloria was frightened – 'what are you talking about?'

'Oh, forgive me, how silly.' His voice was thick with

sarcasm. 'Of course, there have been so many – men I mean – that you would not necessarily know immediately to whom I was refering. Let's sit down, and I'll tell you all about it. Quite an interesting story really, once it gets going. Any chance of a Scotch?'

'For fuck's sake, Peter,' said Gloria, trying to make her anger stronger than her fear, 'you've no fucking right to come barging in here . . . get out. I said, get out.' She stood there, feeling weak and silly in her frilly dressing-gown and bare feet.

'The Scotch lives in here, I believe.' He pushed past her into the sitting-room. Having located the drinks on the sideboard, he poured half a tumbler of whisky and threw himself on to the sofa. Gloria stood helplessly in the doorway, watching.

'I am referring, my dear, to Julian – or rather to Teddy, who incidentally threw himself out of a window this morning. Hadn't you heard? Yes, well, as I was saying, it all began with Julian you see . . .'

'Teddy what . . .?'

'Shush now, there's a good girl, and do let me finish. It's all very amusing really. You see Ted was gay, and so was Julian – but ever so briefly. And as usual with these things, it was all a frightful secret, until some silly little hussy got it into her head to break the news to the rest of the world. For her own revenge, you see. But – and here's the funny part – the man she was aiming at could hardly give a damn, while the other one is so upset that he jumps out of a window. You've got to laugh, haven't you, at the way things turn out?'

'He hasn't . . . Ted hasn't . . .'

'Thrown himself out of a window, you mean? Oh, yes, he has. He most definitely has. Landed very neatly in fact. Quite a feat considering the amount of Scotch inside him.' Peter took a swig of his own. 'And all because of your spiteful little letter to good old Tadfield Rugby Club telling everyone about Julian and Ted. I have to take my hat off to you . . .'

'Peter, I swear,' she stepped forward and gripped the back of a chair, 'I did not write any such letter. It wasn't me, Peter, I swear it wasn't me.' Her voice cracked and she turned away.

There is something about a truthful answer which can be immediately obvious. Peter knew at once that he had made a terrible mistake. He didn't say so straight away, but remained slumped in the corner of the sofa, suddenly feeling shattered.

'He's in a coma,' he said after a while, in a different tone of voice. 'The chances of him recovering are nil.' Gloria came over with a glass and the whisky bottle and sat next to him. She knew that he knew he had accused her wrongly.

'Poor, poor Teddy, I'm so sorry.' They both sat there in silence for what seemed like several minutes.

'I was sorry to lose Julian, I don't deny it. But I would never have . . .'

'I know, I'm sorry. Forgive those things I said, Gloria. I didn't mean any of it. But I'm so very angry – and sad.'

Gloria, still very shocked, went on with her own train of thought: '. . . I just went home to recover for a bit afterwards . . . sort myself out . . . dear Teddy – how on earth could he have done such a terrible thing I wonder . . .'

'The letter was nasty – very nasty – and it got read out to the whole bloody club – stuff about him and Julian.'

'But who on earth could have written it? I mean nobody knew . . .'

'Well, I knew, I suppose. I guessed something ages back. But I never said anything to anybody. It never even crossed my mind to, other people's sexual preferences not being a subject that preoccupies me unduly . . .'

'Oh God, Sids, I think I might know,' she interrupted.

'Know what?'

'The letter. I think I might know who wrote that bloody letter.'

'How can you possibly?'

'Katherine Vermont. I've just remembered. I bumped into her on the train home. It was all so odd. I've never really known her at all, but I wanted so badly to talk to someone . . . I don't think men get like that – not in quite the same way . . .'

'Katherine Vermont?'

'We talked about Julian . . . because she'd gone through something similar it somehow seemed all right to talk to her about him. And then . . . well, I can't remember how it happened exactly, but I told her about Julian and Teddy . . .' She tried to explain how she had wanted to give something, share some secret with this other person who had been so hurt by Julian Blake.

'How extremely indiscreet of you, Gloria . . .'

'Well, how the hell was I to know? I mean, it's not such a big deal – at least not to me – that men sometimes have affairs with each other. So bloody what? How was I to know that that bitch would blurt it out to everybody in some silly letter . . . and that Teddy would be so . . . oh God,' and she started to cry.

Peter put his arm round her and comforted her as best he could.

'Come on now, we can't do anything. You're right, you weren't to know . . .'

'But it's my fault,' she managed between sobs.

'It's everybody's fault. We all had a part in it. Now come on, stop crying . . . I haven't got a handkerchief I'm afraid.'

'It's all right, I've got some tissues.' She got up and went into the bathroom to try and regain control of herself.

Peter, left on his own in the sitting-room, sat thinking about Katherine Vermont. Like some hazy figure in an old photo she had always been there, standing in the background of their lives. As part of Julian's romantic history; as the neat black and white figure at his wedding; as

George's dining companion and heart's love; as the girl who appeared and disappeared on the fringes of parties; hovering in the shadows, but never stepping forward into the light of direct contact. Except with George – apparently. (Peter and Ted had often speculated on whether George wasn't making the whole thing up.) Peter wondered if she could really have nurtured her resentment against Julian for so long, and shivered at the thought.

'I wonder if it really was her,' he said, when she reappeared from the bathroom, looking red-eyed but composed.

'I'm sure of it. I didn't tell anyone else if that's what you're thinking . . .'

'I can assure you I am not.'

'And she was very strange . . . I don't know, sort of thrilled when I told her . . .'

'Thrilled?'

'Yes, I can't explain it exactly, but . . . perhaps it was because of what happened to her brother that she was behaving so oddly . . .'

'Her brother? Now Gloria, I'm afraid you have lost me entirely.'

'Well, the other funny thing was her saying something about her brother breaking his heart – I didn't hear properly – just as I was getting off the train. Then she came to the window, as the train was pulling out and yelled more stuff about her brother . . . I really couldn't hear a thing. You should have seen her – it was so bizarre.'

'It sounds it.' Peter drained his glass. 'I am sorry, Gloria. I have behaved very rudely . . .'

'No, I'm sorry. If it wasn't for me none of this . . .'

'Now don't start that again. There are all sorts of reasons why what's happened has happened. Lots and lots of things – most of which we'll probably never discover – lie behind it.'

'What are you going to do, about Katherine I mean?'

'I don't know. I really don't know.'

'Which hospital is he in?'

'Westminster. They moved him there yesterday afternoon, because apparently they've got more equipment for this sort of thing.'

Gloria shuddered. 'I'll go first thing in the morning. Poor, poor Teddy.' She looked down at her toes. The nail varnish on eight of them had smudged horribly, leaving a purplish-red mess that made her think of blood.

Peter got up from the sofa.

'Don't go please, Peter. Not just yet.'

'Really, Gloria, I— '

'I know you think I'm a complete slut, but I just want . . .'

'I don't think you're a slut. I meant none of the things I said. It was all anger.'

'I do so want some company.' Gloria didn't think she had ever felt so lonely. 'Please stay a little,' she whispered miserably, 'just to talk.' Then the tears really started and Peter put his long arms round her and held on tight. Her emotion was too desperate for him to feel awkward or worry about what he should or should not do. Gloria Croft, attractive, utterly self-sufficient, in tears on his shoulder – it was quite an eye-opener; it made him wish he had thought a bit more about what other people really felt, behind their brave smiles.

'I must call George,' he said, when the strength in his arms had calmed her. 'He'll be lonely – and a little scared too I shouldn't wonder. Poor old George – so unaware of everything. Can't think why Katherine should have picked on him.'

'Did she?'

'Oh, rather. Regular little tête-à-tête dinners. The highlights of George's life. He's mad about the girl.'

Peter phoned the flat to say he was going to be back late, while Gloria put the kettle on.

'Pretty stinking isn't it, Peter?'

He nodded.

'I don't just mean Ted, I mean the whole bloody business – life.'

'Sometimes it is, yes.'

'How can you be so cool and rational all the time? The Iceman. That's how I think of you, you know. Nothing really touches you, does it?'

'That's not true, Gloria.' Peter was more hurt by these words than anything that had been said to him for a long time. 'I feel things very deeply.'

'But you don't seem to mind anything; or at least you don't show it if you do. I mind things horribly, all the time. Mostly for selfish reasons I'll admit – because I'm getting hurt in some way. I'm always bleeding from some wound or other.'

He looked at her tenderly. She did indeed appear very vulnerable suddenly, in her pink dressing-gown with her hair falling in her eyes; quite a different and, he decided, an altogether nicer Gloria. He reached out and squeezed her hand. They were sitting side by side on the sofa, until this point not touching.

'I think I should perhaps show my feelings more,' he said. 'Keeping them back helps me feel secure, helps keep the surface of things sweet, but probably doesn't do any good in the end.'

She held on to his hand. 'What I want to know, Sids, is do people like Julian ever get punished? If people like us let him get away with it, then presumably he'll carry on, doing as he pleases, getting off scot-free forever. Where's the punishment, that's what I want to know. There ought to be a punishment for his brand of crime.'

He thought for a while. 'It's in himself I believe. There's no court of law for hurting people emotionally, but he'll suffer in himself all right.'

'I'm not sure I believe that. He doesn't look or behave like a man in torment.'

'No, but he's not happy either. And I can't see that he ever will be. He'll earn lots of money and he'll have lots of affairs' – he shot her a small look of apology as he said this – 'but he'll get increasingly restless, dissatisfied. Have you ever met his father?'

She shook her head.

'Well, that's Julian's fate. Smooth, charming, successful on the outside and a bloody mess inside. They're their own worst enemies those types. Because it's taboo to mention the discontent, the secret bad side. It's not manly. Not done at all. So it festers inside them.'

'But I think lots of women are like that too, Sids. In fact trillions of people are like that. Everyone hides behind facades all the time. Look at Katherine all these years. Look at Teddy. Look at me.' She hung her head, feeling a new army of tears rallying to attack.

Peter lifted her chin with his finger and kissed her softly on the lips. 'I am looking at you,' he said, brushing back the hair from her face, 'and I'm wondering that I've never looked properly before.'

*   *   *

Of course Katherine had written the letter. It was about the last sane thing she did before collapsing in a gibbering heap on the kitchen floor. The idea had come to her on the train, as Gloria's revelation, Tommy's death and Julian's unpunished crimes churned round in her mind like milk turning sour.

Mrs Vermont's frail defences nearly gave way at the appearance of her daughter as she stumbled off the train at the station. Instead of the usual, neat chocolate-box figure, a dishevelled, smeary-faced woman walked slowly down the platform towards her, as if in a trance.

'My poor darling,' she said, putting her arm round her and leading her to the car. The ridiculously painted face, the absence of luggage, the stunned silence, she put down to shock. When she broke down entirely, a few hours after they got home, her mother saw it as a good sign – some release of tension at least – and put her to bed with a couple of Disprin and a hot water bottle. Katherine's collapse was just part of the way in which their lives had been turned upside down by the crisis. Normality had been swept away, seemingly forever. They barely ate, talked very little and spent many gruelling hours on the telephone. There was so much to be organized, what with the problems of getting the body shipped home, telling relatives and making arrangements for the funeral.

Mrs Vermont's mourning, like that of all the family, was not for the man who had thrown himself off the top of an apartment block in São Paulo. It was for the bright-eyed boy who wrote letters full of cricket and football scores, who teased his sister for her freckles and got through ten jars of peanut butter a term. The pasty-faced, lanky man with a beard and straggly long hair, who had called in one afternoon, after months of hiking round Europe, to inform them of his plans to explore South America, had been a complete stranger. The Tommy they knew and loved had been dead to them for years.

Peter had spoken honestly to Gloria. He did not know what to do about Katherine. The petty desire for finding someone to accuse, for finding the trigger that pushed Teddy out of the window that night, had faded into a helpless sorrow. The more he found out and thought about things, the more he realized that the strands of events and emotions – both concealed and otherwise – that had contributed to the accident were too numerous to unravel into tidy compartments of what had led to what.

It was like some massive spider's web that had them all in its clutches.

In the end it was neither anger nor a desire for revenge that made him decide to contact Katherine; but a vaguely moral feeling that she ought to be made aware of what had happened; that she should be dealt her share of the suffering.

Getting hold of her, however, did not turn out to be as easy as he expected. Having tried to call her flat on several evenings, he finally went to the lengths of finding out where she worked (from a mystified and jealously suspicious George), looking the number up in the book (since George had never been allowed to call her at work) and finding out from her work colleagues that she had gone home for an undefined leave of absence. The secretary to whom Peter spoke was very new and did not herself know the full reason for Miss Vermont's non-attendance. She gave him Katherine's home telephone number with only the mildest resistance and without disclosing any details.

If Peter had got to hear that another man connected with Katherine Vermont had jettisoned himself out of a window the same week that Teddy did, he might have lain awake at night speculating about some grand design of misfortune. As it was, when Mrs Vermont took his call, she told him only that Katherine's brother had died, and not how. (His death, as well as being tragic, was embarrassing somehow: because of it being suicide, because they knew so little about it and because they felt guilty.)

'Katherine's broken down under the shock of the news. Perhaps I could take your name so she can call you when she's recovered.'

'No, no, it's quite all right. I had no idea, I'm so sorry. It was nothing important.' He put the phone down before she could say anything else. Hearing of Katherine's own private misfortune made him feel mean for having thought so badly of her. But it also reinforced his belief in a system of rough natural justice whereby people seemed to end up getting what they deserved.

'A friend of yours called from London,' said Mrs Vermont a little later, when she took a bowl of soup and some toast up to Katherine's bedroom.

'That's not possible,' she replied, pushing the tray away, 'I have no friends in London.'

Katherine's parents and the doctor thought, understandably, that her collapse was due to shock at the news of her brother's death. They could not know that it was much more than that. They could not know how deep the trouble went; that their daughter fell more squarely than anyone into that category – identified by Peter and Gloria – of people who hide their true, troubled selves from the world. A sickness had been festering inside her for years, brewing behind that manufactured image of normality. Within her bright and shiny fortress there had lain a chaos of unexpressed feelings and unacknowledged sadness. As the letter shot like a bullet into Teddy's private world, so the news of Tommy blew a hole in the walls that protected Katherine's. Her breakdown was the release of sorrows that she had been bottling up for years; sorrows that had taken root in that first drowning love for Julian Blake; and which, because they had been forcefully suppressed at the time, had gone underground and multiplied into something far more destructive. Her obsessive, shy personality ensured this. Katherine had needed some sort of breakdown when she was seventeen, but had not felt able – or been allowed – to go ahead with it. Her mind, being forced to maintain control for so long, had literally warped under the strain. With Tommy's death the control finally snapped, releasing malice and madness.

18

Marriage Made

If it is true that how people react in a crisis offers great insight into character, then Veronica should perhaps have watched Julian more closely at the time of Teddy's accident. But although normally quite observant, she was absorbed by the fascinating business of being pregnant and hindered by knowing only part of the truth. When it struck her, as it did more than once, that Julian still had not visited his friend in hospital and had barely mentioned his name, she chose to interpret these things as an indication of the nature of his sorrow. It was a private sadness, she decided, not something she had a right to intrude on. (The memory, still fresh, of the unhappiness she caused by chivvying him to report on his feelings all the time also prevented her from needling him for an explanation). Never once did it enter her head that her husband was displaying some form of guilt-based cowardice. Nor, perhaps, more seriously, did Julian ever allow such an interpretation of his behaviour to form clearly in his own mind. Adopting the convenient pragmatism that his wife taught him, he easily convinced himself that visiting Teddy in his current condition could do no possible good and might disturb some vigil that the relatives were keeping.

Having a pregnancy in the family was as welcome a distraction for him as it was for her. He even went as far as accompanying her on a few early reconnaissance trips to baby shops. The intention was just to look around and get an idea of what they would need nearer the time. But somehow they never stuck to the plan and would stagger home laden with bags of baby-carriers, reinforced tights (Veronica's single fear seemed to be varicose veins), maternity dresses and endless gadgets, clothes and toys for the baby.

The impending arrival of their first child also turned out to be a marvellous excuse to get away for a holiday. What Julian did not tell Veronica was that the idea for this came to him during a telephone call from Peter, who had rung after weeks of silence to ask whether he had dragged himself over to the hospital yet. Julian assured him that he had every intention of going, but that they were both rushed off their feet with preparations for the baby and – as inspiration flashed – a last holiday together as a 'free' couple.

'I'll go when we get back, Sids, I really will. I keep hoping he'll come round you see – then there would be more reason to visit . . .'

'You are an ostrich, Julian Blake . . .'

'I beg your pardon?'

'Never mind. You're fooling yourself if you think he's going to come round. The doctors have all said that the chances of such a thing happening are very, very slim. In other words, it would take a bloody miracle.'

'Poor Ted. I'll go and see him, honestly – just as soon as we get back.'

Veronica was too thrilled at the thought of two weeks in Bermuda to care where the idea came from. All Julian said was that he wanted to give them – and more particularly her – a last treat before the tough business of becoming parents shattered their independence. When he had said this often enough, he too believed it to be the sole motive for going away. A break from Peter and Teddy had nothing to do with it.

Julian was not dishonest in the sense that a thief is; he never deliberately robbed or deprived anyone of anything with the intention of causing pain. In order to be the successful survivor that he was rather than a hapless victim, he had developed a dishonesty that involved lying to himself as much as to others. Such dishonesty comes with the vague desire to be good but without the will-power or commitment to manage it. If he ever possessed a capacity for selfless love and emotional truthfulness it had been crushed by his upbringing – all signs of a soft spirit having been banned both at school and at home. He had learnt to play cruelly with other people's feelings for his own gain; in all his spoilt life he had never been made to see the wrongs of this; indeed he was totally unaware of it. It was fortunate that he had at least had the instinct – or luck – to marry a survivor of equal resilience, who was learning to play the same games as deftly as he.

In everyday terms the deceit practised by Julian involved confusing the relationship between words, thoughts and actions. He had been a lousy actor on stage. But in the larger theatre of life he was a natural. (Just as the opposite could, rather neatly, be said of Teddy.) The key to Julian's survival-kit was doing things for one reason and afterwards thinking up other pretexts for having done them, invariably convincing himself in the process. In the same vein, he learnt to say things that he wished were true, rather than things which really were true. (At the back of his mind lay the half-baked hope that saying something with enough conviction might make it a reality.) The most extreme example of this play-acting came with his behaviour towards

Veronica. Since the Tadfield dinner, her getting pregnant and Teddy's accident, he had slipped easily into the role of the attentive, adoring husband. Playing this part not only involved expeditions to baby shops, it also entailed being generally much more romantic.

'Always you, it's always only been you, and it always will be you. You're all I'll ever want, my darling,' and other such murmurings now took place on a regular basis. Veronica, believing him, loved him more than ever. He almost believed himself. He wanted it to be true. He really wished that he had always always been faithful, and that his fidelity could be guaranteed for the future. But wishful thinking is a flimsy substitute for resolve. The memory of having got away with it once lay safely tucked away. Julian had successfully lied to his wife not only about fidelity, but about other things too – such as the business with Teddy. He had discovered that he could make her believe him when he wanted to. And deep, deep down in a tiny, honest corner of his soul, he knew that such a hidden, potent talent was hardly something he could ignore for ever.

* * *

On the last evening of Julian and Veronica's holiday in Bermuda, while Veronica was rubbing pints of after-sun coconut milk into her swollen brown tummy and Julian was sipping a gin and tonic on the balcony of their hotel bedroom, pretending not to look at two pretty girls, long-legged and sun-tanned, strolling arm-in-arm in the evening sunshine on the pearly-pink beach below, Teddy died.

'Wonderful, wonderful holiday, darling,' sighed Veronica, stretching out and yawning.

'Hmmm,' said Julian, who had secretly been rather bored. He always forgot, between beach holidays, that his capacity for lying under a hot sun without getting fidgety was limited to a few minutes at a time. Unlike Veronica, who was content to roast her body, day after day, seldom showing any inclination to bathe, let alone do anything else. Water-skiing and windsurfing had helped fill the hours on the beach, but the hire of the equipment was so fiendishly expensive that he had felt obliged to ration himself to two measly half-hour sessions of each a day. When squinting at a greasy, dog-eared paperback became truly intolerable he resorted to strolling off on his own, for an ice-cream or perhaps a beer, and the opportunity to admire the prettiest of the female bodies scattered along the sands. His eye was wandering more than usual since Veronica, apparently worn out by the taxing business of sunbathing, had taken to falling fast asleep the moment her head touched the pillow. In fact they had made love only once during the entire holiday – between showering and eating one evening during the first week. And that had not been enormously enjoyable since it was the day when their sunburn was at its very worst – that burning red stage when the skin feels hot and bruised – and every move they made hurt terribly.

'Still, it will be nice to get home,' she continued, 'to get the nursery properly sorted out and everything.'

'Hmmm,' he said again.

'I think I'm the luckiest girl in the world.'

'What's that?'

'I said, I think I must be the luckiest girl in the world,' she called, more loudly this time.

'And I must be the luckiest chap,' he answered dutifully. Here he was, with a good wife, a good job, the prospect of a child, a nice house, a bright future – everything a man should want. And yet he did not feel content. Not remotely. Perhaps having those leggy girls on the beach as well was the answer, he mused. He stood up and leant on the balcony railings in the vague hope of attracting their attention.

19

The Funerals

The funerals of Katherine's brother and her ex-lover's friend took place on the same day, almost at the same hour. But the connections between the two groups of mourners were too tenuous for either party to be aware of the other. The strange parallels in the events that led them to their respective graveyards were part of a pattern that would never be perceived. Julian had known Tommy well enough once; but they had stopped being friends when things went wrong with Katherine. Then Tommy had flunked his A-levels and, as far as Julian knew, taken off on the hippy trail somewhere. As for Katherine, she was completely unaware of Teddy's accident or of any of the reverberations caused by her spiteful letter to the captain of Tadfield Rugby Club. She had been too absorbed in her own disintegration to wonder about anything very much. If Peter had ever got to challenge her on the subject, she would almost certainly have denied writing the letter anyway. Not because she was a liar, but because she remembered very little about anything these days. This was pure self-defence, explained the doctor to Katherine's parents – a way of shutting out reality, so as to try and protect herself from experiencing any more anguish.

It seemed to Mrs Vermont that the traumas resulting from her son's suicide were worse than the fact of the suicide itself. Watching her daughter go to pieces nearly broke her heart. It was so unexpected, so utterly out of character. Not only had her two children not been close for years, but Katherine had always been such a controlled, tough sort of person. Her reaction was the last thing anyone could have imagined. Sorrow, yes; but complete collapse, never.

As if the awfulness of Tommy killing himself wasn't enough, getting the body home had proven to be as prolonged, costly and strategically complicated as fighting a war. The person who called them from São Paulo with the news had been extremely uninformative on all fronts; and the Vermonts had been too shocked to ask any of the right questions. After several days of long fruitless, phone calls, on lines that sounded as though they were being used as fuses at a fireworks party, they contacted the British Consulate for advice on how to proceed with their grisly task. The British Consulate did help – they did their best – but no amount of good intentions could speed up or unravel the bureaucratic intricacies of getting a body shipped from South America to England. It was an expensive, harrowing business that took many weeks. The cost of the telephone calls alone was enough to convince Mr Vermont that he should have followed his initial urge of flying out there himself to make all the arrangements in person.

So in the end Tommy's body arrived in England about the same time that Teddy's decided to give up its ghost of a life; while Julian was sipping his gin and tonic and saying 'hmmm' to his wife. As Peter had found out, events and people are linked in ways more devious and complicated than they can ever hope to realize.

There were very few people at the little Norman church in

Horley since only close family attended. Katherine, looking thin and frail, walked slowly on the arm of her mother. The black veil covering half her face emphasized the plastic whiteness of her skin; but at least it hid the big hollow eyes. It was the first time she had been out of the house for weeks and the spring breezes hit her fragile frame like force ten gales.

*   *   *

When Tommy's preserved body had been safely cremated and potted, Teddy's was lining up to receive the same fate in a spiky modern church in south London. Mrs Charleston had called on Peter to help with who should be told about the funeral. She knew Teddy had lots of friends whom she guessed would like to attend, but she knew very few of them and was not sure of the best way of getting in touch. Peter suggested printing small cards which he could then see delivered to the correct addresses. This was duly done and the turnout was impressive. Ted had indeed had lots of friends; an enormous circle of people who loved his humour, his kindness and his reckless energy. Peter wondered, as he saw all the familiar faces file into the church, that none of them, himself included, had been able to stop Ted killing himself. It did not say much for man's capacity to help his fellow man, he thought grimly, the guilt still sitting like lead on his own conscience. Seeing Julian and Veronica approaching he quickly turned his head so as not to have to talk to them.

The sun-tanned glow of the Blakes' faces was almost obscene amongst the sober black of the costumes and the grey backcloth of stone. Julian's hair, bleached from so many hours under the sun, shone a golden-white in the dim interior of the church. Walking, or rather waddling, proudly beside him was an embarrassingly healthy and pregnant Veronica. She had long since adopted the clumsy gait of the expectant mother, more to revel in her condition than from any real necessity – as yet – to do so. Veronica exuded self-satisfaction; it radiated from every pore in her shiny brown skin. The funeral, the death, somehow made her feel stronger and – although she could barely admit it to herself – happier. There was death, but there was life too, inside her. She felt immortal.

'Oh, Julian darling,' she whispered, once they had settled themselves in an empty pew, 'there are so many people we know here. People we haven't seen since the wedding. We really must have some of them round, keep in touch more, don't you think? Perhaps it's awful of me to think of such things now, but I can't help . . . oh, there's Gloria arriving.'

Julian didn't want to look, but felt obliged to. In the process he caught Peter Sidcup's eye. They held each other's gaze for a couple of long seconds; Peter's stare was steely, accusatory, merciless in fact. Julian crumbled first, shifting his glance uncomfortably to the figure of Gloria, who was nervously pulling at her black gloves and peering round for somewhere to sit. She found herself looking over towards Veronica, forced into it by the strength of her friend's gaze on her. Veronica grinned – she couldn't help it – and Gloria nodded a tight little smile in return. The last person she wanted to be near was Julian, or his wife for that matter, but Veronica was signalling her to join them. Not immediately spotting an alternative seat, she felt compelled to do so.

'You look well,' she whispered, a little harshly, as she slipped into the seat.

'Yes, so do you,' replied Veronica, inwardly thinking exactly the opposite. Gloria's appearance actually reminded her of a used car – one that has had too many coats of paint in an attempt to hide the cracks.

'Poor Teddy.'

'Yes, poor Teddy.'

Veronica turned her head again to study the profile of her old friend. As she did so, she inadvertently caught Gloria staring across her at Julian. As soon as their eyes met – which was only for a split second – Gloria jerked her head back to face the front. But in that second Veronica saw an expression of such hurt accusation that it made her quite scared. She looked at her husband for reassurance, but his head stayed resolutely facing the altar. Veronica started to wonder about the hidden thoughts and feelings of people who pretend to know each other. She started to wonder what went on behind the scenes. She started to wonder if Julian and Gloria had ever . . . but there she stopped herself. She had a stupid imagination. The funeral was making her morbid. It was pointless to speculate about things which had a one-in-a-million chance of being true; things which she could never hope to find out about properly anyway, and which – if she ever did find out about them – would only make her miserable. She preferred being happy. She preferred believing in her husband. She felt for Julian's hand and gave it a squeeze to reassure herself. He squeezed it back and she immediately felt better.

'If it's a boy we could call him Edward,' she whispered shyly, wanting to please him.

At that moment Gloria felt a gentle hand on her arm.

'Come and sit at the back, Gloria – the pews are much more comfortable there, I promise.'

A grateful smile of relief lit up her face. She hadn't seen Peter since the night he stormed into her flat. His terrible accusations had been followed by the most wonderful sense of intimacy she had ever experienced. They kissed just once. Shortly afterwards he left, saying he would be in touch when he had sorted out both himself and the muddle over the letter. She had since worked hard at convincing herself that the closeness they felt that evening had been a fluke – one of those coincidences of mood and feeling brought on by mutual sorrow. All part of sharing a crisis. It was precisely as a guard against this that Peter had held back from seeing her until he felt – in his own mind at least – that the crisis was over. He had phoned her several times to see if she was all right, but that was all.

After rushing round trying to find Katherine and helping Mrs Charleston with the funeral arrangements, Peter felt that his active part in the drama was over. The inactive part – the regret and the sense of blame – would go on for many years yet, perhaps for ever. Meanwhile, it was time to move out; time to move away from Thurloe Road, from Julian Blake, to a new and better life in which he put more store on things like sincerity and kindness. Gloria felt all that new resolve in the golden touch of his hand as he led her down the aisle to the two spare seats beside George.

George was, as yet, the only male member of the congregation evidently trying not to give way to tears. He kept blowing his nose loudly and taking deep breaths. The urge to cry was for lots of reasons. Obviously Ted dying was the worst thing, though he had been as good as dead already from what George had seen. But there were all sorts of other dreadful things which seemed to have happened at the same time. There was the business of Katherine disappearing without telling him anything, then Sids finding out that it was because she had had a nervous breakdown because of her brother dying. Death, hitherto a remote concept, was suddenly very close and it scared him. Then there was Sids announcing, out of the blue, that he wanted to move out of the flat and put some money down on a place of his own. He said George could still lodge with him, which was very decent, but it wouldn't be the same; nothing would ever be the same without Katherine and Ted. The only good thing to come out of it all as far as George was concerned was that Peter, ever since Ted's accident, had been very kind. Gone were those frequent cold moods of his which always made

George feel clumsy and in the way. Now he was quieter maybe, but softer, more considerate.

Snatching an opportunity between George's snorts into his handkerchief, Peter nudged him gently in the ribs to get his attention.

'George, dear chap,' he whispered,' I have a proposition to make. I think in Edward's honour we should have a private bet as to how long our holy father intends to lecture us on this grey, sad afternoon. I think he would approve of such a wager, don't you?'

George turned to his friend, appalled. Then he grinned. 'By Jove, Sids,' he said in rather too loud a whisper, 'I think he would. A tenner says he'll run for at least fifteen minutes.'

Peter shook his head. 'Poor judgement there, I'm afraid. Look at him. Far too modern and nouveau to think he can fool us all for that long. Not a second over seven, I'd say. And what about the theme, George? We must have a fiver on the theme.'

'Happiness after death?' hazarded George.

'A fair choice, dear boy, but I don't fancy your chances. I'll put my money on quite a different matter. I'll put mine on Just Desserts. That's much more the ticket, don't you think?'

George looked puzzled.

'I mean that everyone gets what they deserve in the end, George.' As he said this he linked his arm through Gloria's and held it tight.

Gloria smiled.

'Oh, I see – I think,' said George, smiling at them.

Then they all turned to listen to the vicar.